TOUCHWOOD CHRONICLES

Book 1

The Sun & the Moon

Corin Thistlewood

First edition 2022

Book design by Publishing Push

ISBN (paperback): 978-1-80227-462-2
ISBN (ebook): 978-1-80227-463-9

Contents

Chapter 1

Beginnings

My story is not important
Soon my spirit will leave for the sky-land
What is important is that dreaming is eternal
And anyone who passes on this culture to the people,
Preserving the traditions becomes part of that eternity.
This is of great importance
Sakshi Anmatyerre

A raven leaps from her nest, high up on a cliff face. She gathered the wind as she spread her black wings and glides effortlessly on the updraughts from the cliffs. Her heavy beak, thick neck, distinctive shaggy throat feathers and wedge-shaped tail, declare she is a carrion bird.

She circles the boglands below, her keen eyes searching for any unwary animal, who has met its end, in this harsh environment. She soars in flight, the raged feathers on her wing tips, hardly moving as she circles, in ever increasing radius.

She banked and turned in graceful spirals, leaning against the air currents. Now flying over bogland, now flying over a human farmstead. Her all-seeing eyes note, the neat rows of vegetables, contrasting with the scrub land bushes and black bogs nearby.

The polytunnels housing an array of green growths. She notes the chickens and the ducks, looking carefully for unprotected chicks.

The roof of the house is lined, with arrays of solar panels, reflecting the brilliant sunshine off their glassy surface's. A wind turbine, happily hums away, fed by the persistent winds.

The sun shone brightly in streams, through the plum and apple tree branches. It was a warm autumn day, and the lush fragrance of ripened fruits filled the air. The gentle sounds of geese murmuring, chickens clucking and the occasional bleat of a goat, offers a sound track that sooths body and mind.

This ragtag community is where I dreamed of staying. This is the start, of spending my last years on earth.

This is my story. Born a child of a golden age. An age where men dreamed of flying to the moon. An age when rock music was young, and New Age Pagans were innocent and unhindered, by the shackles of the mind. I have witnessed what most would only dream of now.

As I write this, I am old and long in the tooth. My once long, youthful locks have turned straw like and silver. My long beard, likewise, has silvered. My once glowing, youthful skin is …but enough of this self-pity, I have a story to tell.

By all that is Holy, I confess these things that I have done. I regret none of it, for they were all necessary, to bring about the end result. Which, as you will see as the story unfolds, is a significant one.

I Touchwood, tell you these things, for it is sometimes necessary to understand the workings of smaller magics, that go unnoticed by the masses, who are often blinded and swamped by the greater stories, that are presented daily by the worlds media.

From an early age, I was fascinated by trees. One of my favourite places, in the whole world to go to was, my special tree. It was in a park, very close to my school, so I used to go there on my way home. It was an easy tree to climb, as it had branches low down. And it wasn't very tall either, it seemed quite stunted, as it was growing out of rocks, in a corner where nobody else seemed to go.

But I loved it. I would climb up as far as I could go, then sit in a fork, near the top and just cling there dreaming. The tree would rock me back and forth, swaying as the wind blew. Here I was lulled into a dream state. I would just sit there, for hours at a time.

I remember very clearly one summer, while in primary school, we were finishing up school for the summer break. The teacher declared to the class, that our project over the summer holidays, was to compile a project book, about the trees in your home area.

At that early age of nine, I was a poor student, not known for my diligence with homework. But I spent that whole summer with trees. Collecting leaves, flowers, bits of bark and small twigs, sticking them in my scrap book. I did bark rubbings and even took photos, with my dad's camera.

I drew maps of where trees were, in my area and what types they were. I learned to identify many types of trees, from their canopy, leaves, seeds, and fruit. My project book was bulging. If I was missing from teatime, my mother knew where to find me, I would be swaying in the highest branches, listening to the wind race through the leafy boughs, while the gentle swaying of the branches lulled me to a state of peace.

It was interesting, that when I presented my project book to my teacher, after the summer break, no one else had thought to do any work on this project. But I didn't care, I had discovered trees.

From these early beginnings, it was no surprise then, that in later years I was drawn to various ecological groups, especially if they had tree projects. No surprise either when I discovered there was an alphabet, based on trees, I was hooked. The Ogham lead me to Druidry, the men who had 'knowledge of the trees'.

Born in Liverpool of Irish and Welsh descendants, it was perhaps not surprising, that as a child I was quite psychic. Spirit guides often talked to me and helped me with my schoolwork. There were many things, I just knew without being told, especially in the realms of physics and geography, which I excelled at.

Yet, there were areas of human life, which baffled me, such as why were the other boys so interested in football? Why did they like to fight and play with guns? These sorts of things were beyond my understanding.

However despite this, I was brought up as a very ordinary English boy, whose only spiritual event, was going to church for an hour on a Sunday morning; all be it reluctantly. But it was a requirement of the church, if you wanted to go to the youth club, on a Friday night.

In my early teens, I became fascinated with electronic equipment. I would often find old radios or vacuum cleaners or other electric junk, which had been thrown out. I would pick them up, take them home and dismantle them, to see how they worked. Before long, with the help of my guides, I was able to repair many of them.

In the same way, my guides helped me make new, electronic circuits, with which I was able, to place microphones about the house and switch to different rooms and hear what was being said. I then started to record these conversations, or arguments on an old reel to reel tape recorder I had found and repaired.

Later, I would play back these arguments to my parents. This proved too much for them. They stormed into my room one evening, demanding how I was able to do all this. My parents, who knew nothing about electronics, and they had checked with my school, to see if they taught it. The answer came back, I wasn't taught any of this at school.

Much to the dismay of my parents, I told them it was the man in my head, telling me how to do it. They were clearly horrified by this answer and told me: I shouldn't tell this to anyone!

Up until then, I had thought that it was perfectly normal, to have a convenient little voice helping you out. I though everyone did. But my mother especially, made it clear, that other people didn't and that they wouldn't understand it, if I told it to anyone so, I should keep very quiet about it.

At about the same time I became fascinated by maps. I had been shown an Ordnance Survey (OS) map at school; I was enthralled by it. While other boys were getting football boots for birthdays, I asked my parents to buy me an OS map, of my home area. I would spend hours staring at it. To me, it was like flying over the area, I could relate to the topography and follow the contours, like a bird flying across the countryside. Later on, I progressed to cycling, to interesting old churches that I had found on the maps. And later on still, I read about ley lines and progressed to drawing these on my maps.

It was also quite a common occurrence, that I would get premonitions. So much so that I considered them a normal part of being alive and that everyone got them. It wasn't until I left school and started talking, more intimately with girls, that I realised that it wasn't that common an occurrence. The premonitions were usually concerned with my personal safety and were glimpses into the very near future.

One such occasion, was when I was coming home from grammar school one day. I had the misfortune of being sent to a school, quite a long way from my home, on the outskirts of Liverpool. It was a very good school, but I had to get two different, public transport buses and both where quite long journeys. There was also, a half mile walk to get to the bus stop as well.

Anyway, I must have been fourteen or fifteen, so I had gone this route hundreds of times before. I was walking along the busy road, near to the bus shelter, where I usually waited for my bus.

I knew the bus shelter intimately; it was a concrete framework, about waist height, with a metal framework and glass windows all round.

I was just about to enter the shelter, when I suddenly had a vision of the glass smashing into the shelter; I instinctively stopped in my tracks, startled by this. The vision was so vivid, that I thought it was real. I just stood there, looking at the glass on the floor of the shelter.

As I was standing there, just before the entrance, an older boy was coming up behind me and bumped me sideways, as he said, "Out of the way Thistle!"

However just at that moment, a car, on the busy road, suddenly swerved and crashed into the bus shelter. It was stopped by the concrete frame, but smashed the glass window into the shelter, just as I had seen in my vision. If I hadn't been stopped, for a few seconds by my vision, I would have been in the shelter, when the car crashed into it and the glass would have smashed, all over me. I could have been very badly injured, thankfully my premonition prevented it.

It wasn't until later in life, when I was more confident that I mentioned these premonitions to other people. Many people where fascinated by what form they took and asked lots of questions. The best way I can describe this, is to say it's like this. It's like imagination. Say you have been to an unfamiliar place and some dramatic event happens like a car crash. Years later, you may be able to re-live it, remember it or even visualise it happening again. Perhaps you are in your office, aware of your normal surroundings, but you are also visualising the car crash at the same time. My premonitions are like that.

Towards the end of my school days, my natural abilities in the realms of technical subjects, began to be noticed. I became, what today you would call a physics nerd. But I exceled in a number of technical subjects. Always getting top marks in the technical subjects I loved. And went on to take 'A levels' in several subjects.

One day, a government head-hunter or talent spotter, visited my school looking for students who showed especial aptitude in technical subjects. My headmaster, recommended to him that I should be interviewed, along with a few of my 'nerdy' classmates.

I was very fortunate, that I was chosen to be sponsored by the government, to undergo a technical apprenticeship, and go on to be trained by them, to become an electrical engineer. To my parents' it was a dream come true. Their clever boy, would go through university, paid for by the government.

I took to a career in electronics with gusto and eventually became an aerospace Engineer working for the Ministry of Defence (MOD).

However, there was another side to me; my spiritual side. But in those early days, I was not so fortunate with this aspect of my life. I was passionately interested in the supernatural, and read extensively about it, throughout my teens and twenties. But I needed to meet others who had similar interests, I enrolled on many different personal development courses. These I very much enjoyed, but I came to realise, there were not many people, in these circles with my supernatural gifts or interests. And of course, in those days there was no internet, emails or chat rooms, so it was very difficult to find like-minded people.

My apprenticeship with the MOD was based in South-West England near Bath in Wiltshire. And it was while I was based there, that I discovered what a wonderful place Wessex was. It was literally littered, with stone circles and other megalithic sites, which I loved to visit and of course, I learned to dowse and draw ley lines on my OS maps.

***

'So now you know my early beginnings. Fairly ordinary, for the most part you may think. But it was at this point, towards the end of my apprenticeship, that my story truly starts...'

Wrote Touchwood. He was now writing his history down in a ledger, a large A4 notebook. He had taken his granddaughters advice, to write it all down before he forgot it entirely. He had often told her stories of his early life, when she asked it of him.

But now, he realised it was also better for him, as he could write his story whenever it suited him; for example, when he woke up during the night-time. Also, there was much about his early life ... that he couldn't tell his granddaughter.... not while he lived.

There was a gentle 'Knock, knock' on his door.

"Come in", he shouted as his granddaughter entered, bearing a tray of tea and some homemade cookies. It was Victoria and she was as beautiful as her name. Her eyes, green as grass and long blond hair, tied into plaits with some green material, she had no doubt, found in the seconds pile.

She wore dungaree's, a practical choice, as she had wanted to tend the animals, from the moment she could walk. She had fed them, housed them, and birthed them. Now at the tender age of sixteen, she was experienced beyond her years, at caring for all their needs.

Now her large heart, had taken on caring for him, as he grew older every day.

Victoria set the tray down near her grandfather, then sat down on a large cushion beside the stove.

"So, what happened next, in your story grandpapa?" she asked.

He had been reading to her, the parts he had written so far, it was good that she was interested, so he indulged her a little.

"Well, this is where things stated to get interesting," stated Touchwood as he stretched back in his rocking chair, causing it to creak and groan, as the old chair joints protested to the strain. He picked up his ledger and started reading …

Chapter 2

Starr Hill

Twinkle, twinkle, little star
how I wonder what you are?

During my apprenticeship with the Ministry of Defence, my interest in ley lines became a sort of hobby on the side, as most of the time, I was kept busy with college work. However I talked to several of my fellow apprentices about the subject many times, usually in the pub over a pint or two of beer.

Mike, a handsome chap with reddish brown hair, slightly freckled, with a wicked grin and always impeccably dressed; Girls seemed to be infatuated with him. He was one of my closest friends as we shared a similar sense of humour.

Anyway, Mike seemed very interested in the UFO side of ley lines. He had read that Unidentified Flying Object's where often sighted on or at the crossing of ley lines over sacred sites. He had also read in the local paper that there was a UFO 'flap' going on in Warminster. I wasn't sure what a 'flap' was, at that stage, so he told me that it's when UFOs are particularly active in a specific area ...

"So, why don't we go and see if we can see one, after all Warminster isn't that far away from here," I said to Mike, as we were sat in our favourite Pub in Trowbridge; two pints of Wadworth's 6X sat before us.

Mike was a very bright sort of guy, very quick witted. He kept me on my toes trying to keep up with him, I really admired his intellect.

"Sure thing, why don't we," he said. "The paper said, apparently Cradle Hill is a common place to go for viewing the night sky for UFOs."

"Ok great, I have an OS map of the area back at the house, I'll check out where it is and then we should go out there as soon as we can."

So that was the plan made up on the spot, just like that.

Back at my house, I checked my maps and found several places near Salisbury plain and Warminster that had ley intersections. But unfortunately Cradle Hill wasn't marked on my one-inch OS map. So I thought I would take a trip to Trowbridge library after work, to check out the large-scale maps of that area.

I found some nice old two and a half inches to the mile maps there, and fortunately to the east of Warminster was marked Cradle Hill. I felt excitement building in me.

I asked the woman on the information desk, a lovely old lady in wire rim glasses and her hair in a tight little bun at the back, if I could photocopy part of the map. With her help I managed to obtain an A3 copy of the whole area round cradle Hill. I had no idea at the time, but this photocopied map would become invaluable to our adventures later on.

So the day finally came when we trundled off to Salisbury Plain looking for adventure. There were three of us, Mike, myself, and my girlfriend Sarah; all piled into in my clapped-out old Ford Anglia. I had bought it from one of the older apprentices, who had made it into a project. It was souped-up with bored out pistons, skimmed head and fitted with what must have been some sort of motorbike exhaust system, because it sounded like a cross between a motorboat and a lawn mower. It was overdone of course, as it kept blowing head gaskets, but I loved it to bits, and nursed it back to life each time it blew a gasket.

Oh, how excited we were, striking off in the dead of night into the mysterious Salisbury Plain, which apart from the UFO's, had all sorts of rumours about military experiments and other strange goings on in the 'military exclusion zone'. Which everybody felt was the UK's equivalent to the USA's 'Area 51'.

The photocopied map showed a sort of farm track leading partway up the Hill. Which was remarkably hard to find in the deserted and dark country lanes of Wiltshire, with no signposts to help us.

But eventually we trundled up the track till we came to a farm gate, where we all piled out. To our astonishment there were several people there already. One or two giving us bitter looks as we had blinded everyone with our head lights.

Sheepishly, we went over to the group and asked if this is where we see the UFO's.

"You just missed one," someone said

I felt like we had imposed on them a bit, but after a little while, we all settled down to the sombre business of watching the night skies. We were very fortunate as it was a clear, moon less night, the best for sky watching.

After a few minutes Mike called out, "There's one over there, look," as he pointed to the northern sky. Sure enough something that looked like a star was slowly moving towards us. I was excited.

After a minute or so someone shouted, "It's a satellite."

"Oh really how can you tell?" I asked, totally naïvely.

The guy who had said it was dressed in what looked like some sort of military fatigues. I wandered over to him and asked again more quietly. He looked me up and down; I think he could tell I was a green horn at this, so he answered me in a friendlier manner.

"Most satellites look like that one, average brightness, moving at constant speed, in a linear direction. And usually traveling north- south, in what we call a polar orbit."

This guy seemed quite knowledgeable. I looked at his fatigues and said:

"Are you from the military?"

He just gave a slight nod, then said, "We've seen all sorts of strange aerial activity in this area; you need to know your wheat from your chaff." He nodded to one of the other guys, "See that guy over there, with the hat, that's Arthur, he's a local journalist, he's seen a lot of UFO's, go ask him about them." Then he turned his back, looking up at the sky; I felt I had been dismissed by my Headmaster.

Fortunately, Arthur turned out to be quite a character and knew a lot about this subject. More importantly for us, he was willing to share what he knew. The three of us had a good chat with him while watching the night sky all the while.

Occasionally, he pointed out things we should know, like identifying military helicopters on night manoeuvres; or identifying satellites and other things in the night sky that could be explained.

Suddenly he stopped talking and just pointed up to the sky to what seemed like to me, was another satellite. Luckily along with my map, I had brought a compass which was hanging about my neck. I quickly checked; the 'star' was moving quite quickly from the southwest towards us.

"Keep watching," said Arthur.

As we watched the moving star suddenly went out. The hairs on the back of my neck prickled. Then the light came on again and continued its journey.

"I've been watching that one," said Arthur. "It's blinked out three times now."

We all continued watching until it was directly overhead. Then a very peculiar thing happened. The 'star' suddenly veered sideways, at ninety degrees to its original flight. Then continued its journey in the new direction, blinking off for a second or two every couple of minutes.

"We see a lot of them ones round here," said Arthur.

"Really," I exclaimed, "err …what are they?" I managed, still shocked at what I was seeing

"No idea," came the frank reply. "But it's defiantly not a satellite or space junk, it just can't do that."

"And it's not an aeroplane or helicopters either," shouted the surly military looking guy.

"Who's that?" I whispered to Arthur

"Oh, he's part of the joint helicopter command. Doesn't want it getting about that he's up here looking for UFO's," Arthur whispered behind his hand and winking at me.

I couldn't help smiling, and casually looked over at the military man. All the same, I wouldn't want to come up against *him* on a dark night.

I was still slightly shaking with adrenaline from what we had seen. Clearly this seemed to be an Unidentified Flying Object as these trained observers didn't know what it had been.

The Hills around Warminster sit on the edge of the wide expanse of Salisbury Plain, which is an ancient chalk plateau in the southwestern part England; covering some 300 square miles and largely lies within the county of Wiltshire.

It is famous for its history and archaeology. In the Neolithic period, Stone Age people began to settle on the plain. Large long barrows such as White Barrow and other earthworks were built across it. By 2500 BC, areas around Durrington Walls and Stonehenge had become a focus for building, and the southern part of the plain continued to be settled into the Bronze Age.

The military training area covers roughly half of the plain. The army first conducted exercises on the plain in 1898. From that time, the Ministry of Defense bought up large areas of land until the Second World War.

The MoD now own 150 square miles of land, making it the largest military training area in the United Kingdom. There is a large military exclusion zone, where the public are not allowed in, and this has encouraged countless rumours about UFOs and aliens and is considered something of the UK's equivalent of USA's top-secret base; Area 51.

Warminster in Wiltshire became something of a UFO Mecca in the 1960s, thanks largely to the writings or Arthur Shuttlewood, who was a local journalist. He wrote about UFOs in his local newspaper, so often that he gathered enough evidence to write several books about them: 'The Warminster Mystery - Warnings from Flying Friends' being perhaps the most famous.

The exact locations of these sightings vary but tend to be in the vicinity of Middle Hill; often referred to informally as Starr Hill and Cradle Hill, both to the east of Warminster.

Over a period of a couple of years during the early 70's I went to the Hills of Warminster many times UFO spotting. We saw many strange lights in the sky and met lots of interesting people like Arthur Shuttlewood. On Starr Hill, we met Donald Keyhoe UFO writer (esteemed leader in the field in the 60s) founder of NICAP, National Investigations Committee on Ariel Phenomena. He was in the UK while promoting his books.

We met several military men, a professor from Cardiff University, as well as many other experienced observers and UFO spotters. All of whom were baffled by the many strange aerial phenomena we witnessed.

One other thing that we didn't know at the time, but I only found out years later, was that at the same time period we were there and in the same vicinity, there were a number of crop circle-type effects which were described as circles of swirled down reeds and grass, which in those early days were dubbed as "nests".

There were many other independent witnesses but an excerpt from Arthur Shuttlewood books:

"Reeds and grass have been curiously flattened in what invariably seems to be clockwise fashion, blades swept smoothly inert in shallow depressions ... It is significant that most circles, depressed and clearly formed, measure exactly thirty feet in diameter."

Some months after that first night, we were UFO spotting on Starr Hill, it had been a busy night. There was about eight of us up there and we had seen a number of odd lighting effects. One 'star' had been orange in colour moving much faster than any satellite and much brighter. In fact we thought at first it might have been an aircraft but then it started to zigzag on its course till it was directly overhead, then it just stopped, hanging there in the night sky like a bright orange star directly overhead.

There was no sound at all just the light. I asked one of the army guys that were there:

"Do you think that could be a helicopter?"

"No chance," he said. "There's no sound and they don't have orange lights."

"What about the zigzag?"

"I doubt very much weather any helicopter I know of, can zigzag like that, in such a tight manoeuvre."

So this one did seem very unexplained. We had already seen several 'silver blinkers', but we had seen many of those over the past year and were slightly bored with them.

To the left of the gate where we all congregated, there was a bumpy farm track leading up the hill to a small copse of trees, which was always dark and mysterious. I had wanted to explore up there for a while now and thought lets go tonight. Mike and my girlfriend came with me.

As we approached the copse of trees we heard a Vixen scream, it's a terrifying noise when you're a little bit spooked anyway. Thankfully I had lived in the country cottage for a while and knew what it was. But Mike had stopped dead in his tracks, and I could see he had gone pale. I thought I would spook him out a little.

"What the hell was that; sounded like a scream?" I said, barely containing my snigger. I caught my girlfriend's eye who was behind Mike. She knew I was joking and was shaking her head.

"Do you think we should go and investigate, might be someone in trouble?" said Mike a little shakily.

"Yeah, you go and check it out…. But I'm not going into that dark copse for anyone," I remarked.

Mikes face went even paler. So, I relented and said, "Ok let's all go up." After a few more paces up the track I relented again and said, "You do know, that that was a female fox, don't you?"

Mike looked at me pan faced, but I could tell there was relief there too.

"Bastard," was all he said.

We explored the copse together, there was an old ramshackle farm shed with some old, rusted farm machinery, but nothing of interest. I thought that we might get a better all-round view of the night sky there, but once at the top, there was too much glare coming from the town on the other side of the Hill. The trees were obscuring some of the sky anyway.

After about fifteen minutes, we decided to go back down to the others. Halfway down the track, it seemed to be pitch black after the glare of the streetlights from the top, and we were all stumbling over the loose stones and clods of earth.

Then we heard one of the others from the bottom shouting something at us.

"What?" I shouted, as I couldn't hear what they were saying.

"Look behind you!" they shouted louder.

We all turned in unison. Coming from the direction of the copse, was a low flying light. It was like a head light shining down, but it was peculiar because it was like concentrated moonlight shining down. It was illuminating a small area of the track as it came quickly towards us.

There was no sound at all. We, all of us were rooted to the ground like statues staring up at this 'thing' coming towards us. I had this strange feeling of Deja vu, it was uncanny. The 'moonlight thing' can't have been more than thirty feet up when it went directly over us.

As I turned to follow it, I could see Mike's awestruck face, lit up by the moonlight coming from the craft. The moonlight washed over all of us, then continued down the track. I remember the uncanny thing was that it was completely silent.

The 'moonlight thing' continued down the dark track illuminating the others as it passed over them. I heard one of them give a 'whoop' as it passed overhead. So I knew they had seen it too. Then the 'moonlight thing' carried on over

Salisbury Plain rising higher into the night sky, till it eventually diminished into a pinpoint of light, just like any another star.

No one was saying a word. The three of us just continued to stare off into the distance where the thing had gone.

I was overcome with a myriad of emotions but most of all, an over whelming feeling of loss. Then I realised it wasn't Deja vu I had felt it was a feeling of 'belonging', of 'coming home', of being loved by my family. But now it was gone. And it was devastating. I looked over at my two friends and could see it in their eyes they had experienced the same feelings.

The old man with the silver beard, sitting in his rocking chair, was parched from his reading, so took a last sip from his mug of tea, then pulled a face, the tea had gone cold.

His granddaughter had a faraway look in her eyes as she listened, she said a little dreamily:

"It must have been wonderful to have seen those 'fairy lights' in the sky grandpapa, maybe one day I will see one."

The old man looked down indulgently at his granddaughter and continued reading.

'As I look back now, I realise I was touched that day by something I can't explain. But it was a turning point for me. I realise now that one of the things it sowed in me was that feeling of wanting to 'belong'. The feeling of wanting to 'belong to my tribe.' And I would spend a large part of my life looking to fulfil that feeling again'.

Chapter 3

The Base

And they showed me a world
where I could be so dependable
Oh clinical, oh intellectual, cynical

Supertramp

The old bus wound its way chugging along the coastal road. At sharp corners, the gears would crunch and grind, as the driver struggled to keep the ancient bus on the road and not scrap against the rocky cliff on the right or skid off on to the rocky beach on the left.

The bus was full to capacity, all those people creating a stuffy humid atmosphere within and misting up all the windows. I wiped my hand across the condensation in a bid to create a small hole of clear glass in order to see out the window. My hand came away soaking wet but ignoring this I peered out the hole to view the world outside.

I could see the rocky beach on the left and the dark cold waters of the Scottish loch, sloshing listlessly against the gravel.

Beyond that was a grey mist so thick that the mountains across the loch were but dark grey shadows that looked like some vast beast had laine down to die in the cold waters.

The cold front of humid clouds had descended on the Scottish peninsular after a storm two weeks ago and had stayed there like an unwanted guest.

It was raining.

It had been raining for two weeks solid now, without stopping.

My orange VW beetle had finally succumbed to the incessant damp, and two mornings ago had refused to be roused from its nightly slumber. This is why I was on the bus today.

The tired old bus finally ground to a halt, and the local bus conductor had shouted out: "The base," refusing to even acknowledge its full naval title of RNAD Coulport.

People sneezed and coughed their way off the bus, I too pushed and jostled my way to the front door; I was glad to leave this breeding ground for every flue and cold virus there ever was.

Outside, the air was cool and humid, I took great draughts of it trying to clear my lungs of the fetid atmosphere on the bus. The whole group of us headed like sheep towards the front gate of the base.

The entire admiralty armament depot covered some 1,600 acres, including the reinforced concrete bunkers, housing the warheads, built into the hillside. The whole area was surrounded by a double row of high fences with swaths of razor wire adorning the tops. While security dog patrols, constantly roamed the perimeter between the fences.

I patiently waited in line by the front gate, while dozens of soldiers with automatic weapons stood by watching. Each person entering the base had their pass checked by the security guard's handheld machine; then was briskly frisked. Any shopping bags, rucksacks or bags of any kind were confiscated at the gate.

Having passed the gate security, I was now within the first level security area which housed the site canteen and HR buildings.

To get to my place of work, I needed to pass through three more increasingly higher security levels. By the time I had got through to my work area, my work colleagues and I went straight to our tearoom, downing thick coffees or tea as was personal preference.

"See it's raining again," said somebody.

"Aye its set in for sure," said another.

"Did you see Dundee and Celtic playing last night?" said the first man.

"Aye, was a good match Celtic played; shame about that Dundee crowd."

The 'weather' and 'football' were the perpetual topics; Such was the extent of the conversation in our tearoom. I was glad to down my coffee and head to my work bench.

"Sure, George is keen this morning," I heard someone say as I hurried out. I could feel myself slowly dying if I stayed in there any longer.

The lab I worked in had several benches set up for the assembly and testing of the various electronic assemblies that were to end up in the main Polaris rocket. A companion lab was setup for mechanical assembly.

It was a clean room environment where we all wore white protective jump suits, white rubber shoes and white hair caps. Inside the lab there were no windows only white plastic walls and banks of fluorescent light in the ceiling.

I was also required to wear a chain wrist band which was on a long wire that was earthed to prevent static build-up. I used to jokingly say to my wife I was literally chained to my bench.

At my bench I often daydreamed. Too often, I would question myself, how on earth did I end up here?

***

Touchwood stopped writing a moment, as he remembered the day, he had told his wife. She had innocently asked, "Did they really chain you to your bench George?"

"No of course not Sarah, it was just a little joke, me and the boys had in the clean room." Although it really did feel like it some days, I wasn't really happy there. But let me continue with my story…

'After the halcyon days of my apprenticeship, my juvenile mind had been drawn to the exotic prospect of working in aerospace. 'I would be assembling rockets in the majestic mountains of Scotland', I would think to myself. As my apprenticeship drew to a close, I had married Sarah. We had become a respectable married couple, I needed to knuckle down into a steady job. If we had a house, Sarah was hinting, then we would be in the ideal position to start a family. Also the prospect of being offered a readymade office job and low maintenance modern house, for cheap rent, had persuaded my wife.'

'So, we were both drawn into thinking that moving to the admiralty base in Scotland was the best for both of us.'

'The reality had somehow manifested in a very different way. I had been here two years now and was already planning how I was

going to make my next career move. In the civil service, promotion was only a matter of time, if I kept my nose clean.'

'But the only way 'up' was to 'manage' the clean room, a prospect I wasn't particularly keen on either. So, I just trundled on day after day, not really knowing what else to do.'

'I didn't know it at the time but all that was about to change.'

***

Ding Dong.

It was the front doorbell. "Who on earth could that be?" said Sarah. "Nobody ever calls here, well except the post man maybe with a parcel, and he only comes in the morning twice a week."

I was watching the six o'clock news on TV, it was very interesting as it was talking about Bristol and South-West England. Apparently, they were suffering with a severe heat wave and had gone for forty-five days with no rain! I was wishing we would get some of that here, some chance.

Sarah was in the kitchen washing up the evening meals dishes, "Could you get that George, my hands are all soapy."

"Oh! Ok," I said reluctantly. I didn't want to miss what it was saying about Bristol. I walked awkwardly to the front door, straining my neck round to keep watching the TV till the last minute.

In the hallway I looked toward the frosted glass of the front door. I could see the shape of a tall person in blue. Puzzled by who it could be, I released the catch and opened the door.

It was a scruffy looking guy wearing a blue denim jacket and jeans. He looked to be in his late twenties. He was tall and skinny but wiry and athletic. He had longish, curly black hair.

His face was long and pointy, with a bit of a foxes look about him. He seemed to have smallpox scars on his cheeks but was handsome in a rugged way.

"Hello," I said. "Can I help you?"

"Yes, I was wondering if you wanted some fresh fish. I'm your local fisherman, they were caught fresh this morning."

"Oh!" I said taken aback, he hadn't called before. We had been existing on frozen produce, as there were no fresh food shops on the peninsula. We had to go weekly shopping in the big town, an hour's drive away.

'It certainly would be nice to get some fresh fish', I thought.

"What have you got?" I inquired.

"Come and have a look," he said. "The vans just there."

He led me down the path to his white ford van, parked in the road, and opened the back doors. Inside were wooden trays filled with ice and fish. A strong fishy smell wafted out. There were lots of fish I didn't recognize, but I could see some lobsters and large prawn type things, still moving about.

"Not sure what's, what here," I admitted.

"Well look here's Monkfish," he said pointing at the various boxes, "and there's Mackerel and some Herring too. Do you like shellfish?" He continued, without waiting for an answer, "I've got Scallops there, Brown Crabs and Live Lobster."

"What are those prawn-like things?" I said pointing at the brown crustacean with claws still moving.

"Ah, they are Scottish Langoustine."

"Lang …what's that?" I stuttered.

"That would be Scampi or Dublin Bay prawns, to you," he said patiently.

"Aww! I'd love some of them."

"Ok, how many? Couple of dozen?" he said as he started piling them into a plastic shopping bag.

"What about some fish? Couldn't be fresher, caught only this morning." He said giving me the sales pitch. I wasn't really sure about what fish was good to eat. I had only ever had Cod from a fish and chip shop.

I was procrastinating. I looked up towards my front door, looking for help. Sarah was there in her rubber gloves and tea towel.

"What fish would you like?" I called up to her.

"What's he got?" She called as she walked down the path towards the van.

"What's your name mate?" I said to him, suddenly realizing we hadn't introduced ourselves to each other.

"Oh, my names Hamish Campbell," he said, mock bowing his head to Sarah and giving some sort of salute. "Your local fisher man at your service mam."

Sarah smiled and blushed, then immediately removed her rubber gloves, stuffing them in her apron pocket.

"What fish would you like?" I repeated to Sarah.

"Oh, I like those things with the claws," she said pointing to the Dublin Bay prawns.

"Yes, I'm getting some of them. But he wants to know what fish you want," putting the decision over to her. Knowing full well that she was as ignorant about fish as I was.

Hamish looked at her with a twinkle in his eye, he could see her consternation.

"Meaty monkfish," he said, "are lovely. Just fillet them, give them a quick sizzle in the frying pan. Pop them in the oven. Goes lovely with a lemon and parsley butter sauce. Top fish that."

My mouth was watering at his description, "I think we can manage that, Sarah?"

"Yes, we'll have a couple of them," she said.

"What about smoked salmon?" Said Hamish, as he put the monk fish in the bag. "Smoke it myself, I can let you have it cheaper than the shops in town."

We both loved smoked salmon I knew, but we rarely had it, it was usually expensive. "Yes, I'd love to try some of that, but just a bit, as I don't know how long it keeps."

"I've just got myself a vacuum pack machine now. It'll keep a couple of weeks in the fridge."

"Ok, we will have a packet of that too. How much is all that?" Said Sarah, as she took the bag and disappeared back into the house.

I pulled out my wallet from my back pocket. It actually worked out quite cheap, I was well pleased with my fishy haul.

I caught Hamish eying my long hair and jeans, as he said to me, with a very knowing look:

"Is there anything else, I can get you?" He said conspiratorially as he waved two fingers in front of his mouth. I didn't think he was talking about cigarettes. I looked about at all the houses in the estate. Every window could have eyes looking at what was happening in the street.

"Er... no," I said flatly. "Maybe another time," I hadn't smoked anything like that since my first year as a student. And now working at a top security base I wasn't about to start.

"Never mind," he said unfazed, handing me his card. "If you need any fish for special occasions just give me a call. It's my aunt's number, but she will get a message to me."

"Ok, will do. Thanks again for the fish." I waved goodbye to Hamish as he was walking down to the next house, to sell his fish.

My workaday routine at the base continued. But somehow, I had a new sense of optimism. I was starting to get odd things happening in my dreams too. Or rather when I was in that halfway state, half asleep, half awake.

It was nothing visual like most dreams, but rather I could hear a whispering pipe music that set the hairs at the nape of my neck a tingling. At first, I was convinced it was coming from outside my window. Waking up, I sat up in bed listening hard and strained to hear it again, but there was nothing but the low murmuring of the wind......

This played out over several nights, till I was eventually convinced it was in fact internal. It was always low and quiet just on the edge of hearing. But now I was sure that within it, there were whispered words. Yet in such a fashion that it could only be remembered or thought of except as music; it was like having a new sense.

Then I remembered the guiding voice I used to get when I was young, my mother had told me never to tell anyone. But I clearly remember the voice. So, I tried tuning into it, like when you are at a party and there are lots of voices at once, but you tune into the person you're trying to listen to.

So, I tried tuning to that voice I remembered. After a few failed attempts, I was now able to discern some of the words:

"A …. doesn't whine … don't … way. A …. makes things … way."

It was frustrating. I was missing half the words, but it kept repeating over and over within the pipe music. Eventually I started to develop 'an ear' for the voice. Gradually more words came through, till eventually one evening I was able to discern the whole message: *"A wiseman doesn't whine when things don't go their way. A wiseman makes things go their way"*.

What a strange message I thought. But it was certainly relevant to me, I had been moaning about my situation, feeling sorry for myself, but not doing anything about it. Clearly now I needed to be a 'wiseman' and start to *make* changes happen.

I must '*do something*' to change my daily work struggle at the base. The only thing I could come up with though, was to make an appointment, to have a talk with my boss, to see if he could come up with anything.

It was several days later that the appointment time finally came. I walked into his office and sat down and explained to my boss that I needed a change from the clean room routine. I said I was happy to try working somewhere else on the base. He told me that it wasn't so easy to do this, with the bureaucracy, security issues and paperwork involved. But I might be able to solve another problem he had.

He needed to fill a position with an engineer, who needed to install the various electronic assemblies into the missile body itself. It was a challenging job, working in cramped conditions and required unusual dexterity and precision.

Additionally, the position required an engineer that was more qualified than I was. But he was having trouble filling the post, as it was unpopular because it was so demanding, and the cramped conditions.

"Most engineers with that experience," he said, "quite frankly were older and usually getting a bit Tubby round the waist." He laughed at his own little joke, but I just looked at him, not quite knowing how to react.

He said he had been campaigning for a while now, to allow a younger, fitter engineer to train up on the job, alongside the experienced engineer.

He said a young skinny lad like you, would be ideal for the job, but I would need six months of intensive training before qualifying for the full pay rise.

Then he asked me would I be interested in such a position?

I was a bit taken back as I hadn't expected something so immediate. My current job was actually pretty cruisy, no real challenges, just daily repetition, sat comfortably at a bench. But perhaps that was the problem. Perhaps that was why I was so bored with it; I was young, I needed a challenge.

Before I thought about it too much, I found myself saying, "Yes, I really would like to try for it."

He then said, "Tell you what, I will have a talk to my superiors, explaining my position again and that I now had a young, fit lad keen to train up for the position. Does that sound ok?" he asked. "No promises mind, but I'm optimistic."

He stood up and shook my hand, which indicated the interview was over. Walking over to the door I turned back a said simply:

"Thank you," then walked out his office.

I didn't tell Sarah about my dreams and voices but told her about my optimistic meeting with my boss. Sarah was delighted with the news of possible promotion and immediately decided to have a party.

"Isn't that what young people do, have parties?" she said. "When you were an apprentice down in Bath, we had parties all the time. We haven't hosted one party since we have been here. Don't you think it's about time?"

"I guess so," I said. Then I realized that I didn't really have any friends, in my local area. And there was no one at the base, I wanted to invite. There was no one in the MOD housing estate we lived in that I wanted to invite either.

Sarah worked at the Faslane base, as a clerk in the offices there, so knew a few other women and had a friendly relationship with some of them. So, we both decided to have a small, informal, buffet party with those few friends that she knew.

"Why don't you invite Hamish?" Sarah asked. I think she was feeling sorry for me, as I hadn't invited anyone to our party. I did feel a bit down hearted by it.

"He seems like a nice guy," Sarah probed. "You seemed to get on with him."

"I hardly know him Sarah, I only bought some fish from him," I said sulkily. "But I guess you're right, it would be nice to have someone, that I at least know. Maybe we could ask him for some seafood for the buffet?"

"Ooow!" Sarah enthused, "yes, let's do that. You've got his number, haven't you?"

Hamish seemed quite pleased that I had thought to invite him to our party, I imagine he had not had much contact with people from the base before, except perhaps as customers. To my surprise he actually offered to bring some sea food along for free, but I said I was happy to pay for it.

On the night of the party, Hamish caused quite a stir, when he arrived bearing trays of lobsters and prawns. They looked beautiful, with lovely colors, as they had all been cooked and chilled, so were ready to eat.

Most of the guests had arrived on time, bearing bottles of wine, and the party was well underway. I was beginning to think that perhaps Hamish wasn't going to come at all. But he made a grand entrance, with a flair of the dramatic. All my guests immediately took great interest in the lovely fresh shellfish and the party became an instant success.

After having tasted the smoked salmon Hamish had brought, I was very curious to see how he smoked it, as I hadn't ever seen the process done before. So later on, when Hamish and I were chatting in a corner, over a glass of red wine, I casually asked him the address of where he lived, so as I could come and look at his smoker.

Hamish gave me one of his sideways looks. I thought he was judging me, 'was I to be trusted,' I thought he was thinking. So, I tried to reassure him.

"It's ok Hamish I won't judge you on where you live," thinking he may be embarrassed to let me see his 'impoverished dwelling'.

"It's not that," he said. "But it doesn't really have an address. It's in the woods, you would never find it. But its ok I don't mind driving you up there one day."

"That would be great," I enthused, "I can help you cut up the salmon, or something."

"Tell you what," Hamish said, scratching his stubbled chin. "I don't have any salmon on the go at the moment, but when I do, I will let you know," then he stopped a to think, I could see his face twisting a bit, considering.

After a minute he said, "I tell ye what, have you ever done any rowing?"

"Yeh, sure," I bluffed. "I've done a bit of rowing before," trying to sound experienced. I could see Sarah a little way off, out of the corner of my eye eavesdropping, as she sipped her glass of Martini with a little paper umbrella in it. As I said this, she gave a great snort, of distain. As it was her, I had last rowed with, in a boating lake in Chester. Somehow, we had ended up tipping the boat, with both of us in the water. She wasn't going to let me forget it. My pride bruised; I chose to ignore her.

"Well then," cried Hamish, throwing his arms around expressively. "Come out with me catching the salmon, and I'll show you the smoker after."

"Ok by me, sounds like a plan. When are you going out next?"

"Depends on a lot of things, he said, "I will call you when I'm ready. Give me your telephone number."

So, I wrote it down on a piece of scrap card, I found on the work top. Hamish tucked it into his trouser pocket, then gave me a mock salute.

And that was how we left it. I enjoyed the rest of the party but all the while I was talking to the other guests, I was secretly more excited by the prospect of going out on a fishing boat on a Scottish loch.

I was inside a rocket! I was actually, inside a rocket that would be flying up above the earth's atmosphere.

At the moment I was lying on a blue plastic covered foam bed, that was attached to some sort of mini cherry picker, that could be controlled, to move me up down or forwards or backwards, while I worked on the rocket.

Well, it was the equipment section of the rocket anyway. Which instead of being vertical, like you see rockets, when they take off. It was laying horizontal while it was being fitted out.

Inside, we had to cram in all sorts of control system equipment. There was the accelerometers and a block of high-speed gyroscopes, a software flight control system, a block of auxiliary electrical equipment, the main computer and various power supplies.

You see the problem was, unlike the huge Saturn rockets or Apollo class you see launching on TV. The Polaris was only about four and a half feet in diameter. The equipment section was tiny really. It had to fit on top of the second stage rocket, then on top of that was the payload. All that equipment crammed into such a small space required precision engineering. Mounting the various equipment, onto the bulkhead of the equipment section, was a pain in the arse.

However, I was really enjoying the challenge. Lying face down on the blue plastic covered foam bed, I was able to manoeuvre into the cramped rocket space and fit the power supply without crawling over and possibly damaging other sensitive equipment. It was a genius device really and saved a lot of back problems, I'm sure.

I was surprised how quickly the job change had come about, really. My boss had obviously done a good job of convincing his management to trial me. I was to be given a month's trial on the job, to see if it suited me, and if I had the aptitude for the job. The senior engineer, would be there on the spot, guiding me as to what to do at every stage. If that all worked out ok, I was to get my security clearance up graded. And start my intensive training, which involved three days a week in the high security training facility on the base.

Courses, of such high security, such as this, could not be done at the local Uni or tech collage. All the instructors were U.S. naval offices. In the training facility I was amazed to see they had computer terminals that had video call facility, directly connected to their counterparts in the U.S. This was very high tec indeed, for those days in the 1970s, when the public only had very costly, clunky international telephone links at best.

I was to learn that it was possible to look up a part number, from a blown-up schematic on display. I could then order the part from the U.S.A. and have it flown over to arrive within a day or two. Something unheard of in those days. To me it was totally mind blowing.

I was also to get a tour of the first and second stage rocket assembly, areas and the tour included the reinforced concrete bunkers, housing the warheads, built into the hillside. It really brought home the reality of what we were doing here.

***

'I was involved in constructing weapons of mass destruction! There was no getting away from it'

Touchwood stared at the sentence he had just written in disbelief. But that was the reality of it at the time, he thought to himself. He took off his wire rimmed glasses and breathing a mist onto the lens, before polishing them with his handkerchief. His granddaughter didn't know about this part of his past, in fact no one in this community did. The official secrets act had prevented him talking about it for years and years. And when he was allowed to speak of it, it just didn't seem relevant, to the life he lead now.

He wondered how she would take it, how the others would take it? They only knew him for what he was now. But it was part of his story and he needed to make it complete. He continued writing …

'How had a nerdy physics boy, from the streets of Liverpool, end up doing this? Over the coming weeks and months, it was a question I was to ask myself over and over.'

Chapter 4

The Fisherman

But at night, when all the world's asleep
The questions run so deep
For such a simple man
Won't you please tell me what we've learned
I know it sounds absurd
Please tell me who I am

Supertramp

My boots slipped on squelchy kelp and slimy rocks, as we scrambled down the beach, pushing the little rowing boat into the cold waters of the Scottish loch. She was a beautiful craft, lovingly painted blue and white with a mysterious painted eye at the front. It looked like the eye of Ra; Hamish had told me it was for good luck; I hoped it was working.

We were going out at night, into an icy cold loch that was fed by the ocean, it was almost pitch black, and no one knew where we were. I was beginning to doubt the wisdom of taking up Hamish's offer of coming out with him fishing; to my town dwellers mind it had seemed like a romantic notion and Hamish had described it in lustrous tones.

As the waves started to buck the boat, I scrambled in over the gunwale, seized the oars and set them in place. By now I was pumping adrenalin and my heart was racing

Hamish pushed us out further, before jumping in; sleek like an otter he came over the side. His bare feet and old grease-stained trousers rolled up to the knee were soaking wet. He looked over to me and grinned, happy as a clam.

We were now buoyant and rocking slightly, as the small waves rippled on the shore dragging at the gravel with that timeless swish sound that I loved.

We rowed someway round a head land, past little rocky coves, there weren't many signs of life here, no lights on the shore. Then Hamish called:

"This is it, we'll put the net out here."

I unsteadily rowed, while Hamish sat in the stern paying out the net. He had instructed me to row out slowly at right angles to the shore.

I had caught my breath now and starting to relax, so started looking about me. It was a beautiful still evening, I could just see the resplendent, crescent boat of the moon, low in the western sky. Above me the heavens were encrusted with a billion stars, the belt of the Milky Way flowed clearly across the night sky.

Hamish looked back at me and seeing the wonder in my eyes, called casualty from the stern, "Did you know up here, you can see the Andromeda galaxy with the naked eye."

"I wouldn't doubt it for a minute," I answered without looking down. "If you knew where to look."

It was one of the wonders of the Scottish Highlands, well away from the glare of the cities and streetlights; you could see just how many stars there really were in the sky; something city dwellers never see.

"I can't believe how well we can see," I remarked, as I continued to slowly row. "There are no streetlights, and the moon is almost set, yet I can see the oars and the boat quite well."

"We are seeing by the light of the stars," he said simply. "And you start to develop your night vision when you get away from the city lights."

"Yes, for sure that must be it. What an amazing place to live." I was starting to be quite smitten by the beauty of the place. There was something very primal stirring in me. Being out on an open boat, at the dead of night…paying out nets and hunting for fish…The moon, the stars, the mountains all about us…the loch, had all been here for a million years. And men like us had been going out fishing for thousands of years.

"How did you learn to fish Hamish?" I asked, casually.

He looked back at me with that funny sideways look, assessing me again, then answered.

"Before he drank himself to death, my father taught me and his father before him," he reminisced. "This is his boat, my grandfathers I mean. Its clinker built and strong, it's had countless repairs, but I've managed to keep it going." There was proudness in his voice, but sadness too.

"It earns it's keep, over and over."

"So, your family has been here a long time then?" I probed.

"Yes," he said still paying out the net. "Before 'the base' came and built the road, linking all the little villages along the loch, people round here relied on boats to get what they could catch or get stores from the bigger towns. Everyone knew their place and what was expected or them. We all looked after each other. Many families like my grandfather were fishermen. Now I'm the only one doing it," I could hear the bitterness in his voice.

"I wouldn't want to live anywhere else mind," he continued. "A few winters back, when the conditions were right, I saw the Aurora Borealis. It was magical…there was glowing green lights, flickering under a purple sky…meanwhile the rest of the sky was filled with millions of stars from our galaxy, and I was surrounded by the snow-bound mountains all about."

There was something of a poet's heart in that man, I thought, a man content in his surroundings.

"Right, that's the end of the net," declared Hamish. "Time to turn about and head for shore," he commanded.

Never known to disobey a captain's order, I did my best to turn about and at the same time trying to avoid the line of nets we had just laid. I had only ever rowed a boat on a lake in the park, which was pretty-tame, this loch was connected to the open sea, so it was a tricky occasion for me.

But I got us back to shore safely. After dragging the rowboat up the gravely shore a way; we headed for Hamish's caravan.

"How on earth did you get the caravan here, in the first place?" I asked Hamish incredulously. "There's no road leading down here?"

He laughed seeing the humour in it, "Well, as I said, before the MoD built the road round the loch to service the base. There was a man, Alan Mackay it was, with a barge used to deliver supplies like gas bottles and other stores to the villages all along the loch.

"I saw him one day with a caravan tied down to the barge. He had moored at Kilcregan to get some ciggies from the post office there. I asked him what he was about. Said he was delivering it to a new guy, building a house, further round the loch.

"So, I asked him if he could do the same for me. And he said: 'well, as it happens, I have a van you can have that will never ride the road again, but it will be ok to be static'. We agreed on a price, and I got him to deliver it here. With a few of my mates we got it up the gravel and onto the grass up there."

Hamish went to the door of the caravan and opened it; it wasn't locked. "No one comes round here," he said. "You can only get to this wee geodha by boat, because of the cleit behind us," he pointed up to the rocky cliff, so as I could get the gist of his meaning.

Inside the caravan smelled of fish, Hamish lit a gas mantle, to give us some light then filled the kettle from the tap, and put it on the stove, then lit it with his zippo lighter.

"How do you take your tea?" he asked.

"Oh, milk and one sugar thanks." Then, realizing where we were, I asked, "Do you have milk?"

"Nah, only powder."

"That will do then," I laughed as I sat down on one of the cushioned benches. It was starting to feel quite cosy inside the van, the dim yellow glow of the gas lamp, kettle on the stove, the homely smell of Calor gas, mixed with burnt carbon on the sides of the kettle, a faint odour of fish.

When the kettle had boiled, Hamish offered me a packet of chocolate digestives, along with a mug of tea. As I sipped the steaming mug, I recalled caravan holidays as a kid and how tea, made in a caravan, on a gas stove always seemed to taste so good.

"So, what do we do now?" I asked, stifling a yawn.

"Drink tea, wait, sleep," he said simply.

"When do we go out to collect the fish?

"Just before dawn, a few hours yet. Finish your tea and have a little sleep on that bench there. I'll wake you when it's time to go out," he said, pointing to the bench I was sitting on.

By now, I was feeling a little sleepy, so I finished my tea and settled into a corner and tried to sleep.

I must have gone out like a light, for the next thing I knew, was Hamish was shaking me awake, "W... what? Did I sleep?" Was all I managed, stretching.

"Like a dog snoring," said Hamish with a smirk. "It's time to go out again." Hamish stubbed his cigarette out, then opened the caravan door; a cool breeze blew in as he looked up at the sky.

"Weathers changing, clouds are rolling in, best get out there, could be rain on the way," he stated as he walked out the door.

We crunched our way down the gravel beach, to the little rowboat again. It looked like the tide had come in a bit, as the boat was very close to the water line now. We went through the same procedure as before, pushing the boat out a bit, then I jumped in and maned the oars; while Hamish pushed us out further then quickly jumped in.

I started rowing us out, away from the shore. While we had slept, the sky had clouded over. I couldn't see the moon anymore nor the stars. Hamish produced a torch from his backpack and lit it, then started fiddling about with something in the back of the boat. I noticed the torch had a red filter, or rather a red sweet-wrapper over the lens held on by an elastic band.

"What's the red torch for," I asked.

"The moons gone, so we need our night vision to see by. When our eyes have adjusted, the red filter stops the torch spoiling your night-vision."

"Oh!" I said, I was impressed by his preparedness.

I turned back to my oars and continued rowing. But now I noticed, as I dipped my oar into the salt water, an amazing blueish glow flared out from the disturbance it made. I tried again the other side of the boat; the same amazing light show happened again.

"Wow that's amazing," I said to Hamish, like a kid with a new toy. "Have you seen this Hamish?" As I dipped in the oar again creating a sparkling blue flash.

Hamish had found his baccy tin and was rolling a cigarette with well-practiced hand. He casually glanced at the water.

"Bioluminescence," he said simply.

"Wow, what's that I have never seen anything like it?"

"Fluorescent Plankton, comes in with the tide sometimes." Hamish paused to light up his rollup, taking a big drag, then blowing it out through his nose. "It can often cover a large area round here. A bioluminescent sea will glow when it's disturbed by a splash in the water at night. Pretty amazing really. When we get to the nets it will be interesting."

I continued rowing for a while, Hamish sat in the back puffing away at his roll-up. He was watching me with an amused look on his face. I was still fascinated, like a kid, by the Algae bloom. Every time I dipped the oar, a new light show would occur.

Eventually Hamish said, "Here we are. There's the corks."

I could just make out a line with regularly spaced floaters, that held the line on the surface of the water.

"Row to the end of the cork line George, then slowly row toward shore along the line."

I did as my captain asked, then looked down at the cork line. The little cork floaters were bobbing up and down with the ripples. Through the clear water, I could see vertical panels of netting that hung from the cork line. The net had been weighted at the bottom with lead weights.

As I looked, deep into the clear water, I could see halfway down the net, small bioluminescent sparks, and the dark shape of the salmon, could just be seen. It was quite a magical sight. It stirred in me, some sort of primal instinct or like a memory from another life centuries ago. I kept staring down into the depths, in awe at the mystical scene before me. Hamish was also looking too.

"Amazing sight eh!" he said after a while.

"Totally awesome," I whispered in awe.

"Looks like we have a good few in the net tonight," he said.

"How do you know?" I quizzed.

"I can see the Bioluminescence, all along the line. Look."

As I looked along the line, sure enough I could see little bursts of blue light occurring right along the cork line.

"I'm going to start taking in the net now," he commanded. "You row backwards carefully down the line."

I got my oars ready and attempted to slowly push us stern first toward shore. It was more difficult than I imagined, but slowly I made progress. Hamish was pulling in the net which made it easier to stay in line. As he came to each fish, he carefully disentangled the gills of the fish from the net. Then threw the salmon into the bottom of the boat. By the time we had reached the end of the net, there were a dozen floundering fish in the belly of the boat. It was a beautiful sight, it made me very pleased that I had helped bringing in the catch.

By the time we had rowed back to shore, which was where we had started off, not the caravan bay; Hamish had transferred all the fish to his rucksack. It was one of those frame types of rucksacks, he lugged it onto his back, and we jumped out the boat and hauled the boat up the gravel, beyond the squelchy seaweed. Hamish tied the boat line to the chain that had been tethered to the shore.

"Now it's a'way to our beds," he said. "I'll call round Sunday morning about nine and we can get the smoker fired up."

"Sounds good. See you then," I said waving goodbye.

By now, I was very tired but strangely fulfilled, as I very gratefully headed back to my own warm bed.

Sunday morning came around. My arms and back were still a little stiff from all the rowing. As I jumped into Hamish's van, the smell of fish overwhelmed me; I quickly wound down my window.

"Great smell ehh?" said Hamish with a big grin. "Mingin."

"Yeh lovely," said I sarcastically. We both laughed.

It was early Sunday morning; Hamish had called round as promised. I hadn't quite caught up on lost sleep from our fishing trip but felt strangely excited, by my change in routine.

Off we went down the hill and onto the coast road, the MOD had built for the base. Hamish turned and headed in the direction of the base. I had come this route twice a day for a couple of years now, so knew it quite well. We went through a couple of very small villages, hamlets really, no churches or pubs. In the distance, I could see the imposing view of Knockderry Castle, built of a rocky outcrop. I had been there several times. It had a hotel bar and did a nice meal and bottle of wine; there were no pubs on this isolated peninsular.

We continued along the road a way, then Hamish suddenly pulled into the castle driveway, I hadn't expected this.

"You don't live here, do you?" I asked incredulously.

In answer, Hamish just turned his head and beamed at me, enjoying my astonishment. We continued up the drive, the beautiful round towers with the conical roofs, looked like a Scottish laird's castle. My mind was buzzing with possible scenarios. I had heard all sorts of tales about eccentric Scottish lairds but could not bring myself to believe that Hamish....

We drove through the empty castle carpark, down a little road round the back of the castle, then through an open five bar gate, then up into the forest behind. We continued up a bumpy forest track, taking several turn offs, eventually coming to a lovely little cottage, surrounded by forest.

"Here we are," said Hamish and looked over at me.

"You know for a minute there, I almost believed you lived in the castle." We both laughed and got out the car. Hamish took me round the back of the cottage, it had stone walls and a slate roof, it looked very old.

At the back, was a lean-to woodshed with a neat pile of chopped logs and large plastic rain barrel in a corner.

"I brine the fish first over night with water, sugar, salt and other secret flavourings," said Hamish, as he pointed to the barrel. "Then it's off to the smoker."

I looked in the barrel it was full of mirky whitish water and several scaley fish showed close to the surface. There was an over whelming smell of fish.

"Before we start, let's get a brew on," said Hamish, as we walked towards the back door.

"Is this your cottage?" I asked, not quite sure what to think.

"It was my grandfather's place; he was employed years ago, as game keeper here at the castle. He used to keep the forest stocked with pheasant and grouse on the moor at the top. He also was responsible for the gillnets down in the loch."

By now we had moved into the kitchen, it was like something from a Victorian museum. The stone sink with a wooden draining board. A big old scrubbed wooden table in the centre of the room. An old black range, with big black oven doors and plate racks above it. There were several paraffin lamps around the room, so I guessed the cottage had no electricity. The walls were whitewashed, and the floor was old red quarry tiles, most were cracked. It was quite amazing really.

The only concession to modern living, was a cast iron, two burner gas stove, set on an old cupboard. Hamish went over to it and lit a ring and set the kettle on it.

"I only light the range in the winter," he explained. "It heats the place up lovely."

"You were telling me about your grandfather," I reminded him.

"Yes, he was very loyal to the laird," Hamish continued, "and good at his job. I think my grandfather and him were old friends. When the old laird died, the family moved away. Back to Glasgow, I think. The castle lay empty for years, my grandfather just stayed on as a sort of live-in caretaker.

"When the hotel people bought the castle, my grandfather provided them with smoked salmon, rabbits and pheasant, so they let him stay on."

By now, we were sipping our mugs of hot tea, sitting on hard back chairs round the big kitchen table. I was fascinated by this glimpse of how people used to live years ago. And how they could create arrangements, that didn't involve working in an office or big factory somewhere.

"So how did you get to be here?" I asked, genuinely interested.

"Well, I was never much good with the stuff they taught at school, so I used to come up here and see my grandfather. He used to take me out snaring rabbits, shooting pheasants and he taught me to net the salmon. I loved it, couldn't get enough of it. Ended up hardly going to school at all.

"Anyways, when I was about sixteen, I was having a hard time at home. Dad was coming home drunk all the time. There were lots of arguments between dad and me, we ended up fighting on the kitchen floor." Hamish stared into his mug, looking a bit sad with the memory of it all.

"So, in the end," he continued, "I moved up here with grandfather. When he died, I just took over doing what he was doing." He was looking about him now, at all the things in his domain.

"I don't pay any rent; I do all the repairs myself. I let the hotel have all the smoked salmon and rabbits they need. It works out well for us all."

I was truly fascinated by his life and how he worked it. I had been brought up by parents and school, to believe that the only way to live, was to do well at school, sit exams, get your bits of paper and work for someone who paid you wages.

It was a real awakening to me, to realize that it was possible to have a life outside of all that, if you were prepared to make compromises.

"Anyway, enough of all this," Hamish said loudly, shaking me from my reverie. "We've got fish to smoke. Come on finish your tea and outwith." Before I knew it, he was out the kitchen door; I followed behind like a lost puppy.

"So, like I said, I brine the salmon overnight," Hamish continued, standing over the barrel of brine. "Now we need to fillet the fish and leave the skin on, so that you have two halves connected." With this he grabbed a large salmon out of the barrel and took it to another shelter that had an old stainless sink and tap and a marble slab beside it.

Slapping the fish on the slab, I could see it had been gutted, headed, and tailed before it went into the brine. He grabbed a knife from a rack on the wall and started cutting the fish into slivers.

"What we do is hang them, skin side towards each other over the wooden skewer, like this," Hamish deftly placed the fillet on the skewer. "That's something you can do while I cut the fish, that needs a bit more skill." He handed me the skewer with the bit of fish hanging from it.

"As I cut, you hang the fillets over the skewer. When its full, we then let it dry in that rack over there," he nodded towards a board with lots of holes drilled in it. "It dries in a breeze until the pellicle forms."

"The … what? The pel...what?" I asked like a poor student.

"Before the fish are cold smoked," Hamish stated patiently. "They must be allowed to air-dry, to form a tacky outer layer, known as a pellicle. The pellicle plays a role in producing a better smoke, as it acts as a protective barrier for the food and also plays a role in enhancing the flavour and colour produced by the smoke."

"Oh, I see," I said untruthfully.

Hamish continued cutting the fillets and I hung the fish and put them in the rack, to dry.

After a few hours hard work, my hands were freezing, but we had hung to dry, all the fish from the barrel.

"So, what do we do now?" I asked feeling cold and hungry.

"Why, we warm our hands of course," he turned and walked over to the end of the garden, which backed onto the forest behind. Here was another woodshed full of wood, and next to it was what looked to me, like a wooden outside toilet. There was an old, black, oil drum with a silver flue pipe attached, that went into the bottom of the wooden shed, toilet thing.

"That wooden toilet," said Hamish reading my mind, "is the smoke box." He opened the door, inside was black with soot, but I could just see a series of bars all the way down from the top; so I guessed this is where he hung the fish.

"But at the moment we need to get the fire going, so it can burn down enough, so we can create the right smoke." He turned to the black oil drum: it had a little door cut into the side of it; Hamish opened it.

"My mate Charlie helped me out with this, he's a welder, works in a garage in Helensburgh. Made me a lovely wood stove from this oil drum." As he was saying this, he was feeding old newspaper and forest litter into the door of the stove. Then he lit it with his zippo lighter. As it started to catch, he fed in small twigs from the woodshed.

"Feel that," he said placing his hands close to the metal of the oil drum. I did the same, the drum was starting to heat up, my freezing cold hands appreciated the warmth.

"Ah, lovely," I said, "that's a bit better."

"Oh aye, isn't it just? Mind', you should be here when its Baltic," Hamish laughed. "Ok while that's burning down let's get some breakfast."

Back in his kitchen, before long, toast was cooking under the grill of his two-burner stove, the bacon was sizzling away in a big frying pan. After our hard work with the fish, the smell was tantalising.

While Hamish cracked eggs into the same pan, I asked if I should get the plates. He pointed over to an old Welsh dresser, where there were some plates on a shelf and after investigating the draws, I found some bone handled knives and forks.

"Wow these look old," I said. "They're antique, aren't they?"

"Yeah, they're whale bone. My grandfather found them in the old castle when it was left empty; years old they are. When I was a kid, he used to tell me stories he had heard about the whaling industry in Scotland. It was pretty much the main industry at one time. Apparently, there used to be a lot of Norwegian whaling ships, coming into Scottish ports. There was all sorts of tales of what they used to get up to."

"It's criminal what they did to the whales," I declared. "I think the whole thing is too gross to think about. I'm so glad they stopped doing it here in Scotland."

"Yeh, the whole thing was pretty bad," Hamish agreed. "But I think that things like old fur coats and those whale bone knives need to be treasured. An animal died for this to be made, I think it's a great sin to throw them away or burn them, like some people try to do."

"Yes, we need to treasure them now that they exist," I said looking down at the beauty and craftsmanship of the bone handled knives. "And we need to thank the animal when we use them too," I heard my self say and wasn't quite sure where it had come from. It wasn't something I usually said. But felt my-self changing, just by being in the presence of this young fisherman.

After breakfast we went outside to check the smoker. While Hamish was checking the fire, I went over and looked at the salmon drying in the stiff breeze, they seem to have dried out and the surface looked shiny.

"How is the fire?" I shouted over to Hamish.

"Coming on nicely now, there's a good bed of red coals. I'm ready to put the oak chunks in now, so you can start bringing over the salmon from the drying racks."

I obediently started bringing over the skewers laden with the dried salmon, while Hamish loaded them into the smoker. Before long, we were ready to throw on the oak chunks onto the hot coals.

I looked into the fire and saw the cosy glow of the red coals. As Hamish threw on the oak pieces, the smell of the burning oak wafted up to me, it was a beautiful smell, somehow reminiscent of winter nights sat round the fire.

"So how long does the fish need to smoke for Hamish?" I asked.

"About an hour and they will be ready. Then I need to take them down to the hotel kitchen, they have a big refrigerator I set up in a shed at the back. As I have no electricity here, that's where I bag them too.

"Right that's enough wood chips," he declared. Let's get another tea going and you can be on your way back home."

Chapter 5

Conversation and Whisky

All this, distil. And cask. And wait.
The senselessness of human things resolves
to who we are – our present fate.
Let's taste, let's savour and enjoy.
Let's share once more.
Another glass for absent friends. Pour
until the bottles done.

Ron Butlin

The old black range, with the big black oven doors and plate racks above it, was fired up creating a pleasant warmth in the fisherman's kitchen. Around the room a couple of paraffin lamps burnt with a yellow light, adding to the cosy feeling of the room.

It was late autumn and Hamish and I had become firm friends by now. He often visited us at our house and always brought us some complementary seafood. So, I thought it about time I visited his cottage again.

We were sat at the big old, scrubbed wooden table in the centre of the room. On it a bottle of Famous Grouse, with two fingers left in the bottom. I had brought it over, to thank Hamish for all the seafood he had brought us, in recent months.

Of course, he had opened it straight away and poured us both a glass, a welcome warmer on this chilly, damp evening, he had said. But it hadn't stopped there.

I was now imbued with that inner warmth and glow that only whisky could provide.

It loosened tongues as well.

"…In my own way, I am as different from the folk at the base as you are," I said, feeling a little maudlin. I had been explaining to Hamish that I was not happy with my work situation.

"I don't feel I can fit in there," I moaned. "I'm a stranger here too," I continued, fingers wrapped round my empty glass, staring into the bottom, as if I could find some answer there.

"On this peninsula I mean. No matter how long I live here or how long I try to fit in, the locals won't accept me. I will always be a newcomer, a stranger."

Hamish casually shared out the last of the bottle, his hand wavering, almost missing his glass and dribbling a few drops on the table, then he placed the empty bottle on the old red quarry tiles at his feet.

"I get lonely and so I reach out to you," I bleated. "Because I feel that despite appearances I have more in common with you, than any of them at the base."

I took a small sip from my glass, and continued, "I don't have any friends, you're the closest thing I have to a friend."

Hamish just looked at me patiently, allowing me to talk it out; but was that a look of pity I could see in his eye?

"You know, I envy you Hamish," I continued. "You seem to belong here, to fit in with your surroundings. I have never felt I belong anywhere, not even in Liverpool, not even the town

I was born in. I always felt a stranger there. I was a physics geek, in a world of football crazies. I was into maths and drawing lay lines on maps. While every other boy was into football or dating girls; I would be out walking in the country, following the lays discovering stone circles, standing stones and fairy forts."

"Fairy forts, you say," said Hamish suddenly, with an odd look in his eye. "Ye want to be careful with them now, in case one of the unseelie court catches sight of you."

"Unseelie?" I queried, suddenly drawn out of my maudlin rant. "What's that?"

"That's the unblessed court, the bad malevolent fairies. If you see them before they see you, you're ok. But if they see you first, it could be very dangerous. They can drag you into the underworld and never be seen again."

"Oh, come on, that's just foolish superstition," I blurted.

"I tell you, there's a Fairy fort up on the hill behind here. A few years back, I was up near there; it was All Hallows Eve, and I was out checking my rabbit snares. It was just coming up to dusk when I looked up at the fort and saw a whole host of them trooping along. There was ladies in long gowns on horses, all glowing they were and little children with wings skipping round their feet. I had shivers going up and down my back, I did.

"I found myself frozen to the spot, I couldn't move, the whole time they were there; till they disappeared into the Fairy fort. I tell you; I keep clear of that place now."

I was speechless, I really couldn't decide whether he was just telling a tall tale, or the honest truth.

"I guess I was lucky they were from the Seelie court," he continued. "You know, the aristocratic trooping fairies; they can be compassionate to humans, and always repay a human kindness."

"Do you really believe in all that stuff Hamish," I quizzed him.

"My grandfather did for sure. He used to tell me about the time, back when he was a young man, he found a Selkie maid on the tide line. She had got caught up in one of his salmon lines and was in a bad way, as the tide was going out and she wanted to return to the water.

"My grandfather said, she was the most beautiful creature he had ever seen. She was a young maid, completely naked, he said, with long flowing green hair. Her skin was glistening and multi coloured like a salmons. He said, he just stood there staring at her, couldn't believe his eyes, till she called out to him, pleading for his help. Then he quickly ran over and cut her free from the net with his fishing knife.

"She was so grateful, that Selkie maid, she kissed him right on the lips, he said. Then she quickly picked up her seal skin and ran back into the water. My grandfather said he would never forget that kiss, as long as he lived.

"But you know, he told me, it was uncanny, that after that, his nets were always full of salmon, every time he put them out. It's a funny thing, I've inherited his nets and boat and I've always found the same."

"Well, you certainly got a good catch when we went out together," I said, still not sure what to believe.

"You know," he confided, leaning on the table towards me, "I've not told anyone else this but, you know I told you about my dad being a drunkard, an' all that?"

"Yes, I remember you telling me, I'm so sorry about that."

"Well," he said waving away my sympathy. "I never told you why that was. See, as a young man he used to go out fishing with his da', my grandfather. But one night my dad had to go out on his own, I think my grandfather had the flu or something. Anyways, apparently when he went back to check his nets, he found the selkie maid dancing under the light of the full moon, on the shore, beside his netting anchor. She was a beautiful maid, naked and shiny like my grandfather had told me. Course, my dad knew the tale, as my grandfather had told him also; so, my dad knew what she was, straight away.

"But on seeing her for himself, he was overtaken by desire. So, you know what he did?"

"No," I said, shaking my head, eager for him to continue his tale.

"He quickly runs up and sweeps up her seal skin, then runs off, back to his cottage. She of course, wanting her seal skin back, immediately runs after him. By the time she gets to the cottage, my dad had hidden her seal skin on the way.

"The selkie maid was now trapped. My dad goes up to her and kisses her and says, 'Your now my wife'. The selkie maid knowing she is trapped, reluctantly consents to be his wife."

Hamish gets up from the table, leaving me hanging on the edge of my seat, waiting for the end of the story. He opens the fire box and throws in a couple of dry logs. A great back draught of smoke belches into the room, rising to the ceiling. Then saying nothing, he sits down again in his seat.

"So, what happens then?" I prompt, impatiently.

Hamish was looking at me with his foxy face and half a smirk; the expression I had come to know so well.

"Well?" I say prompting him again.

"My dad and the Selkie maid," he continues at last, "stay together for many years. They even have two children together my sister and …."

"Noooo!........no way?" I exclaimed unbelieving, sudden realisation dawning.

Hamish, on the other side of the kitchen table, is just looking at me with a peculiar smirk on his foxy face. Then slowly, he lifts up his hand with his palm facing me and spreads his fingers. There, in the dim yellow lamp light, I could see small webs of skin going between his fingers. Its largest web is between his thumb and index finger.

I just stare at his hand, in disbelief. I am suddenly aware that my mouth is open, so snap it shut quickly. I'm shaking my head now, in shocked disbelief, unable to think of anything to say.

"Do you want to see my feet?" he says, I can see he is enjoying my consternation.

I'm still shaking my head in shock, as Hamish takes his boot off anyway and thumps his dirty foot on the table. There are webs of skin between his toes as well; if anything, even more pronounced.

"What happened to your sister?" I say stupidly, feeling I needed to say something.

"Oh, she's a nurse now in Dumbarton. She seems happy there," says he flatly.

"So ….so you mum was a…?"

"Yep."

I'm incredulous. Stunned. Still, stupidly shaking my head.

"What happened to her? The selkie maid I mean," I said still feeling I needed more.

"Well, it's a tragedy really. My dad fell hopelessly in love with his Selkie maid. He was actually very happy for years. But one night while my dad was out fishing, I was only about five or six at the time; she just disappeared. My dad guessed that she must have somehow, found her seal skin and went back to the sea. Poor bugger never got over it, he was heartbroken. In the end he turned to drink. But the drink got him in the end, as I said."

I was still shocked, 'a tragic tale indeed', I thought.

Hamish is putting on his boot again. 'He looks a little shaken by his own tale', I thought, 'must be bringing back sad memories'.

"I think, this calls for a dram of the good stuff," he suddenly declares, standing up and walking over to a cupboard, that's built into the stone wall of the cottage. He brings back a bottle and places it carefully on the table.

I lean forward, unsteadily in my seat and peer at it. It certainly seemed like an unusual bottle, it was well rounded and had a waist like a woman's body. The liquid in it was dark like a rum. But what strikes me most is the silver symbol above the label. It was an Ankh, an Egyptian symbol. I knew it was, as I had seen similar symbols of silver, made into necklaces in Indian markets, along with patchouli oil and Indian prints.

But what was it doing on this bottle? I looked more closely at the label. 'Jura Superstition' and 'SINGLE MALT SCOTCH WHISKY'.

"Ah! So it's another bottle of whisky," I said, slurring my words a bit.

"Well spotted," says Hamish a little sarcastically. "But not just *any* whisky. And what's in there, is not what's on the label either," he said with a wink rather mysteriously.

"How do you mean?" I asked intrigued.

"Do you want a taste?" He teased.

"Yes, I'd love to try it."

"Well, you need to hear the history of it first. Because you see, back in the days when the Laird was in the castle here, he was friends with the Laird of Jura. In fact, they were comrades in arms; they both served together in the Highlanders.

"After they left the army, the Laird of Jura, used to send his buddy, in the castle here, a very special single malt whisky. So rare was it, that they didn't sell it publicly, it was the 'Special Reserve' of the Laird of Jura. This secret recipe would, in later years become known as 'Camas an Staca'.

"Anyway, what the Laird of Jura didn't know about, was that some of the Campbell lads working in the distillery, had been stashing away a secret trove of their own. You see during the distilling process of the 'very special reserve', only the 'pure centre cut', the 'heart of the run', the distillates, go on to the 'spirit safe', which even then was controlled by the Customs & Excise.

"The foreshots, and the final runnings have impurities and so are run off and usually recycled through the distiller. But the lads were running some of it off for themselves and taking it to a 'cottage still' up in the hills, that nobody knew about. They were making their own 'special reserve' up in the hills, calling it 'Uisge Beatha'. Storing it in rum barrels that had washed up from a shipwreck, which was fairly common off the Scottish islands.

"Well, sadly the Laird lost all his money and then the distillery collapsed. The lads secret trove, in a cave, up in the hills was never discovered, as only a very few people knew about it. When the distillery collapsed, people moved away or died, the trove was almost forgotten.

"Well, that was over fifty years ago. I can happily say that in recent years, the Isle of Jura distillery has started producing again. Now the Jura whisky salesman, who happened to be the grandson of one of the original crew, who had stashed the secret trove and a Campbell himself, like my grandfather and me, started coming to the hotel.

"When he met my grandfather in the castle grounds, they got talking friendly like. My grandfather invites him back to this cottage for a whisky session. Well, I comes knocking on the door looking for my grandfather, I must have been only about nineteen at the time, they invite me in for a taster.

"As we are drinking, the Campbell salesman notices my finger webs and points them out, brazen like. My grandfather looked a bit affronted by this, but the salesman just lifts up his hand and spreads his fingers, displaying his own webs. Both of us just looked at his hand in shock, not thinking there could be another like me.

"Well, we tell him our story, and he tells us his, which was remarkably similar in many ways. Then he says to us, 'Well I'll tell ye what, next time I come, I will bring you a bottle of some very special whisky. A secret stash'. Then he tells us the story of its making, like I've just told you.

"True to his word, when he came again, some months later, he brought us this bottle. Unfortunately, by the time he came again my grandfather had just died; so sadly, he never got to taste it."

Hamish was staring at the bottle on the table, I thought he looked a little sad, perhaps reminiscing about his lost grandfather. Perhaps reluctant to open the bottle. A minute, or so went by and still he was staring at the strange bottle.

Then suddenly, he seems to pull himself out of it and announces in a stage voice, like he was announcing a famous band:

"Jura Superstition is a good single malt. But this … this is one of the very last bottles left, of that original 'secret stash' of 'Camas an Staca' reworked as 'Uisge Beatha', 50-Year-Old Single Malt Scotch Whisky."

Hamish stands up and fetches out of the cupboard two, single shot glasses, banging them on the table. Then, ever so carefully, poured me a single measure, without spilling a drop.

Looking in the glass, I could see it was much darker than other whiskeys I had had. I lifted the glass to my nose, it smelled sweet and exotic like the oranges and tropical fruit, I had smelled in the markets of Morocco. Yet there was an under tone, not unlike the burning oak from Hamish's cold smoker.

With reverence, I brought the glass to my lips and took a tiny sip; it was rich with subtle flavours. Yes, the zest of orange was there, but more like chocolate orange. Exotic spices came through, mixed with morello cherry. But overall, it was so smooth, no nasty kick of fiery spirit. I took another sip, enjoying the roller coaster of flavour that came through, one after the other. It left me with a malty, orange peel zest.

I was starting to feel its warmth, slowly manifesting in my belly and spreading. Accompanied by, not a heady drunkenness, but a delightful sense of euphoria and wellbeing.

All the while, Hamish's foxy eyes were watching me, waiting to see my reaction. I took the final sip to finish the glass, it was so delicious I wanted more. I could feel its warmth working from my belly, up into my chest, it was like an inner fire. I looked over again at Hamish, he hadn't drunk any yet, in fact he hadn't even poured his glass. He seemed content to continue watching my reaction.

The delicious warmth and wellbeing was washing over me, like I was wrapped in cotton wool, cosy and safe. No cares or worries. I looked around the room, everything here seemed to fit in with everything else. All was very practical but had a simple, honest beauty about it.

The whitewashed stone walls, the old red quarry tiles on the floor, the old black range with plate racks above it, all seemed to be from an age, when practicality and beauty came hand in hand. They had no airs and graces, were not pretending to be something else. They made modern homes and appliances, seem all front and no depth, somehow false gold, that would fade and crumble, almost before your eyes. They had no permanence. Unlike the stone walls and floor of this cottage, which had been around for four hundred years or more.

But there was something else, I was seeing beyond the simple, honest beauty of this cottage. I was grasping to name it, but the name eluded me. Then gradually through the fog of my mind, it came. Soul. This cottage, the whitewashed walls, the old black range, had soul. Or at least this was the closest word I could think of.

I looked back at Hamish, he was still watching me, so I watched him back. In the dim light of the paraffin lamp, his face seemed to morph into that of a fox. Yes, he was a survivor like a fox. He too had a practical, simple, and honest beauty about him. He fitted into this cottage, fitted his lifestyle, fitted his profession. Like the convoluted shape of a jigsaw piece, he fitted perfectly into the tapestry of his life.

So, unlike myself I thought. I did not fit into my life at all. I felt an alien in my workplace, an alien with my work colleagues, an alien in my modern house, none of it was me at all. Even my wife? No! I didn't want to go there. This was too painful. Too unsettling.

I quickly took up the bottle and poured Hamish a glass of his special whiskey. He obligingly took up the glass and sipped. A look of pure delight came over his face. He closed his eyes and lay his head back, in a sort of rapture. After a minute of two, he brought his head back straight and finished his glass. Then looked me straight in the eyes, he knew exactly where I was coming from. I asked him what it was, he could see in my face. But I was sorry I asked him, for he confirmed my worst fears.

"I see a man who is lost, one who doesn't know who he is, or what he wants from life. Your life is a contradiction to your soul." His face was serious, but I could see there was pity there too.

"How long have you known this?" I asked.

"From the first day I saw you," he said simply. "Its why I was drawn to you, in a way. I hoped I could show you another side to life."

"You did that for sure. I thank you for it," I affirmed.

"By the way," he said. "In your face … I can see a fox who is hunted by hounds. But there is a lion also, caged and waiting to be released."

***

'Looking back on that night of Whisky and Conversation, I was at first, taken aback by Hamish's straight talk…'

Touchwood stopped writing for a moment, to take a sip from his mug of warmed milk, with a generous shot of whiskey in it. It was getting cold but still tasted good, so he finished off the rest of the mug. Licking his lips, he wiped his whiskery mouth with his sleeve, picked up his pen and started writing again…

'So few people, I had met up until then, where so honest and straight as Hamish. It takes a true friend to be that honest, and I thank him so much for the honesty that had gifted me.'

'Afterwards, the realisation of what he told me dawned on me and made me very sad, for a while. But he had confirmed my worst fears. In many ways, I already knew it, but was too afraid to face it.'

'However, I didn't know it at the time, but fate was about to change things for the better.'

Chapter 6

Departure

Yes, there are two paths you can go by, but in the long run
There's still time to change the road you're on

Led Zeppelin

Some weeks later, it was a Saturday morning I recall, when I usually have a bit of a slept in. After a shower, I came down to make breakfast for the two of us. I enjoyed cooking breakfast on a weekend and Sarah enjoyed the break from cooking, while she had a lie in. I usually brought it up to her in bed.

I was just walking past the little table, with the telephone on it in the hallway. The telephone books were neatly placed under the phone as usual. But I noticed something else, it was a business card. Not thinking very much of it, I casually picked it up to see what it was. It was the card, of an Engineering section head, of one of the MOD contractor firms I had visited towards the end of my apprenticeship.

'That's odd', I thought, I remembered getting a dozen or so, similar cards from various section heads, of the many firms we had visited during that time. I had just stored them away and not thought about them again. It was years ago now, but how odd that this one, should turn up now. I had no idea what had happened to the others.

Curious, I took another look at the card, it read: C.J. Thomlinson, Section Head, Control Gear Engineering. It had the name of a MOD contractor firm in Bristol. They were involved mostly in computerised control gear, used in aircraft and shipbuilding. I remember the guy quite well and remembered him saying, 'if you get your qualifications from the MOD, I could almost guarantee you a job in this firm'.

'Hum', I wondered if the guy still worked there. I toyed with the idea, that this guy might be able to get me away from the base and down to Bristol; an area of the country I felt much more comfortable with.

On the spare of the moment, I decided to show Sarah, to see what she thought. I ran back up the stairs like an excited child.

"Sarah! Guess what I've found?"

"Where's my bacon and eggs?" she said sleepily.

"Did you find this card somewhere?" I asked her, presenting the card in front of her face.

She squinted sleepily at the card, "No, never seen it before. Where's breakfast?"

"Never mind that," I said holding up the card. "This is a guy from Bristol, who practically offered me a job in his firm, when I visited it a few years ago."

"Really?" I had piqued her interest. "It would be really good to get back down to Somerset and Wiltshire, I loved it round there."

"Thought you wanted to come to Scotland and settle down," I teased.

"I only wanted a home of my own. But although we have a house, I don't feel at home here. It's too far away from my roots in Liverpool."

"So, you wouldn't mind me contacting this guy, to see if he still has a job offer going?"

"Where did you find the card?"

"I told you, it was by the telephone. Are you sure you didn't put it there?"

She looked at the card again, "No, I definitely haven't seen it before."

"Well, it's a bit of a mystery how it got there, and a strange coincidence too. You know what? I'm going to ring him next Monday morning. No point in delaying."

"Yes, make sure you do. Now where's my bacon and eggs?"

Back to work on Monday, I rather cheekily called C.J. Thomlinson, the Section Head using the public phone in the tearoom. Unfortunately, someone else answered the phone. When I asked for C.J. Thomlinson, the guy paused a moment, then explained that he didn't work in this section anymore; my heart sank.

Then he went on to tell me, that Mr. Thomlinson, had been promoted a year ago, to Head Engineer and that I would need to make an appointment to speak to him, through his secretary. Unfortunately, he wasn't able to transfer me, I would have to go through the switchboard.

Hum, that didn't go as well as I'd hoped. I thought about it a moment and realised that he probably would be too busy on a Monday morning, and the best thing to do would be to call him the next day.

"Sarah! Sarah!" I called as I came through the front door; it was Tuesday evening.

"I'm in the kitchen," she called.

"Guess what? That guy from Bristol, I was telling you about. I rang him today and he said he could definitely use a guy with my qualifications. He said it was a strange coincidence, that only last week, one of his engineers had suddenly handed in his notice. They hadn't even had time to advertise the position yet. He said, if I was willing to come for an interview at short notice, and they liked me, they may not even need to."

"Wow, that's encouraging. When's the interview?"

"Friday!"

***

Touchwood looked down on the bowl of steaming vegetable stew, his lovely granddaughter had just brought in for him. Of late she seemed to have lost interest in his reading to her. Apparently, she had been meeting with a boy, from the nearby village and was out a lot more. But that was part of the natural cycle of things, he thought, and there was no point in wishing otherwise.

Although, he was a little saddened by this development, he remembered he was a young man once. Besides, on reflection, if he was to be honest, there was much in his past history that would, let us say ... not be suitable to ears ... that were so young.

He regretted nothing he had done. But sometimes on a magical path there was a means to an end, and we performed rituals that, to the average man in the street, could be …. misconstrued and misinterpreted.

But I am getting ahead of myself, all that was to come…

'…. So, it was a very strange coincidence finding that card by my telephone. It was somehow, almost like it was a message to ring the number. It was odd too, that there had suddenly become a vacancy, the previous week.'

'It all seemed to happen so quick, I didn't even have time to dry-clean my interview suite. The interview went well, Thomlinson had remembered me, from when I had visited before. Said he thought I was a 'very bright lad', even then.'

'In a way the interview seemed like a formality, as there were no other candidates. They asked me to wait in the outer room where his secretary worked, while he discussed it with his section head. I had barely finished my coffee, provided by his secretary, when they called me back in. "How soon can you start?" was the first question they asked.'

'Before I knew where I was, only a month later, I was in temporary digs in Bristol and working at the new job. I barely had time to say my farewells to Hamish, who didn't seem at all surprised at my sudden departure'.

'It was also during my first weeks in Bristol, that another painful and disturbing event happened. I discovered my wife Sarah, had been seeing another man, from her workplace in Faslane. She told me, that she had decided not to come down to be with me in Bristol, after all. And that we should try for separation. The shock of this revelation could not be overstated.'

'*Within a matter of weeks my whole world was turned upside-down. Everything seemed to change all at once. Looking back now, it certainly seemed to be a very fated time. A clearing out of my life, ready for new things to come.*'

Chapter 7

Silbury Hill

We all dance to a mysterious tune,
intoned in the distance by an invisible piper.
Albert Einstein

I was awoken by a chorus of wild chanting. It was very dark; I was cold. I sat up and found myself lying amongst long grass on the earth. The chanting was getting louder, my curiosity buzzing, I crept up out of the dip I was in and peered through the long grass, over to the other side of the mound. What I saw was a strange sight.

There stood seven naked women, illuminated by the flickering fire light of a bonfire. One held up a long sword. My heart began to pound so loudly in my ears, that I was afraid they would hear me. I held by breath, not daring to move. These were witches! I could see that now.

***

Touchwood put his pen down, stroking his silver beard as he read over what he had written. 'Yes, that's how it was,' he thought to himself, then he continued writing …

'Now, I had found myself back in South-West England again. Wessex, a wonderful place with an extraordinary accumulation of megalithic monuments to explore. It seemed to me, in a way, my life was fated, almost out of my control. It had rendered me a single man again, with plenty of time to continue mapping and exploring ley lines.'

'I had visited Silbury Hill several times in the past and always found it an extraordinary place. I had originally discovered it, while drawing ley lines on my OS maps and notice there where several lines converging at that point. So, I had resolved to visit as soon as possible and see what was there. I wasn't disappointed. It had fast become one of my favourite megalithic sites to visit ...'

***

This particular visit I arrived later than usual; as I had been working during the day. The steep climb to the summit was starting to take its toll on my body. However, it was a lovely late summers evening, warm and very still; And the sun was low in the sky like a great golden balloon.

Once on the top, I shaded my eyes and gazed across the calcareous grassland; it seemed to go on for ever. Nowhere was entirely flat, it was a rolling landscape, with gentle undulations of green and ripening cereal crops. Few hedges or trees interrupted the flow of the grasslands. It was a lazy sort of evening, and I was tired from the day, so I thought I would lie down and rest awhile. At the far side of the flat summit, I found a shallow dip and lay in the long grass. Looking up at the blue, blue sky; it was so peaceful and quiet but not silent; for a soft breeze rustled the long grass, where insects buzzed or chirped. It was bliss.

High in the blue, the sweet chime of a lark singing, now above, now far away. Gradually I was becoming aware of the strong earth's energy, healing me; I closed my eyes and relaxed deeply...

I must have fallen asleep, for I was gently awoken by singing. It was now dusk, and the singing sounded like a small choir of about six women. I couldn't hear the words properly, but it had a beautiful rhythm, which seemed to be repeating over and over.

Curiosity overcame me, so I crept up out of the dip, which I found myself in, and peered through the long grass, over to the other side of the mound. What I saw was a strange sight indeed. There were about six or seven figures singing beautifully. They were in silhouette, as the lingering twilight was behind them. Clearly, they didn't know I was there, and I didn't want to disturb them.

They seemed to be women, as they wore long dresses or robes and clearly most had long hair, flowing down their backs. The singing had stopped now, and there was a strange silent anticipation.

One figure now held up what seemed to be a sword, while she was loudly declaring something, and walking round the others. Then another figure, more petit, held up some sort of cup or chalice, holding it up to the sky, making her declaration, in a high-pitched girl's voice. Now she was pouring some of the liquid it contained, onto the ground.

I was fascinated. What was going on here? I wanted to hear the words. I wanted to crawl nearer, but was afraid they would see me, if I crawled out of the dip.

There were more words spoken, by some of the other women, so low I couldn't hear. Then suddenly a fire torch was alight, and was used to light a small bonfire, that I hadn't seen was there. It instantly caught and burned brightly, illuminating the figures; I could see now, that they were clearly woman; wearing cloaks of various colours.

Most looked to be in their early thirties, but one, the lady with the sword, was older, but seemed to have that ageless quality, so was hard to tell. She had dark red hair, plaited, and tied at the back. She now spoke out some words in a commanding voice; then the cloaks were dropped to the ground.

There stood, seven naked women, illuminated by the flickering fire light. My heart began to pound so loudly in my ears, that I was afraid they would hear me. I held by breath not daring to move. These were witches; I could see that now.

I wanted to leave immediately, in case I was discovered, anything could happen. But if I moved now, out of the cover of the long grass and the dip, I would surely be discovered. There was no other shelter on this treeless hilltop: I lay there transfixed by the scene unfolding before me.

The figures were now holding hands and had started another song. But it wasn't a song; it was a rhythmic chant, that seemed much harsher, than the singing earlier on. They had started to circle round the fire now, slowly at first, but building momentum. The chant gradually got faster and faster, as they raced round the fire.

It was a magnificent sight, seeing these powerful women, naked, racing round the fire. I could feel an energy building and building, I could hear them now, they were loudly screaming the words:

"Corn and grain, corn and grain,
All who fall shall rise again.
Hoof and horn, hoof and horn,
All who fall shall be re-born."

The chanting continued over and over, then seemed to reach some sort of crescendo, for they all suddenly stopped circling. Their screaming voices filled the night, their hands raised to the sky, then suddenly they all dived down to the earth, some on all fours and some lying flat on the ground.

I couldn't believe what I had witnessed. They were definitely witches. Slowly I crept back down into the dip, my heart thumping. I suddenly exhaled, for I found I had been holding my breath. Panting now, I lay on my back and looking up at the stars.

I was trapped. I would have to stay here, till they were gone. Looking up at the stars again, my mind started to wander. Surely there is more in heaven and earth than we can comprehend. What were they doing here and why here on Silbury Hill?

I had previously done some research on this megalithic site, apparently it is one of the most intriguing monuments, in the prehistoric landscape of a World Heritage Site, comprising of Stonehenge, Avebury stone circle and West Kennet barrow.

Silbury Hill, is in fact the largest artificial prehistoric mound in Europe, standing at some 30 metres high and some 160 metres wide; and thought to have been built, some 4500 years ago in the Neolithic and Bronze Age.

The original function of Silbury Hill, remains a mystery to science, to this day, although many speculations have been postulated.

At the same time Silbury Hill was built, the whole surrounding area saw intense building activity, when hundreds of people came together, to construct a variety of monuments. As well as Silbury Hill, there was the monumental Avebury Henge, which is over a mile across, together with smaller stone circles and avenues.

Additionally, round about the same time, two large oval enclosures were built at West Kennet farm, these being built out of massive timber posts, which now only survive as buried remains.

Together they all define, one of the richest and most varied areas, of Neolithic and Bronze Age ceremonial and ritual monuments in the country.

But why, was so much effort put into doing all this? When only bronze tools and antler picks where available. Some people have estimated that the equivalent effort today, would be that required to put a man on Mars!

This is no over estimation; it was a phenomenal feat. And beyond any of our modern-day comprehension. As to what they were all used for?

Then I heard that voice in my head, that I hadn't heard since I was a teenager, my guide. I thought he had gone forever…

"What you have been trying to comprehend, is the Great Plan, the 'Tao', the 'Great Dance of Shiva', which others call the 'Web' or the 'Wyrde'. It is simply: 'the Universal dance of nature.' It is and always has been perfect.

"*Some with weak and dark minds, would put themselves apart from it, standing as it where, on the outside, sometimes peering through a tiny crack in the curtain, like small children, not comprehending what they see.*

"*But we, all of us, dance the Great Dance. The dance which we dance, is at the centre and for the dance, all things where made. From the greatest galaxy to the tiniest speck of dust, hear in dwells the Great Spirit.*

"*The Great Spirit dwells within the seed, of the smallest flower and is not cramped, yet the whole universe, is inside her and she is not stretched.*

"*You, my friend, are a perfect being, of the humankind. Although your race appears to rule the earth, and it was for you that it was made, the worlds are for themselves. The sea you have never seen, the fruit you have never harvested, the fire through which your bodies can not pass, the mountain you cannot climb, do not wait for your coming, in order to be perfect; yet they will rejoice when you come.*

"*Only to the darkened mind, does all seem aimless and without plan, because there are more plans than it looked for. The Wyrde, the Web, the tapestry of life, is woven so closely, with fibres so fine, that unless a man looked long and closely at them, he would see neither threads nor weaving at all.*

"*What you have witnessed today, are people who are in tune with the 'Wyrde'. They don't question why? These women just know what they 'feel'. It feels right for them; it is the thing to do, so it is what they do.*

"*This is your path also, your destiny. Although I thought you had wandered away from it, the fates have brought you closer now, than you have ever been.*

"Lying on this dragon path, on this sacred hill, you have witnessed 'an Awakening'. This is your path also, follow it and be joyous…"

The voice went silent, for I must have fallen asleep again. I woke, freezing cold, in pitch-dark and silence. There was no moon, only the blanket of stars, blazing above me, gave me any indication that I was truly awake. I stood up looking around, wondering briefly where I was. I could see the few glowing embers from the bonfire, the only indication that the night revellers had been there. 'So, it was real,' I thought, 'what an experience.'

Getting down from the hundred-foot mound, in complete darkness was another; I would care not to repeat.

***

It was four o'clock in the morning, Touchwood was writing in his ledger by the light of a small lamp.

'… So, it was true then, I had been 'nudged' by the fates, to be in this unique area, to be once again on my spiritual path. Another thing my guide had made abundantly clear to me, I needed to find a teaching group, that could guide me on my spiritual path. One, I could work in and learn about the goddess and her ways. This was now my priority.'

Chapter 8

The Atlanteans

When all the leaves
Have fallen and turned to dust,
Will we remain
Entrenched within our ways.

The Dead Can Dance

'It was almost a year since my encounter on Silbury Hill. I had searched and searched hard for a spiritual group to teach me, but to no avail ...'

Touchwood stopped writing for a moment reflecting on that bitter time, so long ago, when he was so keen to find a mentor, but was also, it seemed to him at the time, eternally frustrated.

He continued writing.

'... I had found places that offered Buddhist retreats, and even a Hare Krishna temple. But these all seemed too eastern for me. I accept that there are many paths, to grow by. But I was only too aware, that to reach the goal of spiritual enlightenment, one has to follow the path with heart.'

'My heart was drawn to the Native Celtic perspective, the often 'secretive' and 'hidden' powers and philosophies and magic of my

native land. It was only later in my quest, that I learned that this included Paganism, Wicca and Druidry.'

'While one can agree with some parts of the philosophies, inherent in Eastern thought and see some correlation, between that and our Native Celtic path. I strongly felt that wholesale following of Eastern ways, can only lead us farther from our Celtic roots & spirituality.'

***

I was in a fit of despair. I thought I would never find likeminded people, or people to teach me about spiritual matters. In desperation, I was searching through the local paper, The Bristol Evening post. I was looking in the classified section for evening classes on photography, which was an interest of mine, when I noticed a curious advert, it said simply:

'Learn to meditate. Free classes.
Every Thursday 7:30pm. The Atlanteans.'

It gave a contact number to ring, for full details of the venue. I was intrigued. Didn't Atlantis fall beneath the waves thousands of years ago? What are they doing in Bristol giving meditation classes?

I had never meditated before, in fact, I wasn't even sure what meditation was. I had heard that it was something, Indian gurus did up in the Himalayas. Apparently, they could live in caves surrounded by snow and weren't affected by the cold.

I also knew that the Beatles went to see a guru in India, to learn to meditate, and they seemed to be quite successful. So, it must be good for you, so I was willing to give it a try. Besides, I was hoping to meet some spiritual people, that might help me start my spiritual journey.

I had to find out. I decided to ring the number straight away, to see what it was about.

A lady answered, she sounded mature and well educated. She wasn't giving much away but told me the address, and that they were meeting this coming Thursday.

"Would you be interested in coming?" she asked. "So I know to expect you."

"Yes," I confirmed, "I'm intrigued, and very interested in what you do."

After I hung up the phone I thought, 'Well, they don't sound completely nutty, so I'll go.' And somehow my mood was lifted. Indeed, I felt buoyant all the next day too.

When Thursday came, I was excited by the prospect of going to see the Atlanteans; whoever they were. But what do I wear? At work I wore a suit, so I was keen to get out of that. But I didn't want to be too casual either; (In those days, you have to remember that being too casual was a social faux pas.) In the end I settled on slacks and an old tweed jacket I had.

The venue was a big old house, up in Clifton. There wasn't any sort of sign outside, but the front door was open, and a light was on in the hallway. Inside there was a lecture easel with room numbers and who was using what room, on each night of the week. It informed me the Atlanteans where in room two, on the ground floor just to the left.

I stood in the doorway of room two, inside there was a very diverse group of people. Some were middle aged women, dressed in cardigans and knee length skirts. There was one guy who looked like he could have been a university lecturer; he had longish white hair, slicked back, a checkered jacket and a dickey bow. There were also several younger people, both men and woman. I would say of the age group, late twenties, or early thirties, dressed very casually in jeans and sweatshirts.

Some people were arranging hard back chairs, in a circle, while others were stood talking in a group. I decided to just get stuck into helping arrange the chairs.

As I was doing this, a young guy holding a chair said, "Hi, I haven't seen you before, welcome, my name is David"

"Oh hi, no this is my first time, my name is George."

We put the chairs down, finishing the circle and as people were starting to sit, we decided to sit also. I sat next to David and asked, "So what is this all about then?"

"Well, it's a nice group, very friendly," he said. "So just relax. I think you will see how we work very shortly, as I think we are about to begin."

Most people were seated by now, except for a couple of ladies arranging some cups, on a table in the corner.

"Welcome everybody," said a middle-aged lady who looked to be in charge of the meeting. "I see we have a couple of new faces tonight, so perhaps we should start with a quick round of names. So, I will begin. My name is Hattie."

People gave their names, in a clockwise direction, which of course I instantly forgot. Nervously I gave mine.

When we got back to Hattie she said, "So, let's start with some simple relaxation exercises and then follow with our meditation. Don't worry about what to do, just follow the instructions I give, and you will be fine."

Hattie continued in an efficient but kindly way. "Now do not cross your limbs. Loosen any tight clothing. Sit firmly in your chair, back straight feet firmly flat on the floor. Now close your eyes. Take a deeeeep breath in through your nose…. hold…...then breathe out through your mouth," here she paused a moment to allow us to follow.

"Repeat this for three breaths." I noticed her voice, gradually getting softer and slower.

"… In order to know how relaxation feels, we must first experience tension… We are going to tense all the muscles of our body, one by one, and keep them tense, until we relax our entire bodies with one breath. Don't clench the muscles so they cramp, just tense them lightly." Hattie continued in a hypnotic sort of voice, very soft extending the length of the word after each phrase.

"Start with your toes… Tense the toes in your right foot ... and now your left foot. Tense your right foot ... and you're left foot.

"Working your way up, tense your right ankle ... and your left ankle…. Continue throughout the whole body, part by part…"

Here, there was a long pause, while we all worked on relaxing bits of our bodies. It was actually harder than it sounds, but I guessed I would get used to it.

"From time to time," Hattie continued. "Remind yourself to tense any muscles that you have let slack…As we work our way up to our heads. Now tense your scalp…. Your whole body is tense … feel the tension in every part. Tense any muscles that have gone slack… Now take a deep breath … inhale … hold … exhale … and relax!

"Relax completely. Let every part of your body go limp. You are completely and totally relaxed. Your fingers are relaxed, and your toes are relaxed and so on, throughout the entire body.

"Keep saying to yourself, 'I am completely and totally relaxed…completely …and… totally relaxed.' Your body is light; it feels like water, like it is melting into the earth. Allow yourself to drift and float peacefully in your state of relaxation.

"If any worries or anxieties, disturb your peace, imagine they drain from your body like water and melt into the earth. Feel yourself being healed and renewed."

There was another pause for a minute or so. Then another voice came in, a man this time.

"It is good to practice this exercise daily, until you can relax completely, simply by sitting down and letting go, without needing to go through the entire process.

"People who have difficulty sleeping, will find this extremely helpful. However, do not allow yourself to drift off into sleep. You are training your mind to remain in a relaxed, but alert state. Later you will use this state for trance work, which will be much more difficult, if you are in the habit of nodding off.

"If you practice this at night before sleeping, sit up, open your eyes and consciously end the exercise, before going to bed."

The man, who I later found out, was called Adrian, continued in that hypnotic voice:

"Now imagine yourself in a beautiful meadow, full of wildflowers…. The sun is shining, you can feel it warm on your back. You can hear the birds singing and the gentle buzz of insects all around you…. you continue walking enjoying the peaceful surroundings… after a while you come to a peaceful lake… the water is gently rippling over a small gravel shore…. It is so warm and peaceful you decide to take off your shoes and socks and paddle in the cool water…. It just feels idyllic…." Here he paused for a moment then went on. "Now I want you to just explore, by yourself for a few minutes, enjoying your environment…"

I was really enjoying paddling in the lake, it was so cool and delicious, the tinny gravel stones seemed to massage my feet, as I walked along the water line. I could see several swans in the water, some way off and there was a heron standing on a dead tree that had fallen in the water; he was intently looking into the water for a fishy breakfast.

I have no idea, how long I was exploring the lake for, but was enjoying myself immensely. But gradually, I became aware of someone calling my name, from a long way off….

I stopped to listen… yes it was definitely calling my name… who was that I wondered. However, the voice started getting louder and more urgent. I could now feel a weight on my shoulder, I looked but nothing was there. Then the weight started wiggling my shoulder and the voice, very near now was saying, "George…George, time to come back to us."

Suddenly I was back in the Atlanteans room again, the lights were very bright. There was a group of people standing in the corner drinking tea, looking over at me. Adrian had his hand on my shoulder.

"Are you alright George? You're coming round now. Jez, you were dug in like a tick. You went very deep. Are you sure you haven't done this before?"

I was still a bit dreamy, but I was slowly coming round.

"Err… Hattie," Adrian sounder a little concerned. "Can we have a cup of tea over here, put in plenty of sugar."

Someone brought over a teacup and put it in my hands. Shakily I accepted it.

"Wow! I think you must be a natural, to have gone that deep first-time round." This was Adrian, bent over me, who I now saw was the lecturer with the bow tie. He still had his hand on my shoulder, it felt warm and comforting, very reassuring; he seemed like a father figure. He then straightened up and went behind me and placed his hands on my shoulders. I could feel a glowing warmth infusing into my shoulders. It felt very healing and reassuring.

"I'm sending you some healing, to balance you up," said Adrian.

I was enjoying the steady warmth, flowing into me, it did feel good. Apparently, this was a fairly normal state of affairs, as everyone else was chatting and drinking tea, not even noticing me anymore.

I went home that night, feeling sure I had encountered something very different, than my everyday experiences. They seemed, a very different type of people, than the average people you meet in the street or at work. Still glowing from the healing I was given; I was also very pleased to have clearly tapped into something spiritual; and found likeminded people.

Their meetings became a regular weekly occurrence for me. In them I was taught how to meditate and how to control the depth I went to, and to be in control of the situation.

I also discovered that I had an aptitude for seeing people's auras; we had regular training sessions. The person instructing, said at first it was easier to 'feel' a person's aura. In pairs, we stood face to face, placing the palms of our hands, about two feet away from the top of the person's head. Then gradually you move your hands towards them. At about six to eight inches away, you will recognize a tiny fluffy effect. The slightest resistance, like when you bring two magnets together of the same pole.

Keeping that distance, slowly move your hands down their body and around the entire body. All the time sensing and feeling that resistance, which varies from place to place. This is the electromagnetic energy, of the body's aura.

Then dimming the lights and lighting candles, we repeated the exercise, but this time with the person backing a white painted wall, this made it easier to view a person's aura. When you're feeling it with your hands, it's easier to learn to view it as well.

The instructor explained that the aura colours, are visible only to a minority of people. The aura consists of seven main colours: red, orange, yellow, green, blue, indigo, and violet. Some people can't see any colours, others only a few colours.

It seemed, that once I had been, 'awakened', to the possibility of seeing auras, I was able to see them at will, in a variety of situations. I was told it was just a matter of raising you vibration to accommodate this new sense.

From time to time, we would have a guest speaker, who would talk to us about an esoteric subject. We had people coming to us from a wide range of disciplines like: Yoga, Alchemy, Anatman Buddhism, Astrology, Egyptian Atenism, Buddhism, Hinduism, ley lines, dowsing, energy healing, tribal shamanism, channelling, Spirit world of fairies and Elementals.

I found most interesting, the guy that talked to us about shamanism. He had been studying and living with a South American tribe in the rainforest. He brought a series of colour slides to show us and talked about how they lived, and what they believed in; it was truly fascinating.

The reader must understand of course, that at that time, there was no such thing as the internet, or indeed very little of these topics on T.V. either. So, these talks where, to me, unique and it opened my eyes to a whole world of esoteric teachings and possibilities, that I had previously no idea existed.

Although I was educated in electronic engineering, which required a person to be very logical and scientific; unusually, I also had a very deep spiritual thirst, which needed quenching. I became very interested in Spiritual healing, as since that first day when Adrian was healing me, I could feel that there was definitely something to it.

I talked to Adrian about this, and he seemed delighted at my interest. And told me that, perhaps I should come along to one of their private, healing sessions, at their teaching centre outside of town. I enthusiastically affirmed I would love to attend and asked how I make that happen. He told me he would have a word with Hattie and would contact me with a time when I could come.

***

    'I remember on the drive home that night….'
Wrote Touchwood, by hand into his ledged book.
    '… I was reflecting on this new and secret world I had discovered. Oh, how excited I was to have found myself a part of it. But even better, Adrian's invitation, I felt, would bring me into some sort of inner circle. I could feel another layer of the esoteric opening up to me, I could almost taste it. So innocent I was back then.'
    'It wasn't long before Adrian rang me, one evening, to inform me that a joint training session had previously been arranged for the Saturday evening in two weeks' time. These private sessions, he explained, where of course chargeable, which I had no problem with. He told me though that Hattie had informed him it was already fully booked, but he would let me come in as his guest.'

Chapter 9

Heart House

All this talk about holiness now
It must be the start of the latest style
Is it all books and words?
Or do you really feel it?
Do you really laugh?
Do you really care?
Do you really smile?

Joni Mitchel

It was like something from the beginning of a 'B rated', horror movie. A lone figure, driving through the pouring rain. It was night-time and very dark. The windscreen wipers, click clacked across the windscreen. It was a filthy night.

I had turned off the main road a while ago, onto tiny, single lane country roads. I was lost.

I followed the deep cut roadway, under the overhanging branches; the rain continued. It threaded and beaded every branch, leaf, and twig. Dripped mournfully, down tree trunks and created little rivulets down the banks at the side of the road. The banks where nearly as high as a walled house and where laced and knotted with enormous, twisted roots, all overgrown with moss and little dripping tongues of fern.

I had been told to look for a small driveway, with a sign saying, 'Heart's House'. 'You can't miss it,' is what Adrian had said. I had driven past it three times, before my headlights caught the tiny white sign, that had been splashed with mud, that all but obscured the lettering.

The gravel driveway, wound about and was lined with overgrown Laurel and Rhododendrons. Eventually the bushes thinned out to reveal the silhouette of an enormous Victorian house; there were no lights on inside.

I half expected that at that very moment, a great flash of lightening followed by an ear-piercing roll of thunder, would momentarily illuminate the scene.

But all I could hear, was the pounding rain on the roof of the car. I drove up to the front door apprehensively, there didn't seem to be anyone home, had I got the right house? Surly this one belonged to Count Dracula!

After searching about under the seats for an umbrella, that I remember seeing there one time, I opened the car door and the umbrella. Then quickly ran up the front steps. Beside the front door was a small sign saying, 'Hart House', thank goodness, at least I had got the right place.

Scanning about for a doorbell of some kind, I couldn't see one, but there in the centre of the big old door, was a very unusual brass knocker. It was a depiction of a great stag with a large array of antlers, looking straight out of the door. Underneath was a brass crescent moon which was the knocker.

Of course! I was thinking the heart in 'Heart House' was a beating heart. Now I could see that it must be spelt 'Hart', so

I checked the sign again and sure enough there it was 'Hart House', I had misread it all along.

The white Deer or 'White Hart', of course are mythological creatures which are considered to be messengers from the otherworld, in Celtic mythology. Very appropriate for an esoteric group.

I grabbed the brass crescent and banged hard on the door knocker, which seemed to echo loudly down the corridor inside. After some minutes, with no answer I banged again, hoping that I had got the right night.

After another minute, or so, I could hear someone drawing the door bolts, on the other side. There seemed to be a lot of them, sliding rustily across the clasps. Eventually the door opened a crack, it was on a chain and a very ancient woman called:

"Who is it?" in a voice that was almost as rusty as the door bolts. Her yellow, wrinkly, old face peered through the crack.

'Oh my god!' I thought this whole thing is getting more and more like that B movie, it was quite bizarre.

"It's George," I shouted above the sound of the rain beating on my umbrella. "I've come to see Adrian, is this the right house?"

"Adrian who?" said the old lady quizzically.

Jeez, I didn't know his second name, I only knew him as Adrian. In desperation, as I was getting soaked standing there in the rain I said, "I'm from the Atlanteans."

"Oh! Why didn't you say so before," she scolded? "They are round the back, we don't use the front door, go round the back." With that she promptly shut the door in my face.

"This is not a movie, this is not a movie, round the back, let's go round the back," I muttered to myself, as I felt my way round the house, in the pitch dark.

But then as I came to the back of the house, there were several cars parked and I could see the conservatory was lite up with bright lights and the pleasant sound of conversation and clinking cups and glasses met my ears.

I could see Adrian with his back to me holding up a glass of wine, and there were several others in there too. In great relief, I knocked on the glass door.

Hattie hastily came to open it saying, "Come in, come in, you'll catch your death out there. What a night? Sorry about the side light, it seems to have gone out in the storm. Here let me take your coat its soaking."

"Yes …yes, I got soaked banging on the front door," I stuttered.

"Oh! We never use the front door, we always use the back; did Adrian not tell you?" She looked over to Adrian, who was looking a bit sheepish.

"Adrian!" She scolded. "You should have told him to use the back door, we don't want to disturb, '*mother*', she'll be in bed by now."

"Must have forgot," he said, smiling cheerfully, as he handed me a grass of red wine, whilst putting his arm round my shoulder, in a fatherly way, as he led me to a vacant corner.

"Apologies about that," confessed Adrian, "they are all a bit superstitious. Apparently, the living go in and out of the back door, only the dead go out the front," he gave a jovial belly laugh, which I was very glad to join in with, as I was quite fazed by the ordeal of getting here. I took a large sip of my wine and was enjoying the comfort of his arm round my shoulder.

"I'm looking for a volunteer for my lecture," he explained. "At the beginning, people are a bit 'shy', to be the first to come forward for healing, so if you're willing, I can waiver the fee on this occasion."

I was more than happy to oblige, as I was still feeling quite shaken, from my journey.

"So, what is this place then?" I queried. "Do you live here?"

"Good gracious no, it's a holistic healing centre. Hattie's mother owns it, but it's used mostly by the Atlanteans, who have various healers using it for healing sessions, or lectures and other private sessions. There's another, bigger place in the Malvern's also. They are mostly channelers there, we have one of them here tonight as a special treat for us all."

I didn't know what a 'channeler' was, but I was more interested in Adrian, "So, what do you do, as a job I mean?"

"I'm in Anthropology. I have a doctorate actually and run research projects in the university and Bristol Museum."

"Really? That sounds interesting," I tried to sound convincing, but I had no idea what Anthropology was. I think Adrian was well used to this reaction, for he went on to explain.

"I specialise in the religious beliefs of tribal cultures, both in the past and today. Did you know that Shamanism is the belief system of all hunter gatherer cultures?"

"No, I didn't," I admitted.

"Shamanism forms the basis, of many more formalized religions, that retain shamanistic elements. Anthropologists have often adopted this broader perspective, seeking similarities among overtly different traditions."

"So, what do these shamans do?" I queried; I was starting to be interested.

"Well, apart from an extensive knowledge of herbal healing. They also heal through spirit intervention, such as protection from malign spirit attack. They are able to travel in the spirit world, to gain knowledge about which healing herbs to use, and how to prepare them. They are able to do a whole array of spiritual healings, such as 'lost soul retrieval'.

"For their tribe, they seem to act as doctor, psychologist and priest all wrapped up in one. Its infinitely fascinating."

"It certainly seems to be. I had no idea," I confessed.

"It's thought that Shamanism began around 30,000 years ago. And has been successfully used by almost every tribe, all over the world since then. Shamanic headdresses and artifacts found at Star Carr in Yorkshire, show us there were shamanic practices in Britain 11,000 years ago.

"In the present day, there are still isolated tribes using it. By comparison, modern medicine, as we know it, only started to emerge after the Industrial Revolution in the 18th century. That's only 300 years, a flash in the pan by Anthropology timescales. And that's only in the western world, many cultures, across the globe still hold to traditional medicines such as herbs."

Wow! I was blown away by this revelation, it was quite remarkable. However we were interrupted by Hattie, who was banging what looked like a dinner gong.

"Attention everybody," Hattie's authoritative voice, caused everyone to quieten down. "Sorry we are running a little late tonight, because of the unexpected storm. But we need to move into the healing room for tonight's sessions."

With that, several people started moving through the doors to the main house. Adrian and I tagged on to the end. We all entered a large sitting room, lit only by candles set about the room. There were several rows of hard back chairs set before a small folding table, which acted as a lectern.

I found a seat vacant at the end of a row on the far side. Looking around, I was surprised to see that there were several more people here, that I hadn't seen in the conservatory, consequently the room was quite crowded.

Adrian went straight to the front table and started sifting through some notes, which he had left there. It took several minutes of scraping chairs and people milling around finding seats next to friends, but eventually the noise reduced to a low murmur of voices.

Adrian picked up a small bell from the table and softly tinkled it. A subdued silence descended on the room.

"So, what exactly is spiritual healing?" Without any preamble Adrian went straight into his rhetorical question about the subject of tonight's lecture.

"Well, that could be answered in many different ways," he continued. "By as many different people. But for me it is a natural, non-invasive treatment, of a patient with the intention of bringing the recipient into a state of balance and wellbeing, on all levels." Here Adrian paused a moment, to allow his words to sink in.

"Sounds fairly straight forward so far, don't you think?" he looked around the room for acknowledgement. "Like any other healing treatment."

There were vague murmurings of soft agreement and nodding of heads, around the room.

"Now here's where it gets interesting," he continued. "Spiritual healing promotes self-healing, by relaxing the body, releasing tensions, and strengthening the body's own immune system.

"Now controversially, this approach is contrary to the philosophy of modern medicine, which generally only treats the symptoms of the patient. It doesn't look for an underlying cause and doesn't treat the person as a whole. It's very scientific in its approach and treats only what is very evident. It doesn't advocate the concept of 'self-healing' and rarely concerns itself with the body's own immune system. So, we are at odds with modern medicine here." Again Adrian looked about the room, to be sure he was grabbing people's attention.

"The next bit is even more interesting," he continued. "Spiritual healing involves the transfer of energy *through* the healer to the recipient. This is the bit that really blows the doctors minds. 'The transfer of energy, what energy?' they say and 'how are you transferring it? Where does it come from?' They ask.

"As far as I'm concerned, I just know it happens, I see and feel the results. I'm not interested in where it comes from, or even, what the energy is called. It has results. Why question it, that's just being anal.

"Of course, once you see and feel it happening, and 'believe' it is happening. It might be interesting to read up about these things. But to let it block you from the start, is just pure foolishness, as far as I'm concerned.

"So, without any more chat, let's move into our first healing demonstration. We have a volunteer already, George would you step up and sit in this chair please."

I rather self-consciously stood up; I was by far the youngest person in the room. Looking around, I could see all eyes upon me, as I walked to the front lectern. I could feel my face warming in a flush. Adrian in a fatherly way, warmly shook my hand and indicated the hard back chair I was to sit on.

Once I was sat down, Adrian asked me to go into a meditative state, the same way that we did every week at our meetings. However, this time I was all too aware that I was the only one doing this, and all eyes were in me. I must admit, this made me feel uncomfortable at first, but I closed my eyes and tried to relax.

Adrian then placed his hands on my shoulders and started talking to me in a slow hypnotic voice. Gently guiding me to my happy place, the one that I had gone to on many occasions at the group sessions. With Adrian guiding me, I was able to go into a deep meditative state with relative ease.

Then gradually I started to be aware of the warmth from Adrian's hands, at first it was glowing and comforting. But then it increased, and the warmth started flowing down my body from my shoulders, through my chest, my abdomen and down my legs. My whole body felt like it was glowing. Then there was tingling all over. At this point Adrian asked me to speak out loud and slowly but clearly describe my happy place.

"I'm in a forest clearing," I start my description, in a slow sleepy kind of voice. "There is a small campfire lite in the centre, with a few logs about it ready for sitting on. It is a deciduous forest with oak and elm and ash trees. But it is coming on to autumn, as the leaves are starting to turn. Even though the sun is shining, it is still cool."

"Very good George, now I want you to look at your own body in this place and describe what you are seeing."

"I am looking down at my feet, they are bare but quite hairy, my legs are tanned and muscular and hairy too. I am wearing a short tunic, of soft brown leather that comes down to my thighs. My hands are not my own. I am wearing a loose shirt, with some sort of tartan weave."

"Excellent George, very good. Now I'm going to send you some special healing and I want you to keep looking at your body and tell me what you're seeing."

At this point I started to feel a deepening inner peace, like a lightening of all my burdens. In my happy place, I looked down at my body.

"I can see a glowing, white energy now, flowing down my chest … it is slowly moving down to my abdomen… At the same time there is a green energy, flowing up from the forest floor … into my feet… It has started to slowly flow up my legs …and now it has arrived at my abdomen … where it seems to be swirling round … mixing with the white energy, coming down from my head… The spiralling energy in my abdomen seems to be expanding now … getting bigger and bigger, spreading right out over the forest… I am feeling a wonderful sense of connectedness, with the whole forest about me… I feel I can communicate with all the creatures living in the forest… I have a wonderful feeling, of belonging to the whole world about me."

I could hear Adrian calmly talking to me now, it sounded as if he were a long way off.

"…Now it's time George, to be coming back to us… Start to bring your awareness back into your body …in the here and now … into this room …into your body."

I was starting to be aware now, of Adrian's hands on my shoulders, they were gripping tighter, making me more aware of them. Slowly, slowly I became aware again of my own body and stretched and ever so slowly opened my eyes.

The sight of everyone in the room, standing in rapt appreciation, startled me; but far less than when they all started to applause. I looked about me, very confused by their reaction.

Adrian held up his hands to the crowd, "Please, please there really is no need for applause. Please be seated."

Gradually, people started sitting down again, but a murmur of low, appreciative voices circled the room.

"Thank you, ladies and gentlemen," Adrian continued. "Now you must all appreciate that George, is one of our star pupils, so not everyone will be able to achieve these depths. But in time with regular practice who knows. Now, is there anyone else who would like to come up here to receive healing?"

Hands shot up round the room.

"Thank you, thank you but we only have time for one more healing, as we have an accomplished channeler visiting, later on. You may go back to your seat now George, thank you."

I went back to my seat in a fog, still not yet fully grounded from my experience. But also, completely befuddled by people's reaction and the things Adrian had said: star pupil? I still considered myself to be a newcomer to the group.

I was deep in thought for some time. But was brought back to awareness suddenly, by Hattie's voice addressing the crowd.

"Thank you, Adrian, for coming tonight. There will be a clipboard circling round. Put you name and telephone number, on the list if you would like to subscribe to a course of treatment. I'm sure you won't be disappointed." This last statement Hattie said with the efficiency and tone of a busy secretary.

But then there was a dramatic pause. She continued with a quiet, quivering, reverent respect, "Now, as a special treat for us all, and without further ado; as we are running late. I will introduce our next guest."

She looked round the room to ensure people were paying attention, then continued. "He has come to us tonight, from our sister healing centre in the Malvern's. I would like to introduce to you, one of the founders of the Atlanteans, channeler for his Atlantean guide, Sir Ambrose Regin," as she said this last sentence, her voice became quiet and almost a whisper.

As someone else extinguished all the candles in the room, except for the one on the lectern, Hattie almost tiptoed back to her seat; leaving the room quiet and atmospheric. A hushed anticipation filled the room, as a solitary figure appeared from behind a small screen, in the shadows of the right-hand corner, that I hadn't noticed before.

He silently sat in the hard back chair, behind the lectern, then closed his eyes. You could see he was taking deep breaths. Then his body started to shake, with some inner effort. His mouth opened and closed, as if speaking, but no words came out.

Then, with what seemed like a massive effort, his whole body suddenly jolted. Then words in stilted sentences came out of his mouth.

"… Many thousands of years have elapsed, since the final sinking, of the island continent of Atlantis. But it's sinking roughly corresponds to the beginning of the early Egyptian civilization…

"… Atlantean immigrants had landed in Egypt, which at that time was known as Khemu, prior to the final catastrophe and had sown early seeds. When they were joined by those Atlanteans, who had left their land, around the time of the great flood, the corner stone of dynastic Egypt was finally laid…

"…Now I will talk about the natural forces, which guide the everyday running of Earth. Those very powers of nature itself, without which, nothing else could manifest. For these, after all, have been the inspiration for many beliefs, past and present…

"…A spirit, has been working through nature on this planet, a spirit of great beauty, great wisdom and great simplicity; it has been referred to as the 'Great god Pan'…

"…is the planetary deva who guides the planet, a being of great evolution, …such a deva, can by its closeness to the Godhead, transmit the love, wisdom and understanding of the Godhead, down on to the planet as a whole…

"…It is like a great beam of light, shining upon the planet, to which those spirits incarnate upon the planet can look upon; but it is rarely anything other than passive…

"This great force, which moves in everyday things upon your planet: the growth of plants, the movement of the seas, the clouds in the air, the wind etc. This force draws the attention of men's minds, to the signposts which point upward, through the beauty of nature; and it has a personality, it is what we call Pan.

"…This spirit heals through nature, because Earth is one of the most beautiful planets, in this solar system and beauty heals. It is Pan, that utilizes the gentle, soothing, balancing force of the tree; Pan that causes grass to rustle and make nature's gentle, restful sounds…."

***

'Looking back on that evening'…
Wrote Touchwood as he stroked his long silver beard,

… 'I now realise that it was a turning point for me. Not only was I learning much about esoteric matters, but here also was a religious aspect, that I had previously not considered. Ambrose Regin's channelling, continued for over an hour, broaching on the subject of nature spirits and the Elementals of planet earth'.

'But what stood out for me most, was the part about the Great god Pan. It rang so many bells for me and lit up so many dark corners of my mind, that it would have a lasting effect on me, for many years to come.'

'To this day, I still cannot work out, weather Ambrose was faking, or if it was a genuine channelling of some spirit. But the words he used, had a kind of magic to them, that felt genuine and true and touched my heart.'

'As for the healing from Adrian? Over the following few days, I felt a hugh releasing of the burden of pain and self-pity, self-doubt and anguish, that I had been carrying with me since my separation from my wife.

'There was pain too, connected with my sudden departure from the beauty and mystique of Scotland. And also, the sudden separation, from my fisherman friend Hamish, who I knew in my heart, that I would never see again.'

Chapter 10

Candra

Father, teach your children
To treat our mother well
If we give her back her diamonds
She will offer up her pearl

The Dead Can Dance

One day, when I arrived at the Atlanteans esoteric group, we were to have a talk by a rather unusual group of women. There were about five of them. They were all wearing long Indian type dresses and wore head scarfs, yet they all seemed to be white, English girls, in their late twenties or so.

Perhaps up until then, I had had a sheltered life, but I had, in all honesty, not seen anything like this before. The women seemed to be quietly reserved and had a spiritual or religious look about them. One slightly older woman, seemed to be the leader of the group and it was she who gave a talk on 'nature spirits.'

It was an interesting talk about Elementals, Divas, Undines, Sylphs and Salamanders. It seemed their community, worked extensively with nature spirits. But what fascinated me most, was this group of women who called themselves the Rhenn's.

When the lecture had finished, and we were all gathered into groups, drinking tea. I went over to the Rhennish group and introduced myself, saying I was interested to know more about their group and what it was about.

The leader, who I later discovered was called Silver, turned her head to look at me, then tilted her head sideways, all the while looking directly at me in a strange way. Then after consideration, she said, "Yes, we can meetup and we will tell you more."

She then handed me a card, which looked very home-made, but had beautiful cursive writing in black ink, and disclosed simply:

Silver Sorority
The Rhenn's
0117 965 4552

Then she told me, "Ring this number, when you feel ready to talk and we can arrange to meet."

I thanked her and said I would be sure to ring soon.

All the way home I was thinking about these unusual women, and what sort of religious group they were. I don't deny it, I was fascinated by them.

My job as a senior, computer hardware engineer, kept me busy most of the day and often I might get called out in the evening also. So, it was over a week later, when I called Silver to arrange a meetup. She answered the call immediately, and remembered who I was, so I was quite impressed with that. Mainly because I wasn't feeling very impressive, in fact I was quite raw, as I was beginning to feel disillusioned with my work life again.

Anyway, Silver arranged to meet me in a pub in Bristol, which surprised me as my protestant upbringing, gave me the impression, that a 'religious person' was someone who didn't drink. Well, I was quickly re-educated about that side of things, when I met them.

In my keenness, I arrived a little early. It was midweek, so the pub was quiet, with only half a dozen local men at the bar. When four women arrived, in this Bristol pub, all dressed in long dresses and head scarfs, and came over to sit with me at my table; it caused quite a stir with the other customers.

I stood up out of respect and offered to buy the drinks, thinking they would probably drink sodas, instead they wanted four pints of best bitter!

They quickly set about those pints, demolishing them in a matter of minutes. Between sips, they had started to tell me about the Rhenn's; each of them chipping in bits of information.

Then they suddenly stopped talking and became silent. Puzzled, I looked round the group of women, one of them, an Indian looking girl, looked straight at me and gave me the, most beautiful smile. Her eyes flicked down to her empty glass, then looked back at me and smiled again. I looked round the table, all the glasses where empty; I got the hint and somewhat bemused, went back up to the bar for four more pints.

By this time, I was getting some very strange looks from the other guys in thc bar. I suppose, having seen these four strangely dressed woman, downing their pints quickly, was a spectacle that didn't usually happen, in this pub, on a Wednesday evening.

Having delivered the four pints, to my eager guests, I noticed mine was still threequarters full. As I picked up my pint and took a sip, I started to take a closer look at their clothing. They all wore those Indian print wraparound skirts with knitted cardigans, or a knitted shawl over a blouse. This was obviously, their more casual look, as at the Atlanteans they had worn long silky, dresses like Saris.

Most of the talk now, was about me and my circumstances. Eventually the oldest woman who was called Silver and seemed to be the leader, said to me that Candra, was willing to be my mentor and to teach me about their ways. She then indicated the Indian girl, who as I looked at her, gave me a shy smile. Silver then asked for my telephone number, which she wrote down and handed the slip of paper to Candra, saying that Candra would contact me to arrange my first mentoring session.

By this time their pints were almost empty again. With a nod to the group from Silver, they all promptly finished their drinks and stood up to leave. I stood up also, saying pleasantries, like thank you for coming, and tried to shake hands, but was refused.

Then they all left the pub, leaving me alone at the table a little forlorn and embarrassed. I looked around me and noticed that every man in the pub, was staring at me in a strange, semi aggressive way, which made me very uncomfortable. So, I finished my pint and left as well.

It was several days later that Candra contacted me. We arranged to meet in a pub that was more local to my house. When we met, it was just her on her own this time, and she seemed more friendly and relaxed, than she had been when she was under the watchful eye of the matriarch Silver.

So much so, that instead of a pint of beer, she asked me to get a bottle of wine from the bar and could we go back to my house and enjoy it, in more comfortable surroundings. Which surprised me enormously, but I complied, and we walked home to my house together.

When we got there, she was very taken with my house, looking round at the lounge and soon found the kitchen. She seemed very excited, by my new gas hob and separate double oven, which in those days was quite unusual and had cost a lot of money.

Immediately, she started opening cupboards and draws looking for vegetables. I found some potatoes for her in the veg rack, by the back door. She set too, preparing something, saying she was very hungry and had not eaten all day, explaining that their members fasted on Fridays, skipping breakfast and lunch; only eating and drinking in the evening.

She then started rooting round, looking for spices. I found some curry powder which she was very pleased with. She told me to go put on some music, so I asked her what she would like, and she said, "Do you have any folk music?"

I found a Fairport Convention album and put that on, and just sat down at the breakfast counter, watching her cook. She seemed happy as a clam, cooking away in my kitchen, so I just went with it.

After a little while, she produced two plates of food which looked delicious, but I hadn't seen anything like it before. There were cubes of spicy fried potatoes, some sort of grain which apparently was bulgur wheat, which she had found at the back of a cupboard, and I had no idea that I had; and some sort of spicy omelette with onions in it. The whole thing was delicious. Considerably better than the beans on toast, which I had made for myself earlier, when I had come home from work.

I opened the wine, which we had with it, and the whole experience was lovely. She was very charming company and a great cook. It had been a long while, since I had sat down to a nice dinner, with a charming woman for company. During the meal she told me about herself.

Candra has very black, long straight hair with tawny brown skin, she was of Indian descent. Her face is very pleasant to look at; but her eyes standout most, as they were a hazel nut color, with a black circle on the outside of her iris. She wore the long dress and head scarf typical of the Rhenn's, but you can see she has a womanly shape underneath.

She is about five foot two inches tall, has a gorgeous smile and radiates a lovely energy; you just want to cuddle her.

The name Candra (pro: CAN -dray), is a Romanized version of the Sanskrit 'Chandra' which literally means 'Shining' or 'moon', after a Hindu lunar deity.

During our conversation, she told me she had been disowned by her Indian family, after having a relationship with a white boy. Fortunately, the Rhennish people adopted her, as she was already very familiar with many of the concepts of Rhennish philosophy and dress.

After we had finished our lovely dinner and bottle of wine, together with Candra's charming company; I was starting to feel quite smitten with her. However, by this time it was getting quite late, and I was all too aware that the buses from my outer suburb, didn't run too late. So, I asked her about this, but she just said:

"That's ok, I can stay the night, do you have a spare room?"

Well, I must admit this did take me by surprise. I thought she was a very forward and brave girl, meeting a relative stranger like this, then coming back to his house and asking to stay the night! Additionally, it was clear by the way she behaved, that she quite liked me, and I admit I liked her well enough.

A scenario like this, in the western culture I grew up in, generally only lead to one thing. However, I was torn trying to decide, if she really was being very forward and giving me a 'come-on'. Or, if she was just very innocent of western culture and the implications.

Clearly these Rhennish folk, were a very different kind of people, so I decided on the latter and to respect her innocence. So, as a good host, I showed her to the spare room that I had, with a bed already made up and showed her the bathroom also. Then left her to get on with preparations for bed, while I went to my own room, to do the same.

Next morning, being a Saturday and no work for me, I was having a lovely lie-in. However, I was rudely awoken by a loud knock, knock at my bedroom door. In a panic, I threw off the bed covers and leaning over the double bed, turned the bedside clock round and saw it was only eight O'clock, way too early.

'Who the hell is that? I live alone,' I thought to myself. Still half asleep I flopped my head face down onto my pillow. "Who is it" I heard myself say?

Someone opened the door, I sleepily turned my head to see who it was, forgetting that in the heat of summer, I always slept naked and had just pulled the covers off me. It was Candra in the door frame, she was fully dressed, ready for the day.

"Candra…what are…?" I managed sleepily.

Unabashed, she was looking directly at me, taking it all in, with a sweet little smile, but her eyes had a mischievous twinkle in them. Then I suddenly realized; I was lying naked on the bed in front of her. So, I quickly shot up, kneeling on the mattress facing her, while franticly fumbling for the covers, that I had just kicked off the bed onto the floor. In a fluster I jumped out of bed, on the other side and found the quilt, holding it over my nakedness.

"Ca… can I help you," I said lamely.

She just smiled with that twinkle in her eye, "Silly boy," she said. "I've been for a walk and found the shops, they open at nine o'clock, do you have any money so I can get us some breakfast?"

"Oh! Yeh …err sure. In my wallet …" I was stupidly pointing at the wallet on the bedside table, near the door. But then scuttled round the bed, still clutching the covers over my privates, and bent down for my wallet.

Suddenly, Candra slapped me on the bottom and said, "Get you back to bed, I will manage."

Then taking a ten-pound note from the wallet, she disappeared down the hallway, leaving me like a fool, still clutching my quilt; not really knowing, just what to make of what had just happened.

From that time on, Candra made it clear that she liked me, but she never led me on, to feel like I should advance on her sexually. In fact, my relationship with her, was like she was a loving older sister. As my initial confusion subsided, in time I got to really enjoy this type of relationship. I could relax into it; the pressure was taken off me.

Outside of my work routine, she made the decisions and organised things for me. It was their way; they were a matriarchal race.

Candra stayed at my house for six weeks. In that time, during the day, Candra became a sort of live-in housekeeper, while I went to work in the day. During the evenings, she taught me about the ways of the Rhennish people and a lot of other spiritual teachings; all were strange and new to me.

She taught me that the Rhennish tradition, is one of the most ancient religious and cultural traditions in Britain and Ireland.

"We worship God as the mother," she told me. "And everything we do is centred around that worship."

Community Rhennish was a matriarchy. The women are called 'maids' to outsiders and 'sisters' to each other. Music and singing are of great importance, an act of devotion. Musical instruments are used by the group and are often handmade by them. She also stressed the importance of crafts, as a path to the sacred.

Apparently, they had several houscholds in cities around the UK, which are sort of scout groups for new members. But they also had a large house with land in Ireland, a community, were there was an emphasis on self-sufficiency and members grow food to feed themselves. This community is called 'Droichead BEO', (meaning the bridge of life).

In this community there is no electricity, no modern devices were used, and plastic is avoided as a pollutant. The community have a strong work ethic, which is an integral part of their spirituality. The Rhennish tradition extends beyond just acts of worship, their spirituality extends to the crafts they practice, their language, their songs and stories.

Candra encouraged me to write down, all she taught me in a notebook, dedicated to their tradition; which I did. I learnt they even had their own type of cursive lettering which was beautiful. I was encouraged to only listen to music, from the pre-renaissance period, music on the pentatonic scale.

One day she went to the library and brought back several vinyl records of pre renaissance folk music, which I was able to copy on to cassette tapes. So from then on, we only listened to this type of music.

She also found a place where I could buy a 'make your own dulcimer kit'. The dulcimer is an ancient musical instrument with two drone strings and one which you fret, I plucked it with a white swan feather that I had found. I made the kit during the evenings, while listening to this lovely ancient folk music. During this time Candra prepared her hand made foods, which were mostly exotically spiced and vegetarian, and total new to my tastes.

Perhaps more importantly, she also taught me to see the goddess within all women. There is no question about it, I was definitely starting to feel more spiritual day by day. I was taught to extend my spiritual practice, into all manner of ways in my everyday life. Like for example, saying a blessing over my food. While doing this, all music and conversation was to be stopped. We paused, breathing deeply placing our hands over the food, breathing in the prana from the food while saying:

> *Lord and lady of all nature*
> *We thank you for this food*
> *Please take it and bless it*
> *That we may be nourished*
> *Blessed be*

After I had made my dulcimer; Candra taught me to play it. She also brought her carving tools to my house and let me use them to carve wood. She picked a picture out of a book, she got from the library, of some sort of ancient church carving, which I attempted to copy. Even though I say so myself, I made a fair effort, for someone who had never carved before. I still have this carving to this day.

One day I asked Candra, if she would like to go to a folk club I knew about. She seemed enthusiastic, as she loved music. So, on the day of the folk club, which I think was a Friday, I drove her to this old country pub outside of town. There was an old barn out the back where the music was playing.

I thoroughly enjoyed the performers music. But Candra didn't like it very much, she said it was too modern for her tastes, but she enjoyed the beer.

When the musicians had finished, we finished our drinks and walked back to the car. Outside, it was now very dark, there were no streetlights as we were out in the countryside. Candra stopped and looked up at the heavens and noticed the new moon quite low in the sky. It was a beautiful, still autumn evening, the sky was clear, and a multitude of stars scattered across the sky. The crescent of the new moon, hung like a boat in the sky. As Candra watched the moon:

"Did you know I was named after the moon?" I turned away from the sky and looked down at her beautiful, innocent face, illuminated by the silver light. Her long, black straight hair and hazel eyes, her Indian shawl pulled over her head. I just looked at her, not knowing quite what to say, the whole scene was just beautiful.

Then Candra, softly offered up a prayer to the moon, which I will always remember.

"Silver star on the waters
That has laughed all the world into being
Beyond all knowing is the splendour of your light
Hold me in the palm of your hand
In this world and all the worlds to come"

Candra taught me about worship. She gifted me with a beautiful painting of a goddess called Inanna, then taught me to set up an alter in my room; and to make devotional, meditation, and worship in the name of the goddess.

Inanna is the daughter of the mother goddess. She is an ancient Mesopotamian goddess associated with love, beauty, sex, war, and justice. Inanna was originally worshiped in Aratta and Sumer under the name 'Queen of Heaven', and was later worshipped by the Akkadians, Babylonians, and Assyrians under the name Ishtar.

I felt very privileged when Candra entrusted me with copies of some of their sacred scripts. They felt very special and sacred and were very highly revered by the Rhennish people. I treasured them and still read them, to this day; they are wonderfully poetic.

Here I reproduce a small section from their Creation Mythos:

1. *Before and beyond all things is the mistress of all things, and when nothing was, She was.*
2. *And having no solid place that Her feet might rest upon, She divided the sea from the sky and made a dance of solitary splendour upon the crested deeps.*
3. *And She was pure force and energy, and therefore pure delight; and the crashing of the waves was the overflowing of her joy.*
4. *And the white force of Her super abundant joy grew so great that it must take shape as laughter; and Her laughter was the shape of all things.*
5. *For each peal of her voice became a Silver fragment, broken from the whole and yet complete in itself. And She loved each fragment with all the joy of Her being, and Her hands knew cunning.*
6. *And She stretched forth Her hands and gave a shape to each fragment, and no one was like any other.*
7. *And she parted the vasty waters that there might be a place to set them down.*
And She laughed.

8. *And each fragment was filled with Her delight and therefore was living. And some grew in the deep earth and were plants and trees; some ran about the ground or flew above it; and those first made that had no place to be set down became fishes and the creatures of the sea. And everything was Silver. And She laughed.*

One evening when Candra and I were discussing the Rhennish spiritual teachings as usual, she said to me:

"We receive a new name during an initiation, to bring us closer to remembering our sacred Divinity. In many cultures and tribes, people take on a new name later on in their life, when their mentor feels they have elevated. So taking on this new name, better identifies with them on a deeper soul level.

"Many times though, a new name is taken or attached to a person, because of a profound journey they have either begun or are preparing to walk upon. A new name, in lieu of this journey, will empower them along the way, by reminding them of who they are and what mission, they are assigned to carryout.

"A new name, opens the soul up to new gifts and will leave definite energetic impressions, on anyone that they encounter and can more importantly, alter the path of the soul that carries the name."

When I heard this, my heart started pounding in my ears, for I had a sense of what was coming next; for I knew it would one day come, and I had been dreading it.

Candra continued, "I have mentored you for some weeks now, and feel you are ready to proceed on your spiritual journey by yourself. I gift you the name 'Corin'. Take it with pride, it means 'Spear' it is a warrior's name. You are destined to lead; I can see that in you. One day you will."

***

'I recall, I was greatly saddened by what she had told me that day …'

Touchwood writing in his ledger had the glint of a tear in his eye. 'Foolish old man', he thought to himself, as he blew his nose on his handkerchief, composed himself, then continued writing.

'… I knew she would be moving on now, to a new student, and I would miss her dearly. That was indeed the last time I saw her. But she had told me early on, that this is how they worked, by choosing people, who they thought, 'had potential'; fertile ground so to speak. So that they could sow a spiritual seed, nurture it and hope it would grow into a mighty tree.'

'For someone, who was brought up as a very ordinary English boy, whose only religious event was going to church for an hour on a Sunday morning. All that Candra taught me was a breath of fresh air.'

'In all, Candra taught me to go about my everyday life, with spiritual focus in everything that I did. The gifts she seeded in me, set the tone of my whole life from then on.'

Chapter 11

The Labyrinth

"I didn't arrive at my understanding of the fundamental
laws of the universe through my rational mind."
Albert Einstein

The old man with the silver beard, sat back in his chair with a sigh. His old bones where aching. Picking up his large notebook to read what he had just written, he recited aloud:

'Candra had taught me so much. I was very saddened when she was ordered to leave me. I believe, in a way, I had fallen in love with her. Perhaps her matron had seen this, so decided it was time to terminate my lessons.'

'But having tasted, what it was like being in the company of a truly spiritual person. Then be left alone, only heightened my need to belong to a similar group. One that could not only give knowledge but be a religious community.'

'I didn't have the heart to return to the Atlanteans. After seeing the genuine and honest, daily spiritual endeavour, Candra followed; the Atlanteans seemed somehow lacking. However, I was grateful for what they had taught me, but felt strongly it was time to move on.'

'Therefore, my desire to find another magical group was stronger than ever. But how to find one, was still a mystery to me. So, like

so many seekers, I decided to go to Glastonbury Tor; hoping to find someone up there to talk to, on this sacred hill.'

***

The drive from Bristol to Glastonbury, took me over the Mendip Hills: an area of outstanding, natural beauty. I had set off early, endeavoring to avoid Bristol's morning rush-hour traffic. It was a beautiful morning. The trees all around were just coming into bud, so many shades of green. As I drove over the top of the hill and started downhill towards Wells, the vista opened up.

Looking down from this vantage point, I could see for miles. Covering the entire wetlands below, was a blanket of early morning mist, which seemed to billow and shift with the heat of the early morning sun. However, rising majestically out of the mist, was Glastonbury Tor, looking for all the world like some mystical island of the fairy; a sight I will never forget. It wasn't difficult to see why so many legends were associated with this mystical place.

Eventually I arrived at the base of the Tor, it was still misty, and the sun looked like a yellow-white ball in the sky. As I began the climb up the spine of the Tor, I started rising above the mist, and could look up and see the top of the majestic Tor. I began to think about the mystery of this ancient place.

Glastonbury Tor is in Somerset, England, and is a cone shaped hill, with the remains of an old mediaeval monastery on the top. There are so many legends and mysteries, attached to this natural looking hill, that one cannot disregard what people have experienced there.

There is clear evidence of a spiral maze, etched into this hill. One that starts at the base and winds its way to the top. Technically it is not a maze, but a systematical labyrinth, a pilgrim path, that leads continuously to the top, with no dead ends.

The grassy spiral has been dated, back to the third or second century CE. During those times, the entire area was full of marshes and shallow lakes; the tor being like an island rising above them.

In the marshes, ancient wooden track ways, have been discovered leading to the Tor. One of these is called the Sweet Track. This ancient track is now known to be the oldest engineered road in the world, estimated to be built in 3,800 BCE.

Many strange phenomena have been attached to the Tor. It is said that it is a place, where there is a portal or doorway, to other dimensions or unseen worlds. Some say it is a fairy hill, an entrance to the underworld, a spot where the 'veil' between worlds, wears thin. Another is that it is the legendary island of Avalon, where King Arthur was buried.

Historical records show, that in 1911, monks from the abbey, declared that they had found the grave of the legendary King Arthur and his Queen.

King Arthur is said to have been injured in battle and taken to Morgan le Fay, a fairy witch who resided on the Island of Avalon. There to heal, in its pure wealth of natural energy. Arthur is said to have never returned from there. Many people believe that such an island did exist, and evidence points to the fact, that Glastonbury was indeed the fabled Avalon.

As I have discovered on my OS maps, there is a web of energy lines converging on the Tor. There are certain times, when these 'ley' lines, as they are called, are stronger than at other times. Many people, including the Mayor of Glastonbury, have seen strange lights striking across the top of the hill and the strange, ping pong ball, type lights, hovering over it.

Finally arriving at the top, I stopped to survey the vista around me. The early morning sun was bright and starting to burn away the mist below, giving way to magnificent views of the surrounding wetlands.

However, I was slightly disappointed, that there was no one else around. But it was so peaceful up there, that I sat down, with my back to the tower and my face to the sun, and decided it was a good place to meditate.

I was a good fifteen minutes, into my peaceful meditation, when I heard a man's voice call, "Did you hear about the walk."

Puzzled, I thought for a moment I was channeling my voices again, so waited to see if anything more was said. A shadow went over the sun, then, "Here, have a leaflet."

I opened my eyes, to see a strange character, dressed in a white robe, with a massive gold chain hanging round his neck, sandals, and a red bandana round his head. He had a green leaflet in his hand, offering it to me, which I silently took; puzzled I looked at it.

It was information about a labyrinth walk on the summer solstice. I looked up to say thanks to the stranger, but no one was there. It was a quiet day, and I would have heard someone walking away. Puzzled, I got up and walked about the top of the Tor, looking for this character, but no one was there.

'That's strange', I thought to myself, then looked down again at the leaflet. It was actually quite interesting, giving information about the mysterious labyrinth carved into the Tor. And information about a group of people organizing a guided walk, following the labyrinth, on the auspicious day of the harmonic convergence.

Apparently, they needed 144,000 people gathered at power centers, all across the globe; naturally the Tor was one of them. It would be the first synchronized, global peace meditation, at a time when Sun, moon and six planets where in conjunction.

On the spot, I decided that this event, was something I must attend. Clearly there was a lot more people connected with new-age spirituality, than I had realized.

On the day of the Glastonbury Tor, labyrinth walk, it was very hot and sultry. The leaflet had instructed to meet at a small marker stone, at the base of the Tor. The stone marks the start of the labyrinth.

However, upon arriving at the Tor, I immediately went to the 'Red Spring' or 'Chalice well' to collect some water for the walk. Cupping my hands under the flowing waters, I drank deeply of the iron tasting water; it was the most delicious water, I had ever tasted. I was so hot that I splashed some water over my head and neck. Then filled my water bottle. The water from this spring, is shrouded in countless tales of mystery, including its magical healing properties.

Refreshed, I walked to the small marker stone at the base of the Tor. There were already about twenty people waiting there, and many more walking past, continuing up to the top.

After waiting around for quite some minutes, for people to arrive, eventually someone in the group, seemed to take control. She was a lovely young girl about twenty years old, with flowing wavey red hair. She went on to tell us, some of the history of the labyrinth, and some of the mystical aspects of labyrinths in general. Apparently, this was part of a pilgrim path.

Our leader had the foresight to bring along a brightly coloured parasol, which on this hot day, everyone was jealous of. But it was also easy to follow. We started our journey bare footed. The path seemed to lead a snaking, spiralling path around the conical hill. I soon realized that this was not only a ceremonial pathway, but I was following a three-dimensional labyrinth pattern, clinging to the sacred Tor. Although there are several flat labyrinths in cathedrals, around the world, there are few, three-dimensional labyrinths.

It was midsummer and the Sun was beating down on us, our little group were all very hot and weary, and our exertions had made us hot and sticky. Most of the guys had striped to the waist. Girls were rolling up trousers to form impromptu shorts, or hitching up long skirts, tucking them into their knickers. Some girls had even boldly removed their tea shirts, sporting only coloured bras. We were looking like a very raga-muffin bunch, as we trod the ceremonial pathway.

About halfway up, our leader stopped, to allow us to rest awhile; we gathered around her. From under her parasol, she tried to instil into us, that many walkers undertake similar pilgrim paths, not only as a spiritual journey, but as an endurance test. A personal journey, a test of spiritual metal, in the company of others, particularly in the summer months. At this point, many of us realised, that it most certainly, did seem to be, a test of endurance.

She told us that this time however, the journey was even more special, as it was preparing us for the harmonic convergence. This was a most auspicious event, where it was required that they needed 144,000 rainbow warriors, to be gathered at power centers, all across the globe, all at a specific time; in order for the fundamental global shift in consciousness to take place.

Eventually we completed the spiral maze and reached the small plateau at the top. Here we were confronted by a massive crowd of people, of all ages and shapes and sizes. Multi coloured dress, it seemed, was mandatory.

There were groups of drummers frantically banging away, other groups were singing or chanting. There were several lap harpists playing, one had even carted up, a six-foot-tall concert harp. There were people dressed as Celtic warriors, others in white druid robes. There were woman from all manner of religious groups gathered, sporting pentangles, ankhs and all kinds of variations of the cross.

It was an impressive gathering of spiritual souls, from many parts of the globe. But I couldn't help but wonder, how they all knew to be here at this time. Clearly, some form of networking was going on, but I couldn't work out what it was. I had arrived by chance. Surely it hadn't been so, for all these people.

Although it was a two-day global event, the climax at Glastonbury Tor, was set for four pm. It was at that time, that we all gathered round the six-foot-tall concert harp, while an elderly and noteworthy spiritual leader, gave us an inspirational speech, about the significance of the event.

At the allotted time the harpist played, while we all meditated on world peace. It really was quite wonderful, listening to the great harp, while deeply meditating, and in the company of so many people. The mystical atmosphere was palpable, but I wasn't sure, if I could feel a connection to people across the globe. But, at that moment, I really did feel connected, to all the human bodies, of the people gathered around me on Glastonbury Tor.

***

Touchwood continued writing with a wry smile.

'... *Returning home from the harmonic convergence, I seemed to be wrapped in a warm glow. It was encouraging and somehow rewarding, to have been part of a gathering, of so many people worldwide, who wished and meditated for peace.*

It was surprising for me too, to know, there were so many people, who had spiritual leanings. Because in my normal day to day life, there was no evidence for it at all. No one else I met, seemed to feel like I did. Or maybe they did but didn't talk about it.'

Chapter 12

The Whisperer

Far away across the field
The tolling of the iron bell
Calls the faithful to their knees
To hear the softly spoken magic spells

Pink Floyd

The significance of the harmonic convergence event was unmistakable. It was the first of its kind, in Britain at least and heartening that two or three hundred people of like mind could gather together in one place and link with people all over the globe, in the name of spiritual peace.

However, the most significant part for me, was after the main climax. I was milling though the crowds of people there, when I came across an interesting figure handing out leaflets for a workshop. I took one, the leaflet said simply:

Talking with tree spirits
Learn how to talk to tree spirits and
how to cut your own healing wand.
Facilitated by a Romanian Shaman

This sounded completely like the sort of thing I would like to learn; I was instantly interested. I caught up with the man handing out leaflets. As it turned out, he was actually the guy running the workshop, his name was Radu.

Radu was stocky, but well-toned, he had short silver-blue hair, that seemed to spike out of the top of his head. His eyes were dark, but kind, with a large nose and generous mouth. He had a short black beard, shaped round the mouth area. And ears that were low and large. He had a nice smile, with a thick eastern European accent.

During our discussion, he told me his father earned a living, as a horse whisperer, looking after and healing horses in Romania. Radu's father had told him to go out into the world and teach people about what they knew. He foretold that there were troubled times ahead and his father was concerned that their way of life and what they knew would die out in the coming years.

Radu also told me, that although he used the word 'Romanian Shaman', on the leaflet, he would rather be known as a 'Nature Whisperer'.

I was convinced, the man was genuine and was very interested in going to his workshop. I thanked him for the leaflet and his honest words and let him continue with his leafleting.

**

On the drive home, reflecting on the day, I was overcome with what an amazing experience it had been. And thanked my good fortune to have bumped into Radu. What I learned about trees and healing from Radu …

Wrote Touchwood, by candlelight. He had woken up at two in the morning and couldn't sleep, so decided to write in his ledged while still in bed, it was often the case.

… I could fill a book with, one day I may. Yet I only learned a fraction of what he knew. I have relayed here, a few of the group highlights and some of the knowledge gained, that happened over several workshops. Blessings Touchwood

***

"A good gardener works with his plants, to create a happy garden," Radu was explaining to us how he works with nature.

"He develops an intuition about the plants he works with and learns to understand what they are trying to tell him."

On the day of the workshop, it was a cool and dry late summer day. Radu had taken us to a woodland a little way outside Glastonbury town; there was about fifteen students in all. We had sat in the little wooded area and created a small campfire and gathered some logs that had been lying around, to create a small circle about the fire. It was here we all sat listening to his background in Romania. And how important it was for him to be teaching others, what his father had taught him, from a very early age.

"If one works with the trees," Radu continued. "Asking their permission, then pruning branches is not an arduous or destructive task. If one is open and receptive, the trees themselves, will even show you where they need pruning; the gardener is mealy the mechanism for their will. It is this same mechanism; we must learn for cutting wands."

Radu had a short staff with him, into it had been carved a small snake, spiralling about the shaft. The wood was some sort of fruit tree and had been stained dark red and was highly polished with use. He lifted it up and pretended to prune it with his fingers.

"When we are pruning an apple tree for example, we are working with the tree, to prune the best branches for abundant fruiting. The tree spirit or dryad, lives within the body of the tree and normally is present within every leaf, branch & bud.

"If a branch is ready for pruning, the dryad starts to withdraw its life force from that branch. So, sensing the trees aura, we look for a branch, whose life force is diminished, or it may have withdrawn, to say halfway along a branch. It is at that point that we cut, just above the node. So, the wood we cut while pruning has no tree spirit within it.

"But when we are cutting a branch, to use as a wand or staff, the difference here being, is that we are requesting, that a shard of the spirit of the tree, be present within the wand or staff we cut. It is desirable to us as whisperers, that we have a wand with a tree spirit residing within it. These can act as an ally to us and aid us in many ways."

One of the girls in our group put her hand up to ask a question. Radu nodded to her to continue.

"Radu, do you have any written handouts," she asked. "For this, so we can look at it later on."

"Our culture," Radu answered. "Mythology, beliefs, and sacred practices, comes from the oral tradition, passed from generation to generation. We aren't that keen on writing. My father was completely illiterate. In that way we are similar to your Celtic druids."

Someone else put their hand up to speak, "How come you're here, if you only pass the knowledge from generation to generation?"

"This is difficult for me," Radu stated. "We live in troubled times; our culture and knowledge are in danger of dying out. I have been given special permission, to pass on some of our practices. Would you like me to continue?"

There was a unanimous bout of nodding and encouragement for him to continue.

"I personally believe," he continued, "that most people can develop intense relationships with trees. Trees have been around longer than humans, they have memories that stretch far back into the distant past. Be aware though, their view of time is different to humans, as they live longer lives and are deeply in tune with the cyclical nature of the seasons.

"A tree is like a memory bank, just like humans and the earth itself. All store, by various means, data from life as it is lived around them. Meditation with trees, is on one level, a way of accessing the wisdom inherent in trees. By working with Trees, their memories emerge, in a process somewhat akin to telepathy.

"Modern people are fixated on the visual and the audible; experiences that can be verified. Trees communicate more on what I would term, an emotional level. In order to understand them, you must be willing to take things at their pace.

"This communication on an emotional level, means that you probably won't hear a 'voice' in your mind. Trees communicate in a holistic fashion, I believe. That is, the way the leaves sound, the way the shadow patterns of the branches change, and the other interaction of animals and birds around them, can be part of their communication.

"Often a 'sense' of something, like a vague feeling of deja Vu, might come over you. Modern people are far too liable to dismiss such things, as fanciful or just an idle thought. Act on your instincts, learn to trust them. After all, it is a way of accessing the web of life; of which we are a part."

Radu paused here. There was silence in the group. Only the sound of the wind through the tree branches above and an occasional bird call, could be heard. I was experiencing an intense feeling of déjà vu now. I knew, I had done this before, in the past, perhaps a thousand years ago. I had done this, sitting about a small fire, listening to a wise one, talk about trees. I felt a chill run down my back. I had a strong feeling of being watched by someone or something; perhaps the trees themselves.

Looking around the group, at their rapt but apprehensive faces, I didn't doubt they were feeling the same.

Radu too, looked around the circle of faces, before saying, "Now the trees have become aware of our intentions, we can start our first practical exercise. Let's stand up."

We all slowly stood up, some people started stretching.

"I find it best, to walk through the woodland for a while," Radu assured us. "To orientate yourself and start to feel comfortable, in this group of trees. Each of you go off, find a tree to work with. Not too far away, as you need to hear me. It is best to work with a tree that you are drawn too, one that you feel comfortable around and one that you feel may be welcoming."

Everyone in our group, started slowly wandering through the trees, each finding their own tree. I found a young sycamore tree, about seven inches across, which I was drawn to.

"When you find your tree, slowly walk towards it," called Radu, speaking a little louder now. "Begin by finding a comfortable sitting position, underneath it, with your back against the trunk. Relax and clear your mind ... smell the earth ... grass and leaves around you ...watch the way the sun plays through the branches ... listen to the wind move the tree."

Radu was silent for a few minutes, while we grew comfortable with our tree.

"Now start your deep breathing exercise, the one we did at the beginning of the class. Allow yourself to slow down ... especially your thoughts ...Trees view time differently from us, they are much more in tune with the seasons, and the cycles of the climate. Remember when you are sitting underneath a tree's branches, you are directly within their energy field; you're in their personal space. When you are relaxed and receptive ... a tree can communicate with you."

Again, Radu was silent allowing us plenty of time.

"Now we are going to start melding with the tree. Feel the tree at your back. Feel the earth beneath you. Take another deep breath. Feel the safety and protection of the tree around you. See if you can feel the life-force pulsing through the tree ... Now take nine deep breaths. Slowly breath in and slowly breath out. With every breath you take, feel yourself move further and further into the tree ... through the bark and right into the centre of the tree. Feel yourself start to 'meld' with the tree."

Again, Radu paused awhile.

"When you reach this point, notice how you feel, being in the centre of this tree. What, if anything do you see there? What, if anything do you hear? What sensations to you detect. Stay there for as long as you can. I'm going to leave you here, for about half an hour, then gently call you back."

I had melded with my tree, gradually feeling like I was a part of it. I was surprised how readily the tree had accepted me. The first thing that I became aware of, was the feeling of my branches reaching up to the light in the sky. I could feel my branches, gently waving in a light breeze, up in the top of my canopy. The light movement of my leaves was like the feeling of my hair gently blowing in a breeze, it was pleasant and stimulating. But most important was the light, I was aware of my leaves, twisting and moving in order to gain full benefit from the life-giving light.

My secondary awareness was of my roots, and how they grew deep into the earth, how they craved to seek out water and nutrients and salts from the soil. And how important they were, to grip firmly to the earth and rocks, to gain stability, in times of high winds and storms. Which I knew I loved, as my branches would wave and blow about, stretching my stiff limbs, increasing my flexibility.

How long I lingered in this state of communion with the tree, I could not say. But gradually, I became aware of a voice calling me back …

"…Take some time, to make sure you are fully back in your body," Radu was saying. "Breathe yourself back into your body, be conscious of your breathing. Breathe deeply, open your eyes, and come back to us in our fire circle. Take your time but be consistent and firm."

I was back in my own body now, looking about me. I could see several of our group coming round now. One girl close by to me, she had long, chestnut, wavey hair but her face looked visibly shaken by her experience, perhaps she had gone deeper into the tree, than I had.

Eventually though, we all managed to come back and returned to the fire circle. Some of our group, looked a little shaken, even afraid, by what they had experienced. No one was saying anything.

Radu started speaking again, "Each tree is an individual, they all have different characters. Therefore, not all Oak Trees, might act the same way, so it's best not to imagine you know everything about Oaks, just because you've formed a relationship with one.

"Each Tree, like each person, has their own role or destiny to fulfil. Some are teachers, some are guardians and others watch. Once you get to know a Tree, or a group of them, their purpose, and how you can help this, will unfold.

"In general, trees love people. They especially love it when we are singing and dancing near them. Despite what you might imagine, they are not static; especially when they are within a forest or wood. This is where you can encounter 'group' communication. While each of them is an individual, they can also act collectively, without any diminishment of their self. When walking in a forest, you can learn to pick up on this background murmur."

Radu paused a moment reflecting, then smiled and gave a little laugh:

"When I was very young, I saw my relationship with Trees, as one where, I was the party who had to give, to aid, and to heal. However, I soon discovered, that when I was feeling vulnerable and upset, I felt drawn to sit underneath them. There they made it clear, that they were there to help me at times; that our relationship was to be one of equality. They enjoyed supporting me, when I needed it and urged me to allow them to comfort me. Trees can be a fantastic source of healing; without even using any part of them for medicine."

Radu paused awhile and looked around the group. Then a young guy with very long brown hair, about the same age as me, put his hand up and asked, "But how do Slavic shamans heal people, Radu?"

"That is a very big question for me to answer," admitted Radu. He looked deep in thought a moment then continued, "We believe that sickness of the body, starts with problems in your spirit or soul. 'Physical sickness' is just a terminal stage, of soul sickness.

"Slavic shamans, whisper to the spirits of nature, they whisper to the water, to enchant it to heal, or they may also whisper, directly into the ear of an ill person, to give their spirit the strength to combat the illness."

"Sorry Radu, I don't understand, what is a whisperer?" It was the same guy asking, with the very long brown hair.

"It is hard for me to explain and is not what we are here to do. But I believe that the power to heal, via whispers, is a gift from the spirit world. Each disease is treated with its own special set of healing words. The words often rhyme and must be said in a single breath, in a barely audible whisper. In this way, we are speaking directly to your soul or spirit, not to you everyday mind. My grandfather could even heal someone, at a distance, by whispering words into the wind.

"That's why, if a Slavic whisperer, whispers a prayer or a chant over an object, it is believed that the object resonates, with the healing energy and its mere presence, can help those suffering from physical or spiritual ailments."

Radu then looked about the group, stopping and catching each person's eye, it felt almost like a challenge. No one asked anymore questions.

Then Radu continued, "There are sacred objects, that shamans use in rituals, which are just used to help them focus and direct their faith and spiritual energy. Other objects are imbued with power, so that they can work later, without the presence of a shaman.

"This is what we are doing today, we are cutting a healing wand from a tree. In later lessons, I will show you how to imbue it with power, and how to use it in healing."

We had finished talking and had moved back to our selected trees. Radu lead us through the exercise.

"Approach the tree, as you did before and meditate. So we are sitting under the tree basking in the tree's aura, while in a meditative state.

"Pose your request to the tree, tell brother tree, what you have come for and what you intend to do with the wand. Wait for a positive answer; remember it won't answer in words, you will know what it is, when you feel it.

"Now, while remaining in your mediative state, stand up and look up into the tree. Feel out its bio-electric field with your hands, like we did in a previous exercise, look for the aura glow about the branches.

"After a while, you may start to see several areas where the life force is diminished, or it may have withdrawn to say halfway along a branch. These are the areas where in time the branch will start to wither and become dead; this is the normal process of self-pruning in the wild.

"What we are looking for, is one of these branches with diminished life-force, but not yet dead. On it look for a small branch or twig which would be suitable for your wand. Remember, we only want to cut off the minimum of wood, just enough to make our wand.

"This is a form of divination or dowsing, least wise we are using similar senses. Look for one you are drawn to; at this stage I often find that I resort to touch; I touch and feel along the branch, till I know I have found what I am looking for.

"Now, look for the node point below the area of your 'divined' wand, this is the area you intend to cut. You should already have your small saw, ready in your pocket. Place your hands around the branch, one above the intended cut and one below.

"Now ask the dryad, to bring a shard of its life force, into your intended wand, give the tree time to react, remembering they have a much slower metabolism than we do. In any case we should have moved and blended into a slower time frame, by this time. When you have sensed the dryad's shard of life force, has moved into your wand, leave one hand below the cut point, with your other get your saw, and cut through the branch quickly and cleanly.

"Do not let your cut wand touch the ground but place it safely in your pocket or rucksack.

Then take some moist earth and rub some of it on the cut to heal it, sending some healing energy to the tree and thanking the tree for the gift it has given you."

When we all met back in our fire circle, there were some very proud faces displaying their newly gained wand. Some people, who were adapt at whittling, were already carving bits off their wand. Radu told us, it was entirely up to us how we fashioned our wand, but one end needed to be worked into a point. He would tell us more about it when we met next time.

***

'Ah this was a happy time for me …'

Wrote Touchwood in his large ledger. As he thought about that wonderful group of tree lovers. We were all so innocent and keen to learn, he thought, as a tiny tear welled up in his eye, but continued writing all the same.

'… without really realising it at the time, I had stumbled upon a genuine worker of the old ways, who had come from a hidden corner of Europe. As an individual, I had learned so much from Radu, and was happy to continue learning from him, for as long as he was willing to teach.'

'As a gathering of like minds we were beginning to cooperate and work together as a cohesive group. Each of us willing to collect

firewood, light fires, arrange food for lunch and many of the daily mundane chores, it takes to run a workshop. We even had a friendly and efficient girl, who volunteered to be our group coordinator. Kate would arrange between Radu and the rest of the group, times and dates for workshops.'

'We had all started off as strangers, from a wide area of locations. But now had come together, for a common purpose, for the love of trees and tree lore. I even dared to think, that perhaps I had found my place in the world, my group of likeminded people.'

'But then a very sad thing happened. Radu left a hasty message with Kate, that his father had suddenly died and that he had been called back to Romania, to be with his family.'

'After that, we heard no other word from him. Our little group seemed to wither and die; without the wisdom and insight of our whisperer Radu.'

Chapter 13

The Gathering

This world is waking up into the New Age revelation
Our spirits are responding to the raising of vibration
We'll use the latest sciences to aid our inner souls
To set the wheels of love and light a-rolling down the road

Steve Hillage

Radu had been a great teacher, whom I felt was very genuine. His sudden return to Romania had been a shock to everyone in the group; personally, I was devastated by it. When I heard the news of his departure, there had already been a workshop planed for the following Saturday, but of course this was now cancelled.

I decided that I would go to Glastonbury anyway, and spent some time in the little wood land, we had been using for the workshops. Perhaps it was my imagination, but the place to me, seemed to be forlorn and traumatized. As if the very trees themselves, were aware of Radu's lose and were sad, that the lovely people in the group, were not coming to work with them again.

I found it hard to stay in the little woodland for very long, the atmosphere was too dark and depressing. So, I instead took a trip into Glastonbury High Street, and wandered around all the new age bookshops there.

In one I discovered a magazine called 'Moonshine'; it was a Pagan magazine; one I had never seen before. It looked very home spun but was full of great articles, from Pagan people all over the UK. I was surprised to find, that there seemed to be a lot more magical or Pagan people about than I realized.

I can't praise the magazine enough, as it opened a window into the Pagan and magical scene in Britain, one which I so badly needed at that time.

In the listings at the back, was advertised, a mini festival, 'a gathering of Pagans' up in Leicester. It was scheduled for a few weeks' time, so I resolved to take time out to attend. It seemed the ideal opportunity, to meet other Pagan/magical people. I became very excited about this prospect, and could not wait for those weeks to pass, so I could travel up to the Midlands and attend.

Eventually the time came, so I travelled up the M5 motorway and found my way to the festival grounds. It was late on a Friday afternoon when I got there, what I found there was a truly wonderful and amazing experience.

As I walked through the festival field, I saw people dressed in cloaks of every color, shamanic looking people, with fur round their shoulders and belts with a myriad of pouches hanging from them. Girls walking round with striped leggings, colorful jester like tops and pixy ears. Pentacles abounded of all sizes. It really seemed that some people, were trying to outdo others, by wearing as big a pentacle as they could.

I walked through the tents, to what seemed to be the central fire, where a great tripod was erected and a massive, black pot hung on chains over the fire. A woman with long black hair stood over the bubbling pot, stirring its contents. She had a black cloak and many chains of silver, sporting all manner of emblems hanging on them. Her makeup was, what today I would call Goth, but it would be many years to come, before that term would be used.

Sat round the fire, were several guys banging drums of various shapes. The whole atmosphere was very tribal. I loved it; it felt like coming home. I sat down on an empty log just soaking up the atmosphere, smoke from the fire, blowing every which way in the swirling wind.

After some minutes one of the drummers said to me, "Would you like a go at drumming?" As he offered me a big round drum, that was about four inches thick. It had some round doweling, in a cross shape at the back, which you held onto, while you banged the drum with an odd little wooden beater, that was shaped like a thigh bone, only about six inches long.

I had not seen a drum like this before, but found I took to it quite well. I wasn't sure what rhythm we were playing too, but it really didn't seem to matter anyway.

After an hour or so of drumming, I began to wonder if I should go and pitch my tent, as it would be getting dark in a couple of hours' time. But before I could act on it, the woman stirring the pot, started ladling out bowls of the broth, she had been cooking over the fire.

I must admit, I was starting to feel quite hungry. The guy next to me had a bowl of the broth, it smelt and looked really good. Then before I knew it, I was passed a bowl of the steaming stuff. Fortunately, I still had my backpack with me, so I rummaged around in it to find my spoon. I found a crusty loaf of whole meal bread, I had brought with me, in there too. So, I pulled off a hunk and offered the loaf to the guy who had leant me the drum. He looked grateful and pulled off a hunk too, thanking me, then passed it to his neighbour. I watched my loaf go round the circle. It seemed everything was for sharing.

I gratefully ate my bread and bowl of vegetable broth, there was a few legumes in it too, not sure what they were, but it all tasted good.

After the food, I stood up and grabbed my rucksack. I wanted to pitch my tent and wondered just were to put it. Then a young lady, with long blond hair and purple cloak came over to the fire. She announced, that there would be a welcome circle happening at about eight o'clock tonight, which wasn't too long off. So, I asked her if she knew where I could pitch my tent.

"Anywhere in this field, we rented the whole field," she said.

I figured it would be best not to be too close to the fire, and so looked at a few tents a little way off and pitched near them.

During the weekend, all food seemed to be shared amongst everyone else, so I was glad I had managed to bring some to share. People seemed very happy to share musical instruments too, so I spent many happy hours round the fire side drumming. The whole concept of all this sharing with relative strangers, was completely new to me; it was quite wonderful though.

As well as the welcome circle, we had several other talking circles, in which a beautifully carved stick, called a talking stick, was passed about to those who wanted to say something. In this way, it allowed people space, to say what they wanted from the heart without being interrupted by anyone else. The talking stick was to be respected and only those who held it were allowed to talk.

The whole weekend was very lovely and interesting and informative. It helped me to feel part of a growing tribe of New Age Pagans. The gathering seemed to be in the very early stages of developing a national network of Pagans. Something which I felt was very much needed, as I had felt very isolated for some time.

Near the end of the weekend, at the closing circle, it was announced that if people wanted to, they could put their name down on a mailing list, to be informed of announcements of future events; I was eager to put my name on the list.

Also, it was asked if anyone could offer lifts to people, who had hitched here or came by bus. I volunteered that I could take two people back to anywhere near Bristol, with their camping gear. Later I was put in touch with two girls, who had come together and needed a lift, back to Bristol.

Natali and Rubi were lovely hippy girls who had attended Glastonbury festival several times before and it seemed, unlike me, were regular festival goers. Both were a few years older than I was, but they were very young at heart. Natali was tall and very thin and lithe with long chestnut hair, that always seemed in a tangle, and dark brown eyes. She wore a long dress with sandals. Rubi wore similar cloths but had reddish henna hair and was well-rounded with a polish accent.

On the drive back to Bristol, the van was filled with the smell of patchouli oil, and bubbly, girly laughter, as we were all in high spirits, after our weekend of connecting and networking with other Pagans; it was quite delightful. The girls plied me with useful information about the alternative scene here in the UK; something I knew nothing about.

Additionally, as it turned out they both lived in Bristol, only a mile away from where I lived. All this time, I had been looking for like-minded people, only to discover there were two, just round the corner from me.

On the drive back, I exchanged addresses and numbers with Natali and Rubi and asked them if they would be interested in meeting up and doing some ritual work. They seemed delighted at the prospect and agreed to meet up some time.

The drawing of ley lines, and the study of one inch OS maps of my surrounding area, was an ongoing hobby of mine. It not only helped me to become familiar, with the megalithic sites in the surrounding district but was a constant source of amusement and enlightenment.

I noticed that not only had churches, been sited on significant leys or intersections, but there were many manor houses and stately homes on them as well. I became increasingly aware that there must have been people, in times gone by, that were aware of this phenomenon and perhaps tried to utilise its power.

For some time, I had felt drawn to the concept of healing the earth. Healing Gaia, of all the damage caused by humanity, in its quest for progress at all costs. I had felt strongly, that to have full effect, the healing needed to utilize the Earths Energy lines or ley lines, at megalithic sites across the country.

I had read extensively on the subject and discovered that the ancient Chinese were aware of Ley lines centuries ago and termed them 'Dragon Lines'. Western people translating the Chinese '*lung mei*' as 'dragon paths'. It seemed, that the ancient Chinese where well aware of the earths energy system, and found it was remarkably similar to our own bodies system. Our connection to the earth is far greater than we realise.

When these 'Dragon Lines' cross each other, their energy spirals into a vortex. If several lines cross at a given point, called a node, it produces a massive vortex of energy. For example, earth energy dowsers have found that, the Avebury circle in England, is where twelve lines meet and go down into the Earth. Many such places across Britain, are where megalithic stone structures were built in ancient times.

Additionally, my research discovered, that if the ley line energy does not flow, or gets stuck, or is damaged by modern structures, the land becomes sick, preventing animals, plants, flowers, and trees from growing properly.

I felt strongly that my path, my fate, was in this direction. Going to sacred sites, to support the ley line structures of the Earth, to power up their energy and support the 'Dragons', in shifting the stuck energy in them and the Landscape.

Additionally, I felt that, if I was going to pursue the path of Earth Energy-worker, it needed a name. Then I remembered what my guide had told me, when I had fallen asleep on top of Silbury hill. He had said I was witnessing an 'awakening'. So in time I devised the concept of 'Awakening the Dragon'.

It was a couple of weeks after the festival, that I contacted Natali and Rubi and asked them, if they would like to come along to Stanton Drew, stone circle and help with some Earth

Healing at the stones. They of course agreed straight away. I also asked them if they knew any friends that would be interested in coming along also, so they agreed to ask around.

I had visited Stanton Drew, several times during my ley line studies and walks, as it was quite close to Bristol. The Stanton Drew stone circles are in the English county of Somerset. The whole complex is considered to be, one of the largest Neolithic monuments to have been built. The largest stone circle is the second largest in Britain, after Avebury.

The Great Circle, was surrounded by a ditch and is accompanied by two smaller stone circles. There is also a group of three stones, known as 'The Cove', in the garden of the local pub, interestingly called the 'Druids Arms'.

Not surprisingly, there are a variety of myths and legends about the stone circles. One such, is that a wedding party was turned to stone. The reception party was held throughout Saturday, but late on Saturday evening a man clothed in black, said to be the Devil, came and started to play his violin for the merrymakers. He continued playing till well after midnight, continuing into holy Sunday morning. When dawn broke, it was revealed that everybody had been turned to stone by the Demon.

On the day we arranged to visit the circle, I was to pick up Natali and Rubi and friends at Rubi's house. Somehow, we managed to squeeze everyone into my old white van. There was Natali and Rubi, and they brought a young couple along, Elizabeth and Adam and of course me, making five in our group.

My old van only had two seats. Natalie voted to sit in the front seat, so all the others were resigned to sit in the back of the van, with no windows. I had thrown a few cushions in the back, to help make it a little more comfortable. But nobody was complaining, as we were 'going on a day out into the country'. I was to learn, that people with no transport of their own, were only too glad, to get out of the city, if a free ride was on offer.

I had already told Natali and Rubi, about the significance of the stone circle and about the legend of the wedding party, turning to stone on a Sunday morning. This seemed to 'seal the deal', so we all agreed that Sunday morning was the best time to go.

It was a grey and damp Sunday morning. The clouds bubbled and scudded across the pale sun, as we passed through the style, into the field, which contained the stones.

There were a significant number of black and white cows in the field, along with a significant amount of cow pats too, which we gingerly dodged, on our way to the stones. There seemed to be stones everywhere in this field. At first it was hard to make out any circle at all.

But eventually after exploring the stones for a while, I was able to discern that the largest circle was Hugh. However, we all agreed to work at the smaller circle, at the far end of the field, which felt the 'right place to work', and we were less likely, to be interrupted by a wandering Sunday morning dog walker.

The five of us stood around a lovely old stone, covered in lichens and mosses. We joined hands in a circle with the stone in the center.

"Close your eyes," I said to the group. "Take a deep breath in, through your nose and hold it for a count of four, then slowly release it through your mouth. Hold again for a count of four, then breathing in again, counting to four."

I paused, everyone seemed to willingly follow my instructions, an expectant stillness descended on the group.

I continued, "Carry on breathing this way, breathing in … hold …then…out. Feel your-self slowing down drifting into a meditative state."

We continued in this way, for about five minutes, in silence. The only sound was the wind gently blustering through our hair. I could feel myself entering an otherworldly state. The state, I go into when channeling my higher self. When I felt the moment was right, the wind intensity suddenly increased, like someone suddenly opening a door.

I heard the words coming out of my mouth, "The best teachers of magic, insist students master the basic skills of meditation, visualization and affirmation. We then use these tools, power it by our imagination, which then becomes a means for channelling spiritual energy into the world."

As if in confirmation, the wind speed increased yet again, blowing our long hair about, every which way. I could feel the energy of the group increasing, people's excitement was palpable, there was a little fear there also.

"True magic," I continued, as the wind slowly subsided, "is the act of spiritual transformation. That is, to imagine the possibilities, to see the future as it could be. Then we invest the energy of hope, choice, commitment, and intention, in order to manifest it in the physical world."

I held onto the hands next to me, a girl either side, I squeezed my left hand tighter. I felt the tightness go round the circle, back to my right.

"Stand solid with your legs apart," I heard myself continue. "Solid as a tree. Feel your legs becoming the roots of a tree, growing … growing deep into the ground, searching for nutrients, searching for the healing Dragon energies of the earth; the empowering telluric energies. See those slumbering Dragon energies getting stronger, awakening. Draw those energies up from deep in the earth, draw them up to the surface, up into the stone and feel it drawing up your legs now. It's a slow sort of energy, quite different from the lightning bolt energy from the heavens.

"Green it is, like a green snake, coiling round your legs. Creeping, it is, creeping up slow, oh so slow. Erotic, tantalizing, filling you with the smells of the forest. Bouquets of forest flowers, baskets full of ripe forest fruits and the pungent but unmistakable smell of deer musk."

We continued to visualize, all this for quite some time. I could feel the green energy getting stronger and stronger, rising from the earth. It seemed to be circling round our little group too.

"Now look to the sky," I declared. "Visualize the lightning bolt energy from the heavens. This is a white light energy much quicker than the earth energy; flooding down from the sky."

As if in answer, there was a low rumbling from the clouds, some way off. One of the girls gave a muted shriek, but we all managed to keep holding hands and visualising white light energy coming down from the sky.

"See the sky energy, coming down into the stones," I said. "Meeting and melding with the green energy of the earth. Swirling round, mixing, and melding, energising the stones. Charging them, and empowering them, to draw up the dragon energies, deep in the earth, by themselves. Allowing them to charge the dragon paths converging on this place, long after we have left here."

We were silent for some time while we continued to visualise.

Suddenly the wind intensity increased again, blowing our hair about. Instinctively I opened my eyes and looked up to the clouds above us, just as droplets of rain started to gently fall on my face. 'Now is the time for energy raising', I thought.

"Now, slowly come back into your bodies," I urged. "And when you are ready, slowly open your eyes."

As everyone gradually opened their eyes, people instinctively looked up at the falling rain.

"Now we are going to do some energy raising," I declared. "Most of us know 'Cauldron of changes' as we sang it at the Pagan camp. We will sing it, in continuous round as we swirl round the stone, in a clockwise direction."

By this time, the rain was coming down more heavily. As we held hands and walked round the stone, in a clockwise direction, we sang:

> *"We are the old people, we are the new people,*
> *We are the same people wiser than before.*
> *Cauldron of changes, feather on the bone.*
> *Arc of eternity. Ringer of the stone."*

Faster and faster, we swirled round the stone. The faster we went, the faster we sang. The faster we sang, the heavier the rain fell. Everybody was soaking wet, there was wet hair and wet skirts and wet cloaks, swirling around in all directions. There was as much laughter as there was singing, everyone was breathless.

Suddenly, there was a deafening 'BOOOM' of thunder directly overhead. At the same time, the sky lit up with an almighty flash of lightning. There were more than a few squeals coming from our group.

The rain suddenly started hammering down. Almost in unison, we all stopped swirling and singing, but still holding hands, we crouched down to the wet earth. Then all together we started a simple chant in unison of 'aaaahhhh'! Which grew louder and higher, as we slowly raised our hands. Eventually reaching a crescendo, of full-throated shouts and screams with our hands raised to the sky.

We all hit the ground together, as if it had been orchestrated.

Silence now; except for the sound of rain hammering on our backs. Gradually people started to sit up, everyone looking round bewildered, by what had happened and how we felt. There was such a wonderful feeling, of camaraderie and joy. We were all soaking wet and muddy, from kneeling on the wet ground, but no one seemed to care. Then a natural moving together, we all just flung our arms about each other, hugging; in one big wet, muddy, loving huddle. It was bliss.

It was unanimously agreed, to adjourn to the pub, to dry off a little. What the landlord of the Druids Arms, thought about a group of wet muddy hippies, trapsing into his pub, and hogging his fire, I will never know. But he served us pints of real ale, with only a few sideways glances, at the girls wringing out their skirts, into the ashes in the hearth.

The pints were very well received and went down very well, with a few packets of cheese and onion crisps. We quickly occupied a corner table, beside the fire and stayed there for several pints, till we all had dried out and were warm again.

***

'It was clear that my training with the Atlanteans and the work I had done with Radu the whisperer, was coming in useful for this sort of Earth healing work….'

Wrote Touchwood, as he penned in his ledger, pausing to stroke his long grey beard, as he thought about those times so long ago. Absently he reached for a piece of cheese, on a small plate beside his elbow. As he nibbled on it, a thought came to him, so he wrote it down.

'… It was almost like, there was a guiding hand, helping me along the way, pushing me into the right training and directing me in this direction.'

'Candra the Rhennish girl had predicted correctly, when she bequeathed me the warrior's name 'Corin' – 'The Spear'.

"You are destined to lead," she had told me. "I can see that in you. One day you will."

'As I went to bed that night, I was contented and fulfilled. So happy to have been part of a small, but lovely group of people, who also were Pagan at heart, and wanted to give some good back to the earth.'

Chapter 14

The Cat Tribe

So, come all ye rolling minstrels
And together we will try
To rouse the spirit of the earth
And move the rolling sky

Fairport Convention

After the success of our first meeting at Stanton Drew, as earth healers. Our ragtag group decided we needed to meet on a regular basis. My house was the obvious choice as I had a large front room that could accommodate a group of people. Plus, all the others lived in shared houses with no extra space.

On our first meeting, we all agreed that we needed to be more organized. We created a provisional telephone tree of all our members, so far. Rubi agreed to write out the list of names and numbers, by hand and distribute one to everyone.

We set out to meet every two weeks at my house, to discuss and practice how our rituals would go. And we all unanimously agreed that few of us, had any knowledge of magical things, and that we should endeavour to learn more and share what we had learned with the group. I declared to the group that I was also moved to recruit more members; with luck we may even recruit someone, who had more knowledge of magical ways than we had.

A few days after this meeting I decided to make a poster. In those days we didn't have publishing software, so all posters were accomplished by photocopying pictures from a book or getting an artist to line draw what you wanted. Then typing out what you needed to say, then pasting it all on to a blank sheet of paper. This was called the master, then you had to find a photocopy machine, this for me was usually the public library. I copied the master onto coloured paper. It was a time-consuming process, but I very much enjoyed it. The poster went something like this:

Awakening the Dragon
Come gather with a group of earth healers.
We meet regularly at sacred sites in the area,
to work with the dragon paths, and magically
awaken the slumbering dragons of Albion.

There was more on the poster of course and a picture of a dragon, but that was the gist of it along with contact details.

Once the poster copies were made, I brought them along to our next meeting. Everybody was very impressed with them, which was wonderfully encouraging. Natali suggested that we magically charge the posters, to give them power to attract the right people to our group. She had seen something similar done at a festival she had been to. Natali told us, we needed to place all the poster copies, in the center of our circle and charge them by singing chants and drumming and raising a cone of power, sending all this energy to the posters, with the intent of attracting the right people to our group.

At the end of the night, I handed out the 'magically charged', Awakening the Dragon posters that I had made, and asked people to hang them in all the bookshops and wholefood shops we could find, or anywhere we thought like-minded people would hang out.

During our meetings and discussions of spiritual matters, it turned out that several people had members of the cat family as a totem or power animals. So that somewhere along the way, we became the Cat Tribe.

Natali had a good idea, she suggested that maybe we should invite knowledgeable people to give talks to the group. It just so happened, that she had a friend who was doing an acupuncture course, that may like to talk to us. I thought that was a wonderful idea and asked her to talk to her friend about it.

Our group were very fortunate, that Natali's acupuncturist friend was very keen to talk to us; in fact she came along to our next meeting, her name was Sherri.

Sherri has a very petite form and stands erect and proud and centred, like a dancer or yoga teacher. She has midnight blue eyes, her wavey blond hair is tied loosely with a thong at the back. Sherri was wearing a silky Chinese style jacket, which is beautifully embroidered and very tight fitting.

Her short, black, pleated skirt, is also made of a silky material, setting off her tanned, bare legs, the type of legs I call 'boy legs' in that they are long and straight, all the way down and not shapely like most women.

At our meeting, we all took our places by sitting cross legged in a circle. After our usual round of names and a short Centering Meditation, I introduce Sherri and invite her to begin her talk.

She starts with a brief introduction about her acupuncture course, telling us she has just come back from her final training and exams in China. Then moves on to the heart of her talk.

"We have an energy which flows around our bodies," states Sherri. "Which is of a vibrational frequency that we are not normally aware of. This energy has been given many different names, such as Orgone energy, Od, Chi, Ki, Prana etc. It is an organic energy, a living energy, which has a spirit of its own."

As Sherri speaks, I am impressed by her poise, as she sits with neatly, cross leges on the floor with a perfectly straight back. She speaks with a refined English accent, which makes me believe, that she probably went to a good private school.

"It flows all over the body," Sherri continues. "But is more concentrated along certain lines or meridians, the acupuncture meridians. This energy is linked to the vital life force, essential to our physical well-being.

"If the channels get restricted or blocked by say, stress or tension, we are starved of this vital life force and become tired, irritable, or depressed. The energy may become stagnant, causing 'black spots' of 'dirty energy' which can lead to illness if not cleared.

"This energy, ebbs and flows from certain points on the meridians, the acupuncture points. The chakras too, are power spots for higher level energies. These power spots or vortex are like tiny black holes and are the links, or gateways, between the various energy bodies which surround the physical body.

"These 'gateways' may become blocked or damaged, again causing adverse effects to the physical body. Manipulation of the acupuncture points can increase or decrease the flow and interaction, between the physical body and its higher vibrational bodies. They can be manipulated in various ways, by needles, heat, cold, pressure, gentle massage, or even laying on of hands."

Sherri's talk continues as she explains about the various meridians and what they are called and briefly how they can be used to heal various ailments. At the end she asks if there are any questions.

I immediately put my hand up and say to her that, we as a group are endeavouring to understand the nature of the Earth's own energy. And can she in anyway, link how to relate what she knows about acupuncture, to the Earth's energy field.

"I believe everything is interlinked," Sherri assures us. "Many of you may well have read about James Lovelocks, 'Gaia Hypothesis' and how he believes that: 'The planet demonstrates all the properties of a living organism'. I sincerely believe that the planet in which we live, 'Gaia' is a living being. This not only refers to the Organic parts, but includes the rocks, the oceans, and the atmosphere. 'Gaia', is in fact the sum of all these things."

Sherri suddenly paused, looking a little uncertain at me and took a moment to look around the circle, to perhaps see if we opposed her. Perhaps, she in the past, had been derided for speaking out in this way.

I smiled at her and nodded, "Please go on," I said.

Sherri seemed encouraged by this and continued, "If for a moment we can use the analogy of an ant colony. Within an anthill, every ant has its own tasks to perform, and depends on all the other ants for its survival. They all seem to know what to do, and when to do it. Yet nothing seems to direct them. This is because they have a 'group consciousnesses', or 'collective spirit', which is no one ant, but the whole combined.

"This is how I see 'Gaia'. She is the 'collective spirit' of all living things within the biosphere of life. She is more than that also, because added to this, is the 'spirit' of the oceans, the 'spirit' of the land, the 'spirit' of the elements, all adding together, to make the collective 'spirit of the Earth', 'Gaia' - the Earth Mother."

"Sherri," I intervened, I could see she was broaching on the religious aspect of what she believed. But I didn't want to be distracted by this and wanted to focus on the earths energies.

"I'm impressed with your awareness of 'Gaia' but as I said at the beginning, we as a group, are endeavouring to understand the nature of the Earth's own Energy. Can you shed any light on that please?"

"Yes of course," she assured me. "The nature of our planet, which is a 'living planet' with a Spirit, and 'energy' which flows across her surface; with meridians, power spots, and acupuncture points, just as we do. And, just as we have meridians which are not straight, so too are the earth's meridians, not straight."

Adam puts his hand up for a question saying, "But I thought ley lines *where* straight, that's the whole point of them."

"Thanks Adam, but the point is," Sherri continued, "is that the meridians are not straight. Nothing in nature, is truly straight, that is a quality known only to mankind. This I feel, is a key point here. Ley lines are straight and are man created, they are not the Earth's meridians.

"Power spots, the places where sensitives can feel the power of the Earth strongest, are natural phenomena and can be felt at many places, not only at sacred sites. These are the equivalent of our acupuncture points or vortices, where energy from other vibrational levels can enter our physical dimension. And, just as our acupuncture points can be manipulated in various ways, to give healing and various other effects; so too, I believe, can the Earth's."

"Wow! Sherri that's incredibly enlightening," I complemented. But went on to say, "I was aware that many thousands of years ago, our ancestors knew of these power spots and held their ceremonies at them. Ceremonies, that put them in touch with the spirit of the land, trees and animals. They also knew that certain trees such as Oak, Yew, Holly and Ash, had a sympathetic resonance with the energies involved and so were encouraged to grow round sacred sites, this led to the creation of the sacred groves."

"They also knew of the power of rocks and crystals in energy work," Rubi added. She I knew, loved to collect crystals, "And certain rocks, containing large amounts of crystals, like sandstone, granite and limestone were placed at sacred sites to interact with the power created there."

"Yes," I added. "This caused the natural vegetation and animals, surrounding these sites to increase, benefiting from the healing energies, and perhaps attracted to them. Our ancestors called these energies, 'Dragon energies' and learnt to work with them."

Sherri, I could see was a little bemused, by all our interruptions and additions to the subject. But determined not to be outdone and trying to reclaim her space came in with, "Our ancient ancestors learnt that standing stones, placed in circles, in certain ways, were able to store this power. They also learnt that the energy could be released slowly or suddenly according to need."

Sherri paused a moment, getting back into her stride, then continued, "They also discovered the ability to direct this energy, where they wanted and so discovered that linking sites together, say in a triangular shape, could spread the beneficial effects to all the lands, contained within the triangle. And so, the system of leys or dragon paths gradually evolved, like a nation grid, of organic energy."

"That's incredible Sherri," I bow to your knowledge of these things, I encouraged. "So practically, how can we work with these Dragon energies?"

"I feel the best way, is to observe our own bodies," Sherri intoned. "You may have noticed that by chanting certain sounds, the power spots and the Chakras on our body, are vibrated and resonated, and so can become activated. Additional rhythmic breathing, into these power spots also seems to affect them. So too does cyclic, repetitious chanting, bodily movement, and dancing. The vibration of rhythmic drumming too has a marked effect on us.

"Looking at native tribal peoples, we see that all these things are present in their everyday lives, rituals and festivals. They are constantly in touch with the natural rhythms of nature and their own bodies. I have been greatly inspired by the teachings of native peoples and tribal cultures from other lands."

Sherri then gave us an indication that she had finished her prepared talk, by placing her hands in a prayer position and bowing her head in the Chinese style.

"Well thank you very much Sherri," I concluded. "For sparing the time to come and talk to us, it was very enlightening and has given us much food for thought."

Moving on to the concluding part of our meeting I said, "We will now move on to our energy raising exercise."

With this, everyone went off to retrieve their musical instruments. During our meetings we all loved to make music with the various musical instruments that people brought along. I now had several bodhrans that people could use. I also had several long plastic tubes, one of which, I used as a didgeridoo, it worked amazingly well. Another heavier tube, I would hit with a drumstick, it made a very tribal base note, which I could vary the pitch of, by hitting at different places along its length; it was very popular with the group.

We would accompany these tribal percussions with loud chanting and whaling. The whole effect was very tribal and shamanic. We learned a lot about raising energy, for use in our rituals this way.

***

'In all, the Cat tribe were becoming quite tribal and shamanic in their workings. We didn't know it at the time, but this type of working magic, in a group, would become known as, 'The Urban Shaman ...'

Wrote Touchwood, in his new ledger book. He had already filled two books with his writings and was now on his third. He looked at the clean, blank pages before him and continued writing.

'There was a surprising development that came from the posters we had put out...'

'Several months later, a man called Ambrose Baldwin, saw my poster in one of the shops in Bristol and decided to contact me about it.'

'He rang me up one evening and told me he was an established author of magical work and had published several books on the subject. When he saw my poster, he was moved to encourage 'the awakening the dragon' work, we were doing in the group.'

'I hadn't heard of him and didn't quite know what to make of this call; was he genuine or just a prank call? I think perhaps that he guessed what I was thinking, when he said that he had a manuscript from his latest book and would I be interested in reading it. You never know, he said it might give you a few pointers. I almost snorted at this, because we needed a lot more than a few pointers, but I was flattered that he would do this for me, so said I would be delighted to read his manuscript.'

'When he asked me for my address to send it to, my initial caution was quickly overcome by the feeling that he was genuine.'

'When the manuscript arrived, I was so overcome with excitement that I couldn't read it at first. However when I eventually read through it, I was disappointed, as it all seemed too highbrow and too high magic for my tastes. It seemed that there were no practical exercises to learn. No how to do it, parts at all. It was all too academic for me.'

'However, when he rang me back to see how I had got on with the book, I tried to avoid any negative comments about it. But I was more direct when I asked him, do you know of any teaching groups or magical groups that I could join to learn about magic and spirituality. He went quiet for a moment, then said he would ask around and get back to me.'

Chapter 15

Samhain

Tell me more about the forest
That you once called home
For the wind cries of late
In the whispering leaves

The Dead Can Dance

One of the wilder members of the Cat Tribe was called Lily.

When I first met her, I remember I was at a medieval fair near Glastonbury Abbey, one weekend. Some battle re-enactors were promoting their troupe, by doing demonstrations with swords and quarter staffs. Lily was among them. I was impressed, by how she was brave enough to take on men much bigger than she was.

At the medieval fair, I was dressed in my cloak and tunic with my long staff; I was doing rune readings, off a blanket on the ground. After the demonstration Lily came over and seemed interested in what I was doing, so I gave her a reading. Afterwards we got talking and I told her about our developing group, the Cat Tribe. She was fascinated by what I had to say and asked for details of where we met.

I told her all the details and wasn't too surprised when she turned up to our meeting the following week. She quickly became a regular Cat Tribe member.

Lily was very much a Tom Boy; her nature was a wild warrior woman. I loved to see her dashing about with her sword and battle cry, that could stun a bull. She has long straight hair that's seems to be light brown, blond or reddish depending on the light. Her hair is as wild as she is, because it is usually blowing about and never tame.

She has piercing blue grey eyes, that warn you not to mess her about. She doesn't wear make up, has a large mouth, with red lips and over large teeth. But is very attractive in a boyish way. Lily had a lovely Scottish accent and loved to tell ghost stories, the more bloodthirsty the better; as far as she was concerned. I greatly admired her as she seemed to know what she was and what she wanted.

It was Samhain; the room was lite only by candles. The Cat Tribe had been gathering for a while now and had settled into a happy routine. As usual we were sat cross legged in a circle, now it was after the main part and at this stage I often would encourage people to tell stories. It was an old Celtic tradition to tell stories round the campfire, on a long winter's night. I endeavored to bring out the bard in each of us.

Lily was very keen on this part of the evening, and she would always have a story to tell. However, this time Lily started by insulting us all, but somehow, as she told the story in her lovely, soft Scottish accent, she somehow got away with it.

"You English are always going on about your Guy Fawkes. But did you know that the bonfires lite on November the 5th in Britain, are really the remnants of the very ancient ceremony of the 'Bone' Fires." Here she paused a moment to allow us to fully understand the gap between 'Bone' and 'Fires'.

She was now fully into her story tellers' character, commanding the room. Slowly, she looked about the circle in a challenging way but, seeing all the rapt faces, satisfied her that she had hooked us, so continued.

"Yes, in the highlands of Scotland, they still remember the old days and tell stories of the hard times, when the big cold came. They needed to prepare for it or die. At Samhain, it was a time to take stock of the food supplies. The vegetables and herbs were stored, cattle were brought down from their higher summer grazing lands.

"They knew, only the strongest cattle, would survive through the harsh winter. So, the weakest or oldest cattle, that they thought would not survive the cold, would be slaughtered. The meat then dried or salted to provide stores through the wintertime.

"So at Samhain, they would have plenty of fresh meat, that couldn't be stored, so they would have a big feast, so everyone could fatten up for the winter."

Lily as always was enjoying the undivided attention of the group. Her face seemed to positively glow, as she mentioned the big feast. With expansive hand gestures, she rubbed her hands together, as if relishing the very memory of it.

"All the bones and waste," she continued, "were amassed into giant heaps, and set alight. These were the original, 'bone' fires and were created to burn all the left-over bones. This is where the word bonfire comes from, literally, 'a fire of bones.

"With all the butchering that went on, this was a gruesome time for the tribes; and blood and gore would be everywhere. Not surprisingly, traditions and stories grew up around it. For it was thought to be a time, when the door to the Otherworld was opened, allowing the souls of the dead, to walk freely between worlds and join us in ours. Ancestor spirits were even invited to the feast, often with a place at the table, laid out for them.

"However, mischievous fairies and evil spirits, could also come through. So in the old days, people would often disguise themselves with strange costumes, as a form of protection from these malevolent beings. Some would also leave food out, on doorsteps to appease the fairies and spirits." Here Lily paused again, looking round the group. Everyone was rapt, eyes wide and shining, in the candlelight, loving her story.

"Many of these old customs," Gary pitched in. "Relating to Samhain, I can recognise in the modern Halloween night traditions."

"Exactly," I said. "A lot of old practices and customs have continued through to modern times. Often renamed and twisted about, to suit the church better, but they are still there if you know the origins."

I looked over to Lily, "Is there any more to your story Lily?" I asked.

"There are stories about what they did with dead people, but it's a bit gruesome. I'm sure you lily livered Sassenach's couldn't take it."

Lily looked about the group with a big grin, enjoying her joke, and the fact that she had insulted us again and got away with it. The whole group were smiling or laughing but, all declaring they would like some more from Lily.

"Well, way back in Neolithic times, they really revered their ancestors. There was like, a cult of the dead; the tribes used to literally worship them. Especial great chieftains or great warriors. The stories tell us, that when people died, some tribes took bodies of the dead and left them in special mortuary houses, well away from the main living areas, until the flesh had dropped from the bones. Only then was the skeleton or a few symbolic bones placed inside a burial chamber or long barrow." Lily paused again looking round the circle and was pleased to see a few faces grimacing, this time.

"Some tribes preferred, sky burials," Lily continued. "This is the practice of placing the dead, on high platforms, where the ravens could pick their bones clean. Ravens were considered sacred to the death goddess and helped the spirits of the dead travel to the spirit world."

"This practice of sky burials," Gary chipped in again. "Is still carried out today, high up in the mountains of Tibet, or by other cultures that still revere their ancestors like the native American Indians, I've been reading up about it."

I smiled at Gary and nodded encouragingly, so he continued.

"Some Neolithic people burnt their dead, till only the bones remained. It is also believed that some tribes practiced the act of…" Gary screwed up his face, trying to remember the word, "Tran… Transumption, in the form of grinding the burnt bones into powder, then adding the bone dust to wheat flour to make bread. This special, 'sacred bread' was respectfully eaten, by all family and tribe in remembrance of the dead ancestor. The book also said that this is thought to be the Pagan origins, of the Eucharist in the church today." Gary looked please with himself, that he had remembered correctly and was contributing to the group discussion.

I noticed also that Lily, was looking at him with a new look of interest, that I hadn't seen before. I felt a warm glow within me and smiled inwardly.

However, I needed to keep the focus on long barrows, as wanted to take the group to a barrow, for a vision quest ritual soon. So wanted everyone to be aware of their use in the past.

"It is thought also," I said, "that selected bones such as the skull and thigh bones were collected and housed within the ancient, long barrows to await regeneration. Some entrances to long barrows, were aligned to faced east, so that the rays of the rising moon on the equinox could flood into the entrance, allowing the spirits of the dead, to ascend to the moon god.

"The symbol of the skull, with two long bones crossed below it, as displayed in the long barrows, became a potent symbol of death, which is used right up to this day, on bottles of poison.

"Shamanic rituals and initiations were thought to be carried out in these long barrows, which often involved talking to dead ancestors through the skulls, interred there. In tribal cultures across the globe, there is an almost universal theme of symbolic death and regeneration, within a cave or underground chamber.

"And just as Lily said, in ancient times there was a skull cult, a practice that was caried right on up, into Celtic times. Amongst the Celts, the human head was venerated above all else, since the head was thought to house the soul," I concluded.

"Lily," I asked. "Do you have anything to add to this?"

"Oh aye! The Celts had a reputation as head-hunters, alright. They cut off the heads of their enemies, slain in battle and attach them to the necks of their horses, as war trophies. They would take them back to their village and display them. This practice was thought to prevent their enemy's soul returning to the other world.

"The story of Brans talking head, is widely considered to derive from the ancient Celtic 'cult of the head,' as it was considered the home of the soul. When Bran, a great Celtic leader, was mortally wounded in battle, he asked his warriors to cut off his head and to return it to Britain. Which they did and buried it in a place called the White Mound. And it is said, that if it is ever removed, Britain will fall in battle. Some say they built the Tower of London, on the same site, so it could never be dug up.

"By the way, did you know that Bran is an old Celtic word meaning Raven," Lily stated. "It's my thinking that in later years, the English mistook the original meaning of the story and thought it was talking about ravens. So, they put a conspiracy of ravens there, in the Tower of London, to maintain the story and keep Britain safe."

Lily gave another big grin as she looked round the circle of faces. Somehow, she had insulted the whole of the English race this time and was pleased that she had got away with it.

Chapter 16

The Temple

"It is entirely possible that behind the perception of our senses, worlds are hidden of which we are unaware."

Albert Einstein

In a dimly lit room, thirteen hooded figures stood in a circle; the silence was deafening. A strong smell of frankincense permeated the air. There was an Alter on one wall, with two beeswax candles, a silver chalice, and an old leatherbound book with a pentangle on the front. In the centre, a small statue of a goddess, with pregnant belly that was covered with crystals.

There were other things too, on that Alter, things I could only guess at their use. Along with objects collected from nature, like feathers, pinecones, and shells. On the walls were ornately decorated pictures, one was of a horned god, another depicted a beautiful goddess, rising from a lake. A strong sense of supressed anticipation filled the room.

Suddenly a gong sounds; reverberating around the room. As one, the hooded figures drop their robes behind them. And there, stood in the dim candlelight, were thirteen men and women, naked before their gods.

***

The silver bearded man called Touchwood, adjusts his desk lamp to illuminate his ledger more clearly. It is late into the night, almost dawn in fact. He has had trouble sleeping of late, after only two hours of sleep, he seems to awaken with a compulsion to write his story in his ledger book. With a slightly wavering hand, Touchwood continues writing.

'… *That was a wonderful time for me, I could hardly believe my luck. I had finally been given the telephone number, of someone in a legitimate coven. Ambrose had been true to his word and asked around and found someone who was willing to talk to me. I was beside myself with excitement.*'

'*Ambrose had told me to ring the high priest of the coven, in the evening, when he is more likely to be in the house. Because in those days, we only had land lines, so we had to be sure someone was in, before ringing. I had been told by Ambrose, it was a Stroud number which is quite a rural area. However, having now got the number, I was feeling too nervous to ring it. How silly was that?*'

***

Eventually though, I did pluck up the courage and rang at about 8.30 pm. Overthinking that dinner would be over and they wouldn't have gone to bed this early.

It rang three times, then a man answered, with a very broad West Country accent. What was I expecting Vincent Price?

"Hello, Doyle speaking."

Ye gods, what do I say now? I thought, I couldn't exactly say, 'Are you a witch?' or 'Do you run a coven of witches?' What if it was the wrong number, what would they say? What if it was the right number and he hung up, thinking it was a prank call. I hadn't thought this through. And now the pause was beginning to be too long, I had to say something, quick.

"Err…do you run a group?" I asked panicking.

"What sort of group?" was the reply.

On no! Now I'm back to the beginning. I was starting to panic. Then inspiration dawned on me what I should say, "Err… I was talking to Ambrose Baldwin … he leant me the manuscript of his new book to read. He recommended you to me, as I was looking for a teaching group."

"Ah yes, Ambrose, yes, good man. And you're looking for a teaching circle, you say?"

"Yes," I answered simply.

"Well, we do run a 'teaching circle'. Occasionally our coven looks out for new members. We have hived off several new covens, over the years."

"Oh! … Err yes. That's what I'm looking for," I'm sure I was sounding too stupid, he is going to hang up.

"Well," he continued, "I know that none of them, are looking for new people, at the moment…."

"But I've been looking for a group for…for years now," I blurted. "And I was on the point of giving up. I started my own group here in Bristol, but …but we are all beginners really. Then I was approached by Ambrose … and he said… he said I was on the right track, and I don't know anyone else …"

I sounded desperate; I knew it. I was desperate; it had been such a long time.

"Well look, I'll tell you what," Doyle said patiently. "We can meet up and have a chat and take it from there. What do you say?"

"Oh! … Really? Oh, that sounds great. Where do you want to meet?" I queried.

"I'm free next Tuesday night. Meet you in the Royal Oak pub, in Church Road about 7.30pm." Then he gave me directions.

"I'll definitely be there," I assured him. "But wait, how will I know you?"

"I will know you," he said mysteriously and hung up.

When the day came, I was completely beside myself. What had I done? I had arranged to meet a real witch, in a strange pub, at night! I could be abducted and held as a human sacrifice! 'No! don't be stupid', I told myself, 'That's just tabloid rubbish, you know it's not really like that. Remember what my guide said, these people honour the earth and the goddess'.

The Royal Oak pub bar was surprisingly busy for a Tuesday night. There was a bunch of young lads playing pool, in a side room and several middle-aged guys discussing football, at the bar. After buying a pint of best bitter, I sat at a corner table facing the door, so I could see who was coming in.

As I sat there, several more people came into the bar, mostly middle-aged couples ordering light snacks. Time was getting on; it was well past 7.30pm now. Already nervous, I was winding myself up into a real state of panic. I was beginning to contemplate; maybe I should go over to one of the couples and ask them. But what would I say? 'Excuse me, I'm meeting a head witch here, are you the one?' Stupid, stupid. I was being irrational, I just needed to be patient. Maybe this was a test of my metal? To see if I would chicken out and leave.

"Hello Corin, would you like another pint?"

There was a man stood in front of me, I hadn't even noticed him come over, in my panic. I just looked up at him. He had shortish wavey brown hair, wore a sleeveless vee necked jumper, with a regular shirt underneath. Average hight, with a bit of a middle-aged belly. He could have been a farmer.

"Oh, Doyle's the name. We arranged to meet. Sorry I'm a bit late," he said in a strong west country accent.

"Oh! …Doyle …yes, I'm here. I mean, we arranged to meet …" I stuttered stupidly. He was so ordinary looking. I looked around, half expecting to see the rest of the coven in tow. What was I expecting? Someone with a pointed hat and broomstick?

Then I realised, I had been staring stupidly at him for too long. "Oh …yes a pint of best would be nice."

He caught the barmaid's eye and called, "Two of the best on my tab please, Lucy," then sat down opposite me.

"So you know Ambrose, do you? How is he these days? Haven't seen him for a few years now."

"Er…. I've been reading his manuscript that he sent me, of his new book. Said it might give me a few pointers. He liked the poster I had put out."

"What poster would that be?" Inquired Doyle.

"Awakening the dragon. We have a small group, we go out to sacred sites, earth healing. But I've been wanting to join a formal coven for ages, and haven't been able to find one, till now."

The barmaid brought over the two pints of best bitter and laid them on the table. She was all smiles and gave Doyle a wink, as she walked away. He smiled back.

"Well you do realise, that if you are accepted into one of our groups, that we require a commitment to attend regularly,"

Doyle told me sounding quite stern. "It may take several years of hard work and study before you would be allowed to hive off, to form your own group."

"Oh yes, I'm completely committed," I enthused. "I've been through quite a journey already. And I'm keen to embark on a proper magical path and to learn more."

"Well, having met you now and Ambrose seems to think you're ok. I'm going to stick my neck out here. In a couple of weeks, we are having a joint ritual, with one of our sister covens. They have a novice too, coming along, so I'll invite you to attend that, and we will take it from there. What do you say?"

"Yes … yes. I would love to do that. Give me the details," I blurted.

"I will need to have a little chat, with my High Priestess first. If she's ok with it, I will give you a ring with the details."

After that we continued to chat about more mundane things, finished our drinks and went to our separate homes.

Back in the dimly lit room, the Wiccan temple. Thirteen figures are standing naked in a circle, the smell of incense is intoxicating, I'm having trouble breathing now. This is my first time in a coven circle. My heart begins to beat loudly in my ears and although the room is warm, I can feel myself shaking. I am terrified, excited, dumbfounded and a hundred different emotions, compete for my attention, as my head starts to swim.

'Ye gods, I think I'm going to faint. Breath; deep breathing.' I tell myself. Slowly, I calm myself and look about the circle; there are naked bodies of every shape and size. Some much older than I, maybe in their fifties with extra pounds, clearly showing. Some only a little older than me, who look in better shape. But I am, without doubt, the youngest there and wonder for a moment, why that is.

A slim woman breaks circle and goes about collecting the discarded cloaks, placing them outside the door in a basket. Another lady takes up the censer and wafts the incense, as she goes round the circle clockwise, muttering something I couldn't quite hear.

When everybody is back in place, a man turns to face east, raising his arms in the blessing position, ready to call the elements. Everyone turns to face the same direction. Out loud he says:

"Ye Lords of the Watchtowers of the East, ye Lords of Air; I do summon, call and stir you up, to witness our rites and to guard the Circle."

As he states these words, he draws in the air a pentagram. Everyone else is doing the same. Then I notice that several are holding a sort of knife, to draw their pentagram. I don't know what to do, so just face the same way as everyone else.

Then a rather trim lady, with dark curly hair, turns to face south holding her dagger up in the air and calls:

"Ye Lords of the Watchtowers of the South, ye Lords of Fire; I do summon, call and stir you up, to witness our rites and to guard the Circle."

Again, everyone has turned the same way and the pentagram is drawn. We continue in the same way round the circle. An older, plump woman calls:

"Ye Lords of the Watchtowers of the West, ye Lords of Water; I do summon, call and stir you up, to witness our rites and to guard the Circle."

Then a tall man in his forties turns to face north and calls:

"Ye Lords of the Watchtowers of the North, ye Lords of Earth; I do summon, call and stir you up, to witness our rites and to guard the Circle."

Many things were done in that circle that night, which I didn't understand, but it was a unique experience, and I will never forget that first time, and the myriad of emotions and sensations, experienced there.

After many years of searching, I had eventually been admitted to a coven. I had to drive thirty miles to attend, but it was well worth it, as at last, I was mixing with spiritual people who knew about the supernatural and worked with a proper structure.

My teachers were wonderful, and I soaked up the knowledge eagerly. It was a Gardnerian coven and so taught in a degree system. The novice like me, just beginning, not fully accepted into the coven. The first degree where you are fully committed and learn all the basics of circle craft. The second degree is more advanced, and you can lead a ritual circle, within the coven. The final grade is the third degree which is more advanced again and once completed, you could run your own group.

As the months went by, I attended many learning circles in the temple, with only a few other neophytes, like myself who were learning the craft of the wise. At these times we were clothed, and we had electric lighting.

It took me a couple of years, but I went through my first and second degree very happily, however, it was much harder work than I thought it would be but loved it.

I learnt things like the three main rules we go by which is, the Wiccan rede:

'An ye harm none, do what ye will'

This is basically saying that in magic circles anything is allowed, providing you don't hurt anyone or yourself.

Another important Law of three is:

'In magic, whatever you do will return to you threefold.'

This is often used to monitor day to day behaviour too. That is, if you send out love you get it back three-fold. If you send out animosity, you get that back three times also.

And of course, the last Law of three, the golden rule:

'Do unto others as you would have them do unto you'

Which is pretty clear and self-explanatory.

I also learned about how to create a proper magic circle and how to close one. How to call in the elements. And how to work with them. And of course I learned the basic concepts of spell craft. Honouring the Lord and Lady of all nature. And particularly, looking for and honouring the goddess in all women.

We Wiccans also believe in taking responsibility for our own actions, which is indicated by those rules, I just mentioned. But also, the belief that, what the universe hands them, is a result of their actions in the past. Conversely, what you may get in the future, is a result of your actions now.

And over all perhaps, is something called 'The Great Work'. This is using your life on this earth for self-betterment, self-examination with a view to personal development, as we go along. Which is hard work and requires dedication. You can't just be a monster all week, then go to church on Sunday and get redemption.

'The Great Work,' also includes acknowledging we have a dark side, which we need to work with. Wiccans understand that 'the dark' is an integral part of life on earth. So 'light energy' builds or creates, whereas dark energy destroys and tears down.

In this physical plane, there is an eternal battle between light and dark: creation and entropy. We work to create a balance between the two. But life is cyclic, the cycle of Life – Death - Rebirth, which we see in nature, in the cycle of the seasons.

Constant growth is unnatural and would ultimately create problems, as of course would constant destruction.

***

'Those were good years for me ...'
Wrote touchwood in his ledger, by candlelight.

'... I was learning the basics of circle craft in a formal learning environment, it helped me to feel legitimate. It felt safe and controlled and organised. It appealed to my organised engineer's nature. Somehow, I felt like I had become a legitimate witch, a proper Wiccan.

The style, contrasted dramatical, with the work I was still doing with the Cat Tribe, which was wild, impassioned and sometimes a little out of control. The Cat tribe didn't feel legitimate, we felt like rebels to society. In some ways, that appealed to that side of my nature.

Both sides of my nature were being sated, I felt satisfied and complete for the first time in my life'

Chapter 17

Water Goddess

My Pagan heart
My Pagan soul
Got to go to the Holy wood
When the sun is good, to the Holy wood
Van Morrison

It was a hot, sultry, summers day in August. We were walking round the edge of a field of wheat. We were a mixed group of about twelve young men and women, all in their twenties or early thirties.

Cat Tribe had accepted an invitation from an Oxford group we knew of though the national Pagan network, for a joint celebration of Litha. We were camping at a privately booked field, at a farm in Wiltshire. It was a sort of mini festival, where we could camp, cook, and celebrate together, in ritual and energy raising.

As we walked, I had been discussing the evenings ritual with Zoey, the leader of the Oxford group. We were getting on well, as we both had similar ideas about rituals and energy raising. And we talked about some of the minor problems we had encountered as Pagans and as leaders of these type of groups

We had been exploring and walking for some time, and we were all hot and starting to sweat. When someone at the front of our group shouted, "Hey look there's a river, lets swim."

There was a general swarm towards the leafy bank. Once people saw the cool inviting water, everyone started stripping off their cloths and tippytoeing down the bank into the water.

By the time Zoey and I got there, there were already several people skinny dipping, in the luscious, cool water. It was a lovely inviting sight. I looked over to Zoey, she just looked back, smiled at me, then shrugged and started stripping off her clothes. Not wanting to miss out, I did the same.

Before long, Zoey was standing there before me, fully naked.

Zoey has very long, black, straight hair. It was almost the black of a native American Indian, although her skin was light, and her face had a Nordic look; handsome not pretty. With deep blue eyes, nicely shaped black brows and generous mouth. Her body was tall, but study like a warrior, she had large pendulous breasts and the thickest, blackest bush, I have ever seen.

I was only half undressed, I think she must have seen me staring at her, for she said, "Come on slow coach." Then she slowly made her way down the bank into the water. So I quickly stripped off the rest of my clothes and followed her naked form down the bank.

The water was deliciously cool, and gently flowing and there was lots of green water weeds growing in it. Before long the scene was becoming like a Waterhouse pre-Raphaelite painting, of water nymphs and water weeds and water lilies.

Gary made a sort of water weed, crown and placed it comically on Sherri's wavey blond hair. Her naked, petite form, immediately took on the stance of a shy water nymph, then suddenly pushes Gary into the water, as she swims away laughing. Gary comes spluttering to the surface, head covered in green weeds and water streaming off him looking like some Undine rising from the deep.

Natali, is swimming through the green water weeds, enjoying the sensation of the water plants, brushing sensuously along her lithe, naked body; her chestnut dreadlocks streaming behind her. She has a smile, so serene with sensual bliss, it quite takes my breathe way.

Noticing Zoey swimming nearby, I decide to join in the fun, as I collect a great bundle of weeds, and shout, "Hey Zoey, I have a present for you."

Zoey obligingly stands in the waist deep water, looking expectant. With the water cascading off her naked breasts, and the sun shining through the droplets of water, creating shimmering rainbows on her skin, I am quite taken aback by her loveliness.

I delicately place the water weeds on her head, arranging them to create long flowing green locks. Clearly, she approves of the new look, as she theatrically spreads her arms wide, palms up, head inclined to the sky, looking like a temple priestess, supplicating to her goddess.

It was quite a mystical moment for me, as I could also see the goddess in the woman shining through. The innocence and the worldliness, in one form.

I fall to my knees, spreading my arms wide saying, "My goddess," in mock worship. But I am only half joking, as she looks so magnificent.

Other people were splashing about and creating strange weedy costumes, in the bright August sunshine. It was a wonderful scene, healthy young bodies, splashing about so innocent and naked, in the bright sunshine, chattering, laughing and happy, playing like kids.

Then I noticed a gradual hush descending on the happy group, so I turned to where people were looking. Descending into the water, through the rushes, a little further down river, was Caroline.

She had been lagging behind the main group, with her husband John, but had now caught up, discarded her cloths and was making her way through the tall bullrushes, a little way off. The water was just above her knees, showing her full nakedness. The sun was behind her, lighting up her long, bronze-coloured hair, forming a corona round her head. Her heavily pregnant body, her bulging belly, her large swollen breasts, and long chestnut bronze hair, was an utterly breathtakingly, beautiful sight.

The whole group of us, now were silent, all holding our breath, not wanting to break the spell, totally awestruck, watching this mother goddess, slowly descending though the rushes, and finally, gently leaning forward to submerge herself, in an elegant slow-motion dive into the reedy waters.

Somehow, Caroline was totally unaware of the attentions from the rest of the group, as she swam upriver towards us.

"The water is so deliciously cool," was all she said; the spell was broken.

Boy, girl started chatting and splashing again, but far more subdued than before, as each was still partially rapt, at the vision of the mother goddess, we had all just witnessed.

It was fully dark now, as we reached a crescendo of energy raising, as several drums banged, twenty young voices chanting, louder and higher. Someone had even brought a large bull horn, that had a bugle mouthpiece attached, creating a wonderfully loud bull call.

We had danced round the fire, holding hands. Cloaks and long skirts, flapping dangerously close to the fire. Someone had branched off, leading a snake line round our small camp, weaving in and out of the tents. Then back to a clear space beside the fire, forming another circle. We had all grabbed our drums or other instruments, for the final energy raising.

What a caterwauling finale it was, as we reached our ear-splitting climax. Then everyone dived to the earth, breathing heavily, sending all our built-up energy, to the healing of the trees in the rainforests.

After our group ritual, we had all gathered round the campfire to eat our evening meal, which had been simmering away, in a great pot hanging on a tripod over the fire.

After our exertions, the spicy, vegetable stew, tasted wonderful, accompanied by fresh wholemeal bread loaves.

We had eaten late, as the food had taken much longer to prepare and cook over the campfire, than we expected. We were all quite tired, after the blistering heat of the day, and the exertions of the energy raising.

It was getting late, and the campfire was burning down; most people had wandered back to their tents to sleep. Zoey and I were the only ones left beside the fire. We had been conversing most of the night. Both of us had had experience working in groups and were familiar with the concept of raising energy and directing it toward a particular cause.

At the moment, we were discussing the different ways that could be used to raise energy in a magical ritual.

We had both worked as solo practitioners with things like meditations, yoga and deep breathing exercises and agreed that these were very good, used on a daily basis, to help raise your vibrational level and increase your awareness.

We had both also worked in groups, energy raising using things like singing & chanting of various sorts. Rhythmic drumming and clapping also was commonly used in groups and we had both done that too.

We then talked about the more exotic practices, of some religious groups, such as the whirling or howling dervishes. Or the repetitive rocking or shaking some people practice. Neither of us had tried these and I admitted, I wasn't drawn to those methods for inducing trance states or raising energy.

When we had Pagan moots or the joining of the clans, we both enjoyed dancing, especially the Spiral Dance. The most successful method we had used, was the combination of chanting, drumming, spiral dance and raising a cone of power. It seemed a very satisfyingly tribal way.

However, we were both aware, that as long as we had two, preferably three people, in the group who were able to orchestrate the raised energy and concentrate on directing it; that would be very successful. This is a role that Zoey and I, had worked with in these groups often and felt we were quite proficient at it.

We were congratulating and complementing each other, on our achievements, when we found ourselves being very close to each other; almost touching. We were both smiling and laughing, then we caught each other's eye. There was definitely, alchemical spark there. A wild chemistry, that we wanted to explore.

As we looked in each other's eyes, I became aware, that we had been dancing round the subject of sex magic. I knew that both of us, had been working with a Wiccan group and that both of us were still at the second-degree stage. So, neither of us had been involved in any way with this form of energy raising. I decided to name it, while the spark was there,

"You know Zoey, there is one energy raising method I haven't tried yet."

"Oh. And what would that be?" Zoey replied, with a wicked smile, as she placed her hand on my shoulder.

"That would be Tantra," I said. "Have you ever tried working with that?"

"No," she admitted, still smiling. "But I would like to,"

"Remember today, Zoey, when we were all splashing about in the river?"

"Yes, it was tremendous fun."

"Yes, it was wonderful. We were all naked, it was sweet and innocent, and we were whole heartedly embracing our sensuality, not our sexuality. I've been reading up about Tantra Zoey, and it stresses that it's important to approach it in the right way. We need to be in a state of 'Oneness' with the goddess or god. Have you ever felt you were channelling the goddess Zoey?"

"Yes, I believe I have done that at times."

"I need to become the god. And you the goddess. I need to see the goddess in you, and you need to see the god in me,"

I said passionately and placed both hands on her shoulders and squeezed.

"Today at the river," she said. "I believe we all were experiencing that. When the pregnant Caroline, entered the water, I swear I could see the goddess in her."

"Yes, me too, it was a truly spiritual moment," I confirmed. "But more than that, I felt at that moment, I was in love with her, or rather more like an Unconditional love. For those few moments, I would have given my life, to save her from harm." I placed both hands on my heart, "That's unconditional love."

Zoey looked at me, with a sort of awe in her eyes, "I feel I could do all that, with you right here, by the fire, under the stars. It feels like a timeless moment."

The moment did seem perfect, so I stood up, removed my cloak, draping it on the ground for us to lie upon. She then stood up also and started to untie the fastenings on my tunic. Heart pounding, I just stood there, in my power and let her do it.

Once my tunic was removed, she placed her palms on my bare chest and started to run her fingers through the soft hairs there. Then placing her cheek to my chest said:

"I can hear your heartbeat, it's getting faster." As she said this, her hands were undoing my belt buckle. Then, after gently undoing my zip, expertly placed her hands on my hips, sliding them down inside my pants and round to my buttocks; she squeezed them hard. I took a sudden, sharp intake of breath, it was exquisite pain, which caused stirrings in my genitals. I felt my manhood throbbing.

Slowly, she slid her hands down my legs, taking my pants with them, till they were round my ankles. As I already had bare feet, I stepped out of them, as she held them in place. She was now kneeling before me. I was naked and she was still clothed. It seemed to shift the power, so she was in control. I felt in some way very vulnerable, yet somehow excited by it.

As she kneeled before me, her face was level with my manhood, she was looking directly at it. Then she slowly leans forward, till she was almost touching it with her lips. I could feel exquisite stirrings in my genitals, my manhood slowly began to unfurl. Then she ever so gently, blew a soft hiss of her warm breath, directly on to my manhood. Which set it stirring into life, becoming more than half erect. Then, she blew again this time harder, and again. My manhood responded, seeming to like this game, and gradually became fully erect.

Zoey now looked up into my face, with a mischievous grin, seemingly pleased with her work. She reminded me of a mischievous imp. She then stood up and removed her cloak, laying it on the ground next to mine. The symbolism was not lost on me.

She now stood there, arms beside her, patiently expectant. I wasn't quite sure where to start, as this was a new game to me. She wore a fur waist coat, which had been made from an old fur coat, I think. And a nicely patterned blouse underneath. Her long skirt was a Laura Ashley print, which fell all the way to her bare toes.

I started with the waist coat, gently removing it, and let it fall to the ground. Then placing my fingers on the top button of her blouse, slowly started to unbutton it. As I did this, I noticed she was wearing a choker necklace, made of earthy Indian beads, with a small silver pentangle in the middle. And a second longer necklace of black leather, with silvery washers, of various sizes; I thought it was most unusual.

Being this close to her, I was now aware of a strong metallic type of smell, about her, which I found arousing. Then moving on to undo the second button, I felt her chest swell, as she sucked in a deep breath of air. Gradually, I worked my way down the buttons, to the bottom. Now there was a strip of bare flesh showing and I could see the rounding of her ample breasts. I slid my hands inside her blouse, at her hips, feeling her warm flesh on my hands, then continued to slide them round the back. At this point, I was kneeling before her facing her navel. I blew on it ever so gently. She made a low moan in her throat, as her head went back facing the stars above.

Sliding my hands slowly, up the warm skin of her back, I then brought them round to the front, to rest on her large breasts, they were surprisingly firm. I could feel her nipples hardening, on the palms of my hands, and her breasts swell and heave as her breathing increased.

As I stood up, I brought my hands inside her blouse again under her arms. I could feel the brush of her underarm hair, then raised her arms above her head, sliding the blouse off her arms and over her hands, in one movement; letting the blouse fall behind her.

I stood back a pace and looked admiringly at my priestess. Her Nordic, handsome face. Her long, black, straight hair, falling across her naked shoulders. Her magnificent, pendulous breasts, still heaving. She was a joy to see.

Stepping forward again, I looked for the tie of her wraparound skirt, finding it on her left side, I undid the bow, then peeled it round her body, till it fell to her feet.

She stood there in her long, white, French bloomers. I had not seen these before and was a little surprised. I looked at her face, she looked back demurely, then shrugged. We both laughed.

They were wonderful things though; I was surprised more women didn't wear them. Kneeling again before her, I slid my thumbs inside the elastic waist band, then slowly lowered the bloomers off her hips. Then, ever so slowly, pulled them down, just enough to expose her resplendent bush; it was wonderfully thick and black and curly. I lowered the bloomers a little more, then blew on to her exposed vagina, making the dark curls move a little.

Zoey took in a sharp intake of breath and started breathing heavily again; she had closed her eyes. I continued to slowly pull her bloomers down to her feet, exposing her lovely long legs. As I held them there at her feet, she daintily stepped out of them.

She was now fully naked before me, as was I. She stood there, straight, and proud of her naked womanhood. The goddess truly shone out of her, as the reflections of the flickering campfire ran across her body.

I too stood tall and straight, endeavouring to become the lord of the forest, the Greenman, Pan the protector of animals. Then I indeed, started to feel something, rush over me, that seemed to both terrify, yet filled me with a powerful calmness and strength.

I think Zoey must have seen it in me too, for she came over to me, embraced me with her warm, soft gentle arms. Then kissed me, full on the lips, with a passion I had rarely encountered. The feel of her warm, naked skin, pressed against mine, was electrifying. We kissed and embraced for several minutes.

Then I could feel Zoey's hand on my manhood, her hands warm and soft. She kneeled before me again and took my member, gently in her hands and drew the foreskin back, then up again. She expertly, started pumping again and again, till my spark took life in her hands and I threw my head back and groaned, "Mmmh, yes!"

But she instinctively knew the exact moment to stop, just before I was about to burst forth. She then took my hand and lead me to the cloaks and guided me to lie down on my back. She then straddled me, with her knees each side of my hips. Taking my fully erect member in her hands again, she then gently lowered herself on to me. I could feel the moist, warm place between her thighs, was ready as a ripe peach, as she guided my manhood into her dark and inviting place.

Slowly, ever so slowly, she rode me, gently moving her hips, back and forth. Sometimes round and round, with me inside her. She was in control and manoeuvring her body to gain maximum pleasure. Her eyes closed, her head back, a soft moaning in her throat. Her pendulous breasts, swinging with the rhythm.

'She truly was a goddess', I thought.

Slowly she encouraged her god, for the remainder of the night, taught me how to unlock the power and passion in a woman, the secret ways of Love and ecstasy.

As our bodies and minds merged as one, for a while at least, I had known the mind of a woman. And realized my own gentle, feminine nature, the creative, emotional, inspirational, and intuitive self. For a brief moment, I knew what it was to be a whole person - a true man.

Chapter 18

Earth Dragon

"The ancients knew something,
which we seem to have forgotten."

Albert Einstein

Everything was painted silver by the luminous light of the full moon.

An ancient, long-barrow lay concealed under the neatly clipped grass. Before it laid a low, stone slab, that could have been an altar. Its sides heavily carved with swirls and spirals; in the centre, a curious triple spiral design demands our gaze.

Behind the slab, amongst the jumble of boulders, a huge stone had been moved to one side revealing a black entrance wide open, gaping like the mouth of a corpse; its dark depths stood as a challenge to any who sought to enter.

Nervously I walked over to the entrance, standing there knowing I must enter. There was no doubt about it, this was a very spooky place at night. There was a prickling on the back of my neck, and I felt a shiver go down my back, as I knelt before the entrance, asking permission of the barrow guardian, if I could enter this sacred place. Feeling no sense of rejection, I slowly and reverently entered the darkness of the barrow.

At one and the same time, I was attending the Wiccan coven and learning all that they had to teach me and continued meetings of the cat tribe. Here, we were all learning together, but now I could see, that members of the group seemed to accept me as their leader. After all, we were often meeting at my house and usually, I was the only one with transport when we went out to sacred sites.

The Cat Tribe had been 'Awakening the Dragon' at several stone circles already; during the daytime. But, for some time, I had felt we were ready for a more in-depth, vision quest. I had been to this barrow many times, on my own in the daytime and knew it for a place of power.

Now the plan was to do ritual inside the barrow, build the energy with drumming and chanting and spend the night inside, hoping perhaps for significant dreams or visions.

In a previous ritual and meditation, I had created a sigil, that represented a personal logo, and spirit name for myself. This spirit-name was 'Earth Dragon'. It was intended, to not only state I was an earth healer, but also to add power to our earth healing rituals.

A sigil is a type of symbol used in ritual magic. The sigil refers to a symbolic representation of the practitioner's desired outcome. The magician acknowledges a desire, he lists the appropriate symbols and arranges them into an easily visualised glyph. Then, by force of will, hurls it into his subconscious, from where the sigil can begin to work unencumbered.

After charging the sigil, it is considered necessary to repress all memory of it: often by burning it. In modern magic, when a complex of thoughts, desires and intentions, gains such a level of sophistication, that it appears to operate autonomously from the magician's consciousness, as if it were an independent being; it is called a servitor.

The sigil looked like this: a dragon's egg half buried in the earth; represented by a straight line. Out of the egg, a coiling line, representing the dragon emerging and pointing to the sky.

Part of the ritual in the barrow, was to charge the sigil as much as we could, then ritually destroy it, releasing its power.

I entered the gaping mouth of the barrow. Inside the walls were smooth and silver grey. The rock is encrusted with millions of large and small crystals of quartz, glistening in the reflected moonlight. Looking closer, I could see that the rocks also contained many fossils of the spiralling Ammonite type. These could be seen covering the roof above and on both side walls.

As I walked further into the darkness, I could just make out carvings of intricate spirals and zigzag patterns. I knew that the spirals represented the spiralling earth energy, and the zigzags represented underground water.

Not wanting to profane the sanctity of this place with my battery torch, I produced a candle and lighter from my leather hip pouch. Shakely my hands lite the candle wick, which spluttered into life, illuminating a small area around me. But at the extremities of the light, out of the corner of my eye, deeper shadows shifted and moved, forming grotesque, ghostly shapes that seemed to gather all around me.

I swallowed the lump forming in my throat and continued along the passageway, until I entered a larger vaulted room.

Knowing this chamber to be the end of the barrow, I placed the small candle on a nook in the stone. Satisfied, I walk back down the passageway to the entrance, where my Cat Tribe members were waiting.

Sherri, had previously prepared a green sage, smudging stick, picking the leaves from a bush in her own garden; in readiness for our ritual tonight. She now lights it from the flame of a zippo lighter that Gary has produced. Together they blow and wave the smudge stick, till its pungent smoke fills the night air.

Sherri wears a peat-coloured cloak, with fur hand stitched, around the hood. Her straw blonde hair, has been braided in several thin plaits, decorated with coloured silks and beads, on one plait hangs a bird feather. On her forehead, she has drawn a small spiral in eyeliner, and a thicker straight line from her lip down her chin. She looks for all the world like a shamanka.

Her midnight blue eyes, look up at me expectantly, as she offers me the smudge stick. Reverently, I take it from her, along with the long, white, swan's feather, which I waft around the burning herbs to keep them alight.

Sherri drops her cloak in readiness. Underneath, she has a suede waist coat with many tassels and dangling beads, shells, and hag stones. Her petite form is well suited to the light tan, chamois leather wrap skirt, setting off her bare legs and a hint of thigh, through a slit at the side. She stands there erect and proud and centred, as I smudge her from top to bottom. Then as she turns, presenting her back, I cleanse and purify her from bottom to top. Paying attention, to her wavey blonde hair which is tied loosely with a thong at the back.

Sherri is now ready to enter the barrow. I turn now to Gary, who is next in line. He is wearing a simple blue tunic down to his thighs, tired round his waist is a long leather belt which has no buckle but is tied with a clever knot. Over this, he wears a brown, sheepskin shoulder wrap, his long black locks falling down onto the fleece. Into his belt is tucked a black handled athame. His baggy, simple tartan pants complete his look.

As I finish smudging him, front and back, he asked me if he should ask permission to enter the barrow. His light grey eyes looked at me as he said this, I can see a hint of fear in them. To reassure him, I place a hand on his shoulder.

"Yes," I say. "Ask with genuine respect in your heart, then wait at the entrance, till you feel any animosity clearing."

Then I turned and proceed to work my way down the line, there are six of us in all. The last girl was Lily. After smudging her all over, she offers to smudge me in return, so I stand straight and true in my power, as she fans the pungent sage smoke, over my whole body. She seemed to pay particular attention to my back, but eventually she is satisfied. Lily and I then turn to enter the darkness of the barrow entrance.

Inside, I notice that several candles have been lite in the large, vaulted room at the end. As we entered the end chamber, the others had formed a rough circle, which Lily and I joined. Everybody had their own drum now, which most had brought out in readiness.

I feel it is important to inform the barrow guardian, of our intent for the evening. So as we all join hands in our circle,

204   The Touchwood Chronicles (Book 1)

I make a statement to the borrow guardian, but at the same time, making it clear to all, what we had committed to do this night.

At this point, I bring out the Earth Dragon sigil, that I had previously prepared and show it to the group. Telling everyone I wanted to charge it up, with the energy we raise tonight, to make it a powerful symbol of earth healing. I then place the paper with the sigil on the floor, in the centre of our group.

All the drums come out now, and we all start beating with a slow but regular heartbeat. Gradually all the drums become synchronised, into a powerful earthy heartbeat. The sound ricochets off the walls, reverberating round the chamber, till it appears, that there are many other drums, all beating together. The acoustics of the large, vaulted room seemed to almost, be designed for this type of drumming.

As the drumming heartbeat continues, I start to feel an otherworldly feeling come over me, till I'm aware, that I have started to chant, along with the rhythm of the drums. The chant has no words, but seems to be coming from a primal place, inside of me. A deep soulful mourning sound.

"Haya haya haya …. hay haya hay … haya hay … haya haya haya …" repeating over and over in continuous round.

Gradually, others join in with the soulful chant. The drum rhythm shifts, and changes as does the chant, but the soulful mourning theme continues. It sounds like the wailing of the very earth itself. It was completely unlike, anything else we had done before, inside my house, or in a stone circle. Perhaps, intuitively we were singing the song of the barrow itself.

After some time, the chant gradually faded, and we all took a break from drumming. But it was only one of the many, energy raising sessions we would be doing that evening.

Some of them would be wild and ecstatic, where we would stand up and dance about, while drumming and shouting. All the while charging up the barrow, with our songs and wild drumming.

Inside the barrow was a timeless place, we could see no moon, we could see no stars, but eventually our enthusiasm for drumming ran dry, and a weary sleepiness steeled over us. As one by one, people crawled into their sleeping bags. Till only Sherri and I were left.

I was about to pull out my sleeping bag when Sherri came over to me and put her arms around me. In our group, we often hugged each other, especially after an earth healing ritual, but somehow this seemed different. She was so petite, somehow, she seemed like a child afraid, yet she was only five years younger than I was. With her head nuzzled into my chest now, I bent my cheek to the top of her head. I could smell the sage smoke, in her soft blond hair. Placing my hand on her bare shoulder, to comfort her, it seemed so skinny and slight, but warm and soft and feminine.

I wasn't really sure what this was. Was it a proposal, did she want me? As if she was reading my thoughts, she shifted herself, raising her head and looked up at me. Her midnight blue eyes, in the candlelight looked like black pools, her face pale, her lips a light red.

She reached up and kissed me on the lips. Ever so softly at first, but then more passionately; her lips were soft and responsive. Although I was a little taken aback by this new development,

I couldn't help but respond, to her amorous advance. Delightful feelings flowed through me, I put both my hands, on her warm, bare shoulders; as she was wearing a sleeveless, suede waist coat. She was warm and responsive, but as she squirmed and shifted to reach up to my lips, I could see that her knee length, chamois skirt, had ridden up high, exposing her deliciously, thin, and tanned legs. I couldn't help but be aroused, by this highly intelligent and strong woman, who was very sexily, kissing me as well.

I could feel my manhood stirring, sending delightful feelings through my body. Then Sherri moved a hand down to the bulge in my trousers and started massaging my manhood. I really was convinced now, that she really intended to seduce me, right here in the barrow, with the others not that far away!

Then suddenly, she stopped kissing and buried here head in my chest again; I could feel she was shaking and sobbing now; I could hear little whimpers coming from her. I embraced her slight body with my strong arms, to comfort her. I could hear her sobbing, but then she whispered through her tears.

"I'm sorry Corin, I don't know what came over me. It's my boyfriend, we have just broken up, after a year together. He was very angry with me, I thought he was going to hit me."

I couldn't believe what I was hearing. How could anyone, be violent with this lovely, clever, and sexy girl? I could feel a paternal protection, for this woman, wash over me, like a wave. At that moment, I could have battled this angry boyfriend, with swords and not care for my own life, so long as I could protect her.

"I just can't seem to help myself," Sherri admitted into my chest. "If I like someone, I just feel I want to kiss them. I've kissed several girls as well."

At that moment, several conflicting feelings, battled for attention in my mind. It was very confusing. I didn't know whether to answer or not. But eventually I said, "So it was you, who went with someone else?"

"Yes," she continued. "I had been chatting with his best friend Mike, who had called round to my flat, to see Tom, that's my boyfriend's name. Anyway, I found that I was enjoying the conversation, I began to like him. Suddenly I was kissing him."

She sniffed and dried her tears, on a tissue she produced from somewhere. Then continued, "But Tom had finished work early, and came round to see me, he had a key and found us. He was very angry Corin, he punched Mike in the stomach, who quickly ran out. Then he turned on me, he threw the key at me, hit me on the cheek, look there's a mark." She looked up at me, like a lost child and tried to kiss me again. But I brought my hand up and placed it on her lips.

"No," I said firmly, "you really mustn't seek comfort from people that way, it can get you into trouble."

"Yes, I know, it's happened before," she admitted. "But Corin, I'm scarred to sleep in this barrow alone. I don't think I could sleep, alone."

Having heard her story, I wasn't willing to have her get me all worked up again, no matter how appealing she was.

"Look," I said. "I will tell you what we will do, I will unzip our sleeping bags like this," as I said it, I did it.

"Then lay mine on the floor and with yours over us. We can snuggle up together, I can hold you and keep you safe, how does that sound?"

She immediately lay down on the sleeping bag. I lay behind her, spooning together. I put my arms protectively round her and pulled the other bag over us. She wriggled and snuggled into me, wiggling her lovely bottom into my groin.

'Ye gods, this is testing me,' I thought.

"Look," I said. "Stop all that stuff. Just relax, I don't want to do that, just cuddle, lets sleep."

Sherrie went quiet then, I thought she might be sulking, but in a very short time, I could hear her breathing slow, then a very faint snoring sound; she was asleep.

I woke up, to the faint hint of dawn light, shining into the cave. The stone walls looked golden in the early morning light. I can hear, the low steady breathing of several members of my tribe, sleeping nearby. There is a woman beside me, dressed in animal skins, my arms around her sleeping form. I can feel the soft leather of her tunic and the warmth of her naked legs. Under her head is a bundle of soft fabric, with a fur pelt.

For a long minute, I am confused about where I am and what I'm doing here. Who is this woman beside me and who are the sleeping forms close by?

Then I remember, we are part of the work team, building this cave. We have been guided and instructed by the wise sorcerers, who call themselves the Draoidh. They wanted a special cave built, to house the bones of our dead ancestors.

Our dead, would be laid out on special platforms, so that the goddess of death, could send her ravens to pick the bones clean. Only selected bones where collected, such as the skull and thigh bones. These would be housed in the special cave we are building. The rest of the bones would be collected and burned in the bone fires.

I have seen other caves, they were magnificent, the rocks of the chamber were covered with earth, then covered over with white, chalky flint stones, so that from a distance, with the sun shining on it, it resembled a giant white egg, half buried in the earth.

In our cave, we built a long thin passageway, linking the central chamber with the outside entrance. The Draoidh took great care, to make sure the entrance faced a certain direction. They used strange instruments, long notched poles, and long lengths of pig's intestine and flat discs, made of gold, with many mystic marks upon them. Much magic and incantations were performed, so that the cave faced exactly, toward the rays of the rising, winter solstice Sunrise.

I saw it with my own eyes, last winter when we were still building. On that day's dawn, a long shaft of sunlight, penetrated into the womb of the earth and illuminated the chamber with glowing, golden light.

I have heard say, that in other caves, the Draoidh perform strange, macabre ceremonies. They collect the bones from the bone fires, then take them into these special caves, were they grind the burnt bones into powder, adding them to wheat flour, to make bread. This special bread is thus eaten, by family and tribe, in remembrance of the dead ancestor.

I find this practice distasteful and am fortunate that my tribe does not practice this ritual.

However, my brother's wife, has a brother who was apprenticed to the Draoidh. He told me of the ceremonies of the Draoidh, in a cave many miles away.

He told me, that on the longest night, a dozen holy men and women, would wait in the darkness, waiting for the return of the Sun. They had told him that no fire or light was allowed into the Holy chamber, of the special cave. But water in great stone bowls, was heated by hot glowing, egg shaped stones, that were heated in a fire outside. As apprentice, that was his job, to keep the stones heated and the fire going.

Repeatedly all night long, he would bring in the glowing stones, to place in the stone bowls of water. The hot stones, would heat the water, creating steam that filled the chamber. Every time he went in, it would make him sweat profusely. But not only that, the air was thick with the aromatic smoke, of the shaman's mushroom, and other vision herbs.

All this allowed the Draoidh, to talk to the spirits of the dead and contemplate the past and contemplate the future, of the tribe. And on the dawn of the longest night, through this hallucinogenic haze, of smoke and steam, would penetrate the golden shafts of sunlight. Illuminating the chamber and refracting through quartz crystals, they had hung from the roof and reflecting from the water basins, creating a carnival of light and colour.

Then great whoops and shouts could be heard from inside the barrow. Then the sound of great bronze horns, would fill the dawn, alerting all about that: the new Sun has been reborn

... rejoice and celebrate. The Sun has graced our land again... Happy Suns return... many happy returns of this day.

The woman beside me was stirring now, she was turning her body to face me. As she looked at me, I did not recognise her. Gone were her dark skin, black matted hair, and thick set bones like the rest of my tribe. This woman had the face of an otherworld creature, with strange, coloured eyes of blue, she had pale hair and pale skin and a small, flat face ...

"Corin? Corin?" She said to me, "Why are you looking at me like that? You seem very strange."

I looked at this strange woman, not knowing her, but there was something familiar about her ...but I couldn't place it... not from my past ... but somehow from my future...

My vision became blurred, then all my peripheral vision, came drawing into the centre, leaving only a white vertical line. Then this line expanded again, and it was like the right side had swapped over with the left side of my vision.

"Sherri? Is that you?" I managed to utter.

"Of course it's me silly. You looked very odd there, for a minute. Did you have a dream?"

"Sherri! Oh, thank the gods," I put my hands each side of her face, and kissed her on the lips.

"I thought you said, you didn't want me anymore," she protested.

"Never mind that. You won't believe, the amazing experience I've just had."

***

'To this day, I still can't explain the experience I had had in the barrow that night...'

Touchwood paused writing, reminiscing about that adventure. It was nothing like any of the other visions or dreams, I have had since then, he thought, then continued writing,

'... Somehow, I had gone back in time, to when the barrow was being built; which is estimated to be some six thousand years ago. It was like, I had inhabited a man from those times, and I knew all his memories. What it revealed to me, I certainly know, I had not read about beforehand. Even though since then, I have researched extensively, I can find no writings, to confirm or deny what it revealed about the life and ceremonies of the people of those times.'

'The other strange phenomena, was the earth dragon sigil, we had charged up. I found the remains of it next morning, it had been trampled into the dirt floor of the barrow, by our leaping and dancing, not much was left of it, so I left it there.'

'About a week later, I was walking past a newsagents stand, when I noticed on one paper, a minor headline, telling about the latest crop circle, that had been found. At the time they were big in the news and often featured on slow news days.'

'Along with UFOs I was interested in crop circles also. I casually picked up the folded paper and opened it up to find underneath the sub headline, was a photograph of the crop circle in question. I could hardly believe my eyes, for there was a crop circle depicting exactly, the earth dragon sigil I had drawn.'

'I read through the article, to see where the circle was, and found that it was within a half mile of the barrow, we had use for our ritual. Clearly, there are strange forces at play in these old barrows, that modern science knows nothing about.'

Chapter 19

Hazel

I was made to love magic
All its wonder to know
But you all lost that magic
Many, many years ago.

Nick Drake

At this point in my life, I was working hard with two challenging spiritual paths, and holding down my professional job as well; with the energy and dedication that only a thirty-year-old could muster.

However, it was very interesting for me to see the different ways of working. In the Wiccan coven, we worked in a formal, more disciplined way. There was a clear and definite structure. And a clear hierarchy and levels of achievement, that you needed to work your way through.

On the other hand, working with the Cat Tribe seemed more democratic, we each contributed what we had learnt. However we tended to be more chaotic and wilder, but non the less reached higher levels of intensity and emotion. None of us realised it at the time, but we were working in a shamanic way.

The contrast between the two ways of working was clear, but I enjoyed both ways and could see pros and cons in each.

As time wore on, I had become interested in researching and reading up about the history of UK Wicca. I was surprised to learn, that Wicca originated in the early twentieth century and was considered a NeoPagan religion. Even though, traditional witchcraft went back to medieval times or beyond.

On the other hand, the use of formal magic rituals, can be traced back to early Egyptian times. But what really interested me, was magic as used by my own native culture, which brought me back to before the Romans, to the early Celts.

The Celts fascinated me. I read extensively about them, finding that their magic rituals were facilitated and performed by Druids. If we look right back, to those very early days of the Celts, the Druids were more like medicine men or shamans. They didn't seem to have indoor temples, but worked their magic outdoors in nature, often at sacred sites, wells, and megaliths.

One day, while attending my Wiccan coven as usual, we were visited by another high priestess. She had hived off from this coven a while ago, and started a group up in north Wales, where she lived. She was attractive yes, but at least ten years older than me and certainly, more mature. But she had something about her, that I couldn't quite define, I found myself drawn to her.

After our main ritual, we usually socialised for a while, so I went over to chat with her, she told me her name was Hazel. The conversation soon led to me talking about how I had been working at sacred sites, round Bristol and Wessex where I lived. I was relating to her how I was excited and stimulated, by those ancient megaliths. Hazel seemed to agree with me whole heartedly, and said she had grown up on Anglesey, where she was surrounded by ancient megaliths.

She told me that there were many, old sacred sites that are virtually unknown and rarely visited. Then she casually mentioned that such places, would be the ideal place to work a third-degree ritual.

I said that it was an interesting coincidence, that she should say that because, I had been studying hard and that my third-degree, graduation ritual was due within the next few months. Oddly, she didn't sound very surprised by that, but only said, "Oh really," in a very casual way.

We continued talking for quite a while. I found I had started to feel quite an affinity for this very wise, woman and wondered about this.

It was only later on in the month, that I discovered that Hazel had talked privately to my High Priestess and Priest about me. They had discussed my working with my own group in Bristol, at sacred sites, something I thought I had kept secret from them, for you were supposed to be dedicated to the Wiccan path. But of course Doyle, somehow knew about it. He also told Hazel that he thought I was a promising student, especially so, if I was able to achieve all this.

The three of them, had also discussed my imminent third-degree initiation. Hazel had somehow convinced my High Priestess and priest, that I could benefit enormously by allowing Hazel to take me under her wing, to prep me for that initiation. The dedicated, one to one training, they all agreed was a great boon. Even though my High Priestess felt, it was an unconventional approach, everyone agreed, that if I was willing, I could work my third degree with Hazel, at one of those sacred sites.

Unusually Doyle phoned me up one evening. I was puzzled by this as he had never phoned me up before. But he said he had something important to discuss with me, that couldn't wait. He then told me about Hazel's proposal, and what they had discussed.

When I heard this, I was surprised and intrigued, but wasn't so sure about it, as it felt like a really big step. Leaving the coven and only having one dedicated teacher, felt a little strange. I would certainly miss the social aspect. But then realised that if I passed my third degree, I was expected to leave and form my own coven anyway.

I had of course worked outdoors before, in a Cat Tribe way, but not in a Wiccan way. All our rituals had been indoors in a purpose-built temple, I wasn't sure they could be worked outdoors. But Doyle convinced me that this was a wonderful opportunity for me, and Hazel had been one of his star pupils, and really knew her stuff.

Also, Doyle said, that Hazel would rewrite the ritual and adapt it for outdoors, at a sacred site. She had in mind an old, long barrow, in Anglesey, that wasn't locked up and hardly anyone went there; this did sound really quite exciting. Doyle somehow won me over, and he said of course, that I could returned to his coven again, to say my goodbyes to all the wonderful people I had worked and studied with. I would also be allowed to visit any time I wanted in the future.

Hazel lived in North Wales, so there was quite a distance between us. But Hazel was prepared for this. We started communicating by letter. She sent me great tombs of writing, with suggested exercises to do, books to read and photocopied sections from books, she had herself.

The letters at first, were a little over whelming, but where incredibly informative. But as time went on, I began to look forward to them. We also met once a month, for face-to-face tuition, at her house or sometimes in nature, on long country walks.

Hazel had long black frizzy hair, to her shoulders; a few strands had turned silver, a tell-tale of her maturity. She usually wore, very red lipstick and had a pale Celtic complexion. She has olive green eyes, that are very kind and knowledgeable. She is petit and slim and has well-proportioned body and limbs.

Hazel always seemed to wear black clothes, often with black lace attached. Today she would be classed as a Goth, but there was no such thing, at the time when I met her. She always seemed to wear lots of clunky jewellery too, with gemstones and beads. She is very attractive in that timeless and mysterious, gothic way. She always held a quiet poise, but when you got to know her, she was very knowledgeable and wise.

During our once-a-month, teaching circles, Hazel had insisted, that in these advanced classes, we needed to work in a circle and be sky clad.

By now, I was used to working sky clad, so just shrugged, and went along with it. We had met for several sessions already, going over things I needed to improve on. But this session turned out to be breaking new ground.

"Hold the Athame out ahead of you … like this," Hazel took her own Athame in her right hand, held the knife out, stretching her arm fully horizontal. I noticed she was supporting her right arm with her left hand.

Hazel and I were in circle, in one of her spare rooms, she had converted it to a small temple, with a lovely Altar, dressed in leaves and other seasonal objects, foraged from the forest. We were both naked, standing in the candlelight.

"It's not only the Athame that has to cut," she continued. "It's your own mind, you have to think it. So try this, put your mind out at the very tip of the Athame. Now concentrate, focus your mind. Don't think about anything else, think about the Athame tip. That is where your consciousness needs to be."

She suddenly came up behind me, grabbed my arm and stretched it out straight. In doing so, she lightly touched, the sensitive skin on my back, with her naked breasts. I felt a stirring in my genitals, a tingling, and my phallus twitched and slightly unfurled.

I think she noticed, because she moved away and said, "Stop, relax, don't force it, your gripping it too tight. Take a break, take some deep breaths, you need to keep your mind on what you're doing here."

I let my arm fall to my side, I was a little confused, so closed my eyes and took several deep breaths, counting and holding, like I had been shown.

Now, feeling so much more centred, I opened my eyes. I saw my priestess was now cross legged on the floor, back straight, looking directly at me. I felt very self-conscious suddenly, like she could see into me, and knew how I had been aroused.

"This magic work," she said. "It's about taking control, not only of your mind, but of your body too. You will have heard the term: 'the energy flows where your mind goes', we use it a lot. And sexual energy is the same thing, we need to be able to control it."

I could feel my cheeks getting hot and knew they must be flushed. I'm almost wishing the earth would swallow me up.

"In more advanced work," she continued. "You're going to learn to control different forms of energy, it's essential."

She took a deep breath then said, "So let's try this, while I'm looking at you, you stand there and try sending sexual energy to your phallus."

I thought my eyes were going to pop out, "What! you can't be serious?"

"You managed it happily just now," she said smiling.

Suddenly, my cheeks were burning, my face must be turning an even brighter red, "But it did it by itself …," I mumbled.

"Exactly my point, you have no control over it," she scolded. "You need to be able to control it and eventually other functions as well. So let's try again. Close your eyes, if it helps. Try sending sexual energy to your phallus".

So feeling like I had no other choice, I kept my eyes tightly closed, not wanting to see her looking at me. Then, I concentrated on my genitals, sending sexy thoughts. My traitorous phallus dutifully unfurled.

"That was easy," she almost laughed. "Now the hard part. I want you to feel the sexual energy, draining away from your lingam. Really concentrate".

I could hear all those locker room jokes about 'once the beast is released....' Reinforcing, how men have no control, over these things. This was new territory for me, but I was determined to progress.

So I concentrated really hard, imagining that pent up sexual energy, flowing away from my groin. flowing up my spine and into my head. I could visualise it now, as a snake slowly uncoiling from the very base of my spine, flowing up the vertebra one at a time. I felt shivers up my back and my neck; then the energy entered my head. I felt lightheaded and felt my awareness slowly rising to the ceiling.

Somehow, I was looking down on myself, I could see my young body standing naked in the circle, back straight, and my phallus slowly drooping down, back to a flaccid state.

My priestess gave a quick clap of applause and giggled. That brought me crashing back into my body again.

"Very good!" She congratulated, "Bet you didn't know you could do that."

"No ... no I didn't," I managed to say, but oddly I felt very proud of myself. And stranger yet, I had opened my eyes and didn't feel embarrassed by the event.

"Now do it again," Hazel commanded.

I just looked at her, but I could see she was serious about me doing it again. So, less reluctantly this time, I closed my eyes, took a deep breath, and concentrated on sending sexual energy to my phallus again. This time it rose quickly, becoming fully erect, firm and hard. I heard Hazel take a quick in breath, but not wanting to be distracted, I ignored it and thought, 'how am I going to undo this?'

"Now draw the energy away again," she instructed me.

So, once again I imagined that pent up, sexual energy flowing away from my groin, up my spine and into my head. I felt buoyant and lightheaded again but, managed to stay in my body and gradually felt my lingam go down again.

"OK, that's very well done Corin, but I think that's enough of that for today. I suggest you practice this exercise at home in front of the mirror, this will give you clearer biofeedback. Now back to the Athame."

Hazel who had been cross legged on the floor, rose to a standing position, in one smooth motion, which was impressive. Then she took her Athame once more from its sheath, which was attached to a cord round her waist. She held it out again, pointing to the south.

"Now, follow me again, hold your Athame in your hand, but loosen your fingers, don't strain towards it, you're not about to engage in battle." She looked over at my extended arm and Athame and smiled approvingly.

"Now feel with it very gently, you're attempting to create a portal, in the fabric of the universe. Think about the Athame tip. That is where your consciousness needs to be. You're looking for a spot, where the veil is thinnest. Looking for a gap, so small, you could never see it with your own eyes, but the Athame tip will find it, if you put your mind there. Feel along the air, till you feel the smallest gap, you could miss it, if your consciousness wasn't at the end."

I tried hard to do as she instructed me. Over the years of my Wiccan training, my Athame was a tool I had used often in circle, to invoke the Elemental Lords, of each of the cardinal directions, and ask them to witness our rites and to guard the Circle. But never had I been instructed in this way. This was new and different.

I tried hard, to project my consciousness to the tip of my Athame. Pushed my focus to be completely one with my knife. Imagined the molecules of the metal, densely fused together at the tip, while the molecules of air surrounded it, where more spaced apart.

Nothing happened.

I tried a different tack. In my mind, I tried to summon the ethereal feeling, I got at sacred sites, where I could feel the veil was thinnest. Then I suddenly realised, this was like dowsing! In dowsing you used a tool like a pendulum, or metal rods, to find water or whatever you were looking for, even lay line energy. When I found it, there would be a minute twitch of my muscles and the metal rods would move. Only now, the tool I used was the Athame.

I tried to put my mind into the same state, as when I was dousing. Slowly, slowly, I moved the blade through the air, searching, this time for a portal in the fabric of the universe. It took a little adjusting to set my mind, as normally I was outside in a field, with my clothes on. But gradually, I relaxed into the familiar dowsing mind set. And yes, suddenly, I felt a minute twitch in my arm.

"Yes! Yes, I think I've found one," I exclaimed.

I was suddenly aware of Hazel, standing at my side. "That's good," she whispered in my ear, like we were stalking an animal.

"When you find one," she whispered, slowly and concisely. "Push your Athame … slightly forward … then twist … like you are prying open a door …Then draw your Athame to the side … like your tearing open a sheet of paper …"

As she whispered, I could feel the hairs on the back of my neck stand on end. Something 'special' was happening here, something spooky and magical at the same time.

"In traditional Wicca," she continued to whisper in my ear, barely audible. "… We draw a pentacle shape …but in reality … we can make any shaped doorway… The important thing is … to visualise the doorway shape … as your making it."

Again, I tried to do as she instructed, but the whispering in my ear was incredible arousing also. But at the same time, it seemed to be talking to a part of me, that was deep inside my subconscious. However I needed to take control of my body's reaction, as in the previous exercise, and overcome it.

It was hard going, but after quite some time I managed to control things and find the doorway with my athame and open it up into a small square. It was a little like the heat haze you get on a hot road in summer, which seemed to shimmer in the air a moment and then vanish.

"Well done," said Hazel in her normal voice. "Now you know what you're looking for, try it again and again, till you can do it every time."

When at last, we stopped for a break. We got dressed and went into Hazel's kitchen. Over tea, I half-jokingly remarked to Hazel, that I thought she was a very hard task master, and that she must have a very disciplined mind, to achieve all that we had been working on.

"I have discovered," she retorted, sounding a little offended. "That discipline of the mind, in a way, seems to free you. In magic, it's important not to let your emotions control you, or they will just take you off, in all sorts of directions, other than the one you're after."

"Yes, I suppose I can see the sense in that," I replied thoughtfully.

"As we found in our earlier exercise, you cannot let your body control you"

"Oh! You mean when I was … er … you know, controlling my erection," I stumbled.

"Exactly," Hazel slightly giggled at my embarrassment. "Non magicals, are totally driven by their bodily needs and often, conflicting emotions and desires. Of course advertisers know this, they have psychologists working for them, they tailor their advertising, to exploit this."

"Really," I wasn't aware that advertisers did this, but was starting to get where she was coming from. Thoughtfully I took a sip of my tea, then said. "I had no idea. So the ability to be in control of your mind and body, not only helps make a magician, but also helps you to be free and live outside the system and government control."

"Yes, exactly" she said earnestly, "I feel as free as a bird."

I couldn't help but look at Hazel with a sort of awe. I was constantly being surprised by her.

"Part of the function of a magical person," she continued, "is to become free. For if you don't win your freedom, it follows that you will spend your life in a sort of prison.

"There are many ways you can be trapped, for example emotional restriction i.e. you find yourself trapped by circumstances, or confined by religious customs, or local cultural customs or even by your family.

"Or you can be restricted by lack of cash, meaning you have to suffer a boss, telling you what to do, where to go. The way out, is to identify what is restricting you, there could be many things, all interlinked, into a sort of knot. Some people look at that knot and sort of give up; they are giving away their power. Or they complain about the restrictions, expecting someone else to fix it for them.

"A magical person starts untangling the knot, one fibre at a time. Gradually, there becomes space for you to grow your power, so you can then tackle the harder restrictions. Eventually the knot starts to unravel more easily, allowing you to obtain your freedom."

***

'I didn't realise it at the time, but meeting Hazel turned out to be a very significant event in my life. She was to influence me for a very long time to come. Her slight form, contrasted with her high intellect and vast magical knowledge. She somehow seemed to continue to surprise me, no matter how many times we met.'

Bright blessings Touchwood

Chapter 20

Of Coloured Paints and Clay

"The intellect has little to do on the road to discovery.
There comes a leap in consciousness, call it intuition or what you will,
the solution comes to you, and you don't know how or why."
Albert Einstein

It was a heady time for me. Fate and the spirit world, seemed to be taking hold of me, using me as a channel for its works. Some things just seemed to fall into place, allowing a certain path to go ahead unheeded, while other paths seemed to be blocked.

My soul was calling out to me, to leave my engineering work and take up a full time, spirit path; perhaps in personal development. But my everyday financial commitments, seemed to outweigh any income I could gain, from running personal development workshops. It was a dilemma, that I could not resolve myself. However the fates, seemed to be directing me in other directions. Meanwhile, the income from my professional career, supported the spiritual path I was on.

It was long before I had met Hazel, that the Cat Tribe, embarked upon our monthly sweat lodges. I had of course told Hazel about our lodges, and invited her to attend, but she had insisted, that it was Cat Tribe business and that I should pursue this path on my own.

The idea of a sweat lodge had been voiced, some time ago, by Natali and Rubi at a Cat Tribe meeting. They had attended sweat lodges before, at some of the festivals they had been to. I liked the idea and voiced that if we all worked together, it could work. But where would we do it?

Shortly after that particular group meeting, I consulted my Ordnance Survey maps of the Bristol area, with the ley lines already drawn in. I was dowsing the map, using a pendulum, asking the question, 'find a suitable site of power, for the Cat Tribe sweat lodge'. I held in my mind that it needed a small stream and woodland, containing hazel trees, that had been coppiced and now growing many new branches. It needed to be secluded and it also needed to be reasonably close to Bristol, so people could get there relatively easily.

Additionally, we needed parking for a few cars off road, so as not to attract unwanted attention. It was a big ask. Looking back now, I am amazed that I was able to find such a place. But at the time of asking, I went into the task with youthful, innocence and faith, that the universe would provide.

We also needed a tarpaulin and suitable stones for the fire pit. They came to me in unexpected ways.

A friend of a friend, unexpectantly came to me and asked, 'could I look after his bender tarp, while he was traveling abroad,' so I graciously accepted. He never came back to Bristol. The stones where easy too.

One day, I stopped in the Avon gorge to watch some climbers on the rocks above, as I was a keen climber at the time. As I was watching them, I heard one of the climbers suddenly shout, 'BELOW' as several rocks gave way under his foot. Rocks banged into rocks, causing a mini avalanche. Several rocks hit the slope below, and continued rolling over to where I was standing. I quickly jumped out the way, but I was more concerned for the climbers above. Both were clinging to the rock face like ivy. Fortunately, they both seemed ok and eventually continued up the rock face.

So I instinctively went over to the rocks that nearly bowelled me over. They looked like they had fossils in them; yes, they were Carboniferous limestone, perfect for a sweat lodge. I had no idea that the rocks, I needed for the lodge were here in Avon Gorge all the time.

Meanwhile, the map dowsing came up with a few possible sites for our sweat lodge. One was at an alternative community in Swindon, that was too far away, and they would charge us. Two others nearer Bristol, seemed to be in wood land areas. So next opportunity I had, I went off to check them out.

The first one, didn't work out, as it was used by a forest school during the day, so we could only have it after about 5 pm and we needed the day to set it up. So all hopes were on the last site.

It was a fine sunny evening, when I eventually found the small dirt track, leading to the area of forest, indicated by my dowsing. It looked very overgrown and unmanaged. I jumped out the car and took my dog Toby for a walk, to see what was there.

Further up the track was a five-bar gate, which had been locked with a rusty old chain and padlock. It was plain this gate had not been opened in years. To the side of the gate, the old box wire fencing had been breached and flattened, presumably by an ambitious walker. But the path was overgrown, no one had been this way for some time.

I continued through the long grass and entered the forest. It was a mixed wood forest, with plenty of new growth, much of it seemed to be hazel trees, that had been coppiced some time ago, so there was plenty of new shoots that looked the perfect size for a bender, sweat lodge.

Encouraged, I continued along the overgrown path for a short way, then came to a small clearing. Toby my dog suddenly ran off, chasing a rabbit into the undergrowth. I continued looking round in wonder at the clearing. This would be ideal, for a sweat lodge. There was plenty of fallen trees, we could use for the fire. There was coppiced hazel, on the pathway here. The small dirt track could park a couple of cars, off road.

Just then I heard my dog Toby barking, then he suddenly burst through the undergrowth. He came up to me, waging his tail and shook himself all over me. He was soaking wet, and now so was I, but I didn't mind, he had found water!

I strode off in the direction he had come from, I could see the flattened grass where Toby had run. Not far in, was a little flowing stream!

"Good dog Toby," I congratulated him as I patted him heartily. "You have found the missing ingredient!"

On the many walks I took around the area with my dog Toby, exploring woods, quarries, and canal paths, I had noticed quite a lot of red clay but never thought much about it.

But one day I noticed near the riverbank, where part of it had been washed away, there was a layer of white clay, exposed in it.

I remember reading a book about the history of Bristol, and that potters used this white earthenware clay, to make clay pipes years ago, so was fascinated by it. I took up a lump and rolled it in my hands, making a clay ball, which was very satisfying. But I also noticed, it stained my hands white. Interesting I thought. So wet it a bit with some puddle water nearby, then taking a finger, drew a white zigzag up my forearm; it's like tribal paint I thought. Knowing I could find red clay readily enough, that would give me two colours, I thought. Cat Tribe could use it as body paint, before the sweat lodges.

However it would be nice, I thought, to find other colours too. Anyway I went back to the car, to collect something to put the white clay in. The only thing I could come up with was a plastic shopping bag, which would have to do. So having collected two shopping bags full of the white clay, which I thought were surprisingly heavy as I staggered back to the car.

On all my walks after that, I looked out for coloured clays. I found and collected a deep reddish-brown clay, easily enough; and took that home. But I hadn't noticed any other colours, in all my walks around the area.

Perhaps I should concentrate on the riverbanks I thought. So meditated and called out a message to the universe, 'I needed blue clay. I'm looking for blue clay'.

The universe answered my call in the best way it could, for one day, there in a riverbank was a seam of blue-black clay. So thanking the universe and my guides and helpers, I collected two more shopping bags of the blue clay.

When I got it home, I immediately started to work with the blue-black clay. However I found it contained tiny, sharp stones, which wouldn't be very safe to paint bodies with. So puzzling what to do, I went to bed that night, with this on my mind. Sure enough, I dreamed about the blue clay and before dawn, the method of what to do, came to me.

What I needed to do, was dissolve the clay in a tub of water. The stones would fall to the bottom, and I would have a suspension of blue-black clay. So then I could syphon off the clay in suspension, to a clean bucket. If I left it for long enough, the clay particles would fall to the bottom, leaving clear water on top. Then all I needed to do, was syphon off the clear water, and be left with very squidgy clay, in the bottom of the bucket. I could then take this wet clay and spread it out on a flat board, to dry in the sun.

So this is what I did, a soon as I could. However it took many days for the tiny clay particles to fall and produce the clear water above it. But having made batches of beer and wine, I knew that patience was a virtue when crafting things. My patience paid off. What I was left with was a beautifully, silky-smooth, blue-black clay.

This of course made me realise, that the white and red clays were in fact quite coarse too. So I had to go about repeating the same process with these as well.

However I still wanted a bright blue colour, so having gone through a lengthy procedure already, I decided to cheat a bit and added some non-toxic, blue poster paint to the white clay which ended up with a dark blue clay, body paint.

Once Cat Tribe had worked out all the various material needs, to create a sweat lodge. We set about devising a ritual for the actual ceremony itself. We all agreed that we didn't want to copy, the native American Indian model.

Our research had found that there are examples of ritual sweating in many other cultures. For example the hot Roman baths and steam bath, Scandinavian sauna, the Slavic Banya and Turkish baths are a few. Many indigenous people around the Bering Strait had sweat baths, the northern Finns, and Laplanders, as well as the ancient Greeks, all have references to them.

Our research showed that often prayer and songs may be involved with rituals in the sauna, and even we found acknowledgement of a spirit-being, who lived in the sauna. We also found that Vapour baths were in use among the Celtic tribes and there are still stone, corbeled sweathouses found in Ireland, to this day.

So Cat Tribe were convinced, there could well have been a Celtic sweating ceremony in days gone by. So we set about devising our own ritual, using what we could glean from our Celtic culture.

The ritual we devised was based on the wheel of the year, a symbol of the eight Sabbats celebrated by many Pagans and Wiccans. We of course brought in the four Elements, then we added some of the trees from the Celtic tree alphabet.

In all the ceremony we conceived, enabled us to relate wholeheartedly, to the sweat lodge experience, using terminology and symbols that we as Celtic Pagans, could relate to on many different levels.

***

'Having spent much time and effort gathering recourses and information, for our sweat lodges ...'

Touchwood was writing in his journal. He looked up out of his window, at the snow gently falling onto the vegetable garden outside. He gave a little shiver and shuffled closer to his stove. Then thought how agreeable it would be, to be good and hot in a sweat lodge right now. It would warm his old bones through and through.

Perhaps, he mused, this could well have been one of the driving forces, why a tribe would create a sweat house in the first place. He continued writing.

... Cat Tribe went on to hold regular, full moon, sweat lodges throughout the year. Word soon spread amongst friends, so we often had seekers from outside Cat Tribe, who were intrigued to come and see what we were about.'

'I remembered reading in a Pagan magazine one time, the article was discussing the revival of the Celtic tradition. In many ways it said, we are at a disadvantage, as there are so few written records about ancient Celtic tradition and ceremonies. Whereas something like the native American tradition, the ceremonies are passed down through family lines.'

'In the native Celtic tradition, we need to be our own grandfathers, devising rituals that we can relate to and feel right for us, in some ways this can be an advantage'.

'One such ceremony we had; I will describe in the next chapter.'

Chapter 21

Sweat Lodge

And on those special occasions
When we hit that cosmic chord
The spirit of the Holy Octave
Comes passing through to you

Steve Hillage

Cat Tribe members had arrived at the sweat lodge site by mid-afternoon. We spent most of the day cutting hazel poles, for the building of the lodge and collecting firewood for the fire to heat the stones. We also needed to fetch the stones and tarpaulin from the van and cart them into the woods. Other tribe members were at the stream, collecting local stones and creating a lovely plunge pool, for us to use later on.

Dusk had started gathering around us; all our tasks had been done. The stones had been placed in the fire. We had drummed for a while, to encourage the fire elementals to burn bright. But now we were sat round the fire relaxing and chatting, waiting for the stones to heat up.

"Animism is older than its name," I relayed.

The conversation had wandered onto an old favourite of mine, "Many scholars consider animism to be the basis of all religion. In fact, even the three monotheistic religions contain animistic elements. Even today, animism is incredibly widespread, in reality most of the world is made up of animists. Western culture is very naïve when it states that the major religions are monotheistic.

"In actual numbers and geographic spread, belief in 'nature spirits', is by far the most practiced worldwide. Almost all of Africa, Southeast Asia, rural China, Tibet, Japan, rural Central and South America, indigenous Pacific Islands. Pretty much everywhere is dominated by animistic beliefs, except of course Western Europe, the Middle East, and North America."

"And that is only the picture today," Lily added. "Modern man has been around for 200,000 years. Animism, is considered to be the very earliest form of believe system, so is potentially that old."

"We have talked about this many times but to reiterate," I felt it best to clarify for the new people present. "Animism is the belief that objects, places, plants and creatures all possess a distinct spiritual essence. Potentially, animism perceives all things, animals, plants, rocks, rivers, and perhaps even weather systems, as having its own spirit life spark."

As if in agreement to this, one of the stones in the fire gave off a load 'CRACK', which made everyone jump, followed by nervous laughs. It brought us all back into full focus.

"Thank you, the stone people," I exclaimed. "As they remind me, to bring us to perhaps the hardest for us to comprehend; the Elementals."

"These of course are quite separate and distinct from the periodic table of elements," Sherri clarified.

"Absolutely. Thanks Sherri," I nodded to her approvingly. "The ethereal Elements of earth, water, air, and fire which we have worked with, in our circle and rituals, also have entities associated with them. Does anyone know what these are, let's say for Earth?

"The Gnomes of the Earth," called Sherri.

"What about the others, anyone?" I queried.

"The Undines of Water," called Rubi.

"The Sylphs of the Air," said Bradley.

"What about fire?" I asked.

"Aren't they Salamanders?" said Gary a little unsure of himself.

"Yes, absolutely, well-done Gary."

"So, in the sweat lodge, we are working with all four elementals. The stones of the earth, we heat those to a high temperature with fire. We take those red-hot stones full of salamanders, into the lodge pit. We then sprinkle them with living water from the stream. This immediately transforms into steam, which is very hot air.

"The very nature of the sweat lodge is a hidden dark space, a womb space. We shed our outer skin, our clothes, a symbol of our past selves. Rendering ourselves vulnerable and naked as a baby. We enter the lodge through a tiny hole, like the birthing canal of the mother. By doing this, again we are vulnerable and humbled, as we need to crawl on the earth, to enter into the womb space."

"Why are we calling it a womb space," asked Alice.

"The concept of the female Vulva or Tantric 'Yoni' of the goddess," answered Rubi. "As a sacred shrine and gateway to an Otherworld, is common to many cultures."

"Many initiation ceremonies," I continued, "enact the process of entering into a womb space. It may be a cave or underground chamber, a sweat lodge or similar."

Alice was nodding, but still looked a little unsure.

"Ritually," Lilly was enjoying sharing her knowledge. "The initiate goes through the Alchemical process, of transformation from one state to another. They enter into the cauldron of the womb, the 'cauldron of changes', where this much needed transformation can take place.

"To bring this about, the initiate undergoes some sort of ordeal, staying for a transitory period, before we can return renewed and transformed. Then coming out of the narrow doorway or birth passage, we are reborn into the material world anew. It is the caterpillar in the crystallise, being reborn as the butterfly." Lily concluded.

"What ordeal are we undergoing in there?" Asked Gary, a little nervously. Although he regularly attended Cat Tribe meetings, he had conspicuously not attended one of our sweats before.

"We must enter the lodge in a meditative state," I answered. "Symbolically moving from our world to the otherworld. Inside the lodge, we are sitting naked on the earth, it is cramped, pitch dark, we are not able to move much, the heat can be oppressive, some people find it hard to push through that. It's very humid, we sweat a lot.

"We will be calling in the four elemental directions, to help us in our transformation and chanting too. It can be very emotional for some people. Especially, if you feel you really need to push through, some problem you are having. It is important to fully participate and allow your barriers to fall away and become vulnerable. However it is a safe place, away from normal society. In the dark, no one truly knows who is going through what. You can feel safe to let go, no one here will judge you."

It was almost time to prepare to enter the lodge. It had become a tradition for Lily to announce this, and for us all to cast off our cloths and body paint in preparation. All the regular tribe members quickly stripped and paired up, and where now busy with the coloured clays and painting each other.

As I was striping off and looking around at the wonderful scene, I noticed that the new girl, Alice had been left on her own and was looking slightly lost. She looked quite youthful, probably in her early twenties. She had light chestnut hair which she wore in dreadlocks. Her hair was thick and there seemed to be many strands, and some had beads of red, green, and gold threaded into them.

Unusually, she wore no makeup; she seemed completely natural that way. Her skin was fair but slightly flushed. Her eyebrows unshaped, where light brown. Her lips were a delicate shade of rose pink, full and slightly parted, revealing her front teeth, which were slightly large for her petit mouth, but none the less quite endearing. And she had a small, circular, silver piercing in one nostril.

Her eyes though were remarkable, they were well spaced and like a clear blue ocean, not a Mediterranean blue, but the dark blue green of an arctic sea, in fact her whole look was Nordic. She was tall and her naked body was very lithe and elven, her small breasts were barley formed, with very pink nipples that were erect and showed she was excited by the whole event.

However what struck me most of all about her, was the hazy aura of blue and purple, that surrounded her, which was much more vibrant and visible than anyone else there.

As my role of tribe leader, I didn't want her to feel left out, so I went over to her with some blue clay and asked her if I could paint her with the clay.

She confidently looked straight into my eyes and affirmed, "Yes, I feel I can trust you."

I noticed she had a strong accent, possibly German, and wondered who had brought her, but I said to her, perhaps too directly, "People seem a little scared of you."

"Yes," she said, "I'm fully aware of the power of my body."

A comment I found a little surprising, coming from one so young.

Then she said, "Yes, I would like the experience of being painted. You have an amazing group here."

"Yes," I said proudly. "I feel it is very special,"

When I came close to her, to start painting, I noticed there was a strong metallic type of smell about her, which I found very agreeable. I started painting her arms first, applying the blue clay, creating several spirals at the top and a snaky wave down to her wrist.

"Have you been to a sweat lodge before, Alice?" I asked casually.

"No, never. But I have wanted to for ages,"

Alice seemed to be relaxing into the experience now, so I picked up a pot of red clay. Painting my hand red and kneeling before her, I applied it to her belly, then heard a sharp intake of breath.

I looked up at her face, but she just smiled down at me, "That's cold," she said giggling.

"Yes, sorry about that," removing my hand, there was now a lovely tribal hand shape, below her belly button and just above her full bush of hair.

Moving on to her legs now, I put a simple blue zigzag, down her thighs. Then stood back, yes, she was looking quite tribal now. Turn round I said, and I will do you back. So she turned round displaying her lovely, rounded bottom in the fire light. The sight almost took my breath away, it took a moment of deep breathing and energy control before I could proceed in a professional way. But she really had the loveliest bottom I had ever seen.

With a brush now, I painted a blue spiral on her sacrum at the base of the spine. Which caused her to shiver, and she said, "Wow, that really tickles."

"Yes," I said. "It's your sacrum, the seat of Kundalini energy. Symbolised by a coiled snake; like the spiral I'm painting now."

I then continued painting the blue snake, zigzagging up her spine with a snake head at the very top.

"There," I said. "You're finished. You look amazing."

With that she turned around and looking straight into my eyes smiled. Then said, "Thank you. But what about you? Don't you need painting?"

"Yes, I suppose I do," I confessed.

With that, she immediately took the pot of blue paint from my hand, and with the brush started to make lines round my right arm; I needed to hold my arm straight out horizontally. As she did her painting, she came in very close to me. Her dreadlocked hair, brushing against my chest was tickly and tantalising. The hair on the top of her head was right under my nose now. However, she seemed completely unaware of her close proximity to me. I could smell an exotic perfume from her hair, possibly patchouli oil.

Suddenly, she seemed dissatisfied with the wide brush in the pot and went over to the pots of paint on the ground, a little way off. Bending over the paint pots, she seemed to make much of selecting a small width brush. At the tantalising sight, I took a sharp intake of breath, and my traitorous heart started beating faster.

When she came back, she stood before me with her head cocked to one side, like an artist surveying her canvas. I could see her eyes sweeping over my naked body, appraising me. It was a little unnerving.

I could see in her face; a decision was made. She then came over and knelt before me. Then started to apply paint to my belly. She set about creating an intricate knot design, with blue paint. The brush strokes where deliciously tickly and blended with the cold of the paint, it created a myriad of sensations within me. Not least, was the awareness of her face and hair, in close proximity, to my manhood. Desperately I started practicing the energy control exercises, Hazel had taught me.

However every now and then, I could feel her warm breath on my phallus, as she breathed out. Which despite my exercises, sent delicious sensations, whirling about my groin. My manhood started to respond by unfurling slightly. Surely, she was aware of the effect, she was having on me, I thought.

As if in answer, her brush slowly worked its way down to the base of my manhood. Unbelievably, she brought the blue line, right on to my manhood, which now started to throb and bob up and down.

This only made her giggle. Then she looked up into my embarrassed face. "I wondered at what point you would react," she said and giggled again.

She had been playing with me. Playing with my emotions. She knew exactly what she had been doing. The Cunning Little Vixen.

By this time, all the others had finished painting each other, and where now standing round watching us. I looked around, we had an audience, and could see that some of them were openly giggling or sniggering. It occurred to me that Alice, in her innocent playfulness, had put me in a difficult position, all be it unknowingly.

'I must be very careful, how to end this', I thought, 'I could lose standing in the group and effect the delicate balance, as a group we achieved'.

Alice stood up, and looked around self-consciously, suddenly aware of her audience.

"Ok, ok you got me," I called to Alice. And reached over to her, throwing my arms about her, giving her a lovely bear hug.

"You got me Alice, you got me good. Come on everyone, group hug."

It was clear that the group, didn't need a second invite. As one, they came and embraced us in a group huddle of naked flesh, and wet paint. Everyone hugging everyone else. Being in the centre, I could feel the power of the group mind and was warmed by the love, projecting out from all the young souls present.

Someone started a low chant of "Aaaah." Others joined in, till we had a continuous drone, it sounded like a swarm of giant bees. We were still hugging, so I could feel the bodies next to me vibrating with the chant, which seemed to go on for quite a while.

My head was swimming with the power of it. It was like being transported to some heavenly realm, where I was wrapped about by angels' wings, where I felt safe and warm and loved and whole. It was the most wonderful feeling in the world.

After our group hug, I gathered everyone about the fire. By this time, it was dark, and the fire was burning down, the stones in the fire where glowing hot. Our group of ten stood 'sky clad' round the fire, in a circle holding hands. Alternating boy, girl.

We stood in silence, firelight flickering over naked bodies. Bodies that were daubed with coloured clays. Blue snakes, red spirals, white stripes. Primal memories stirred from deep within, this was timeless, this could be 3000 years ago.

How beautiful, those young bodies looked. The young men with firm flesh and wild hair from a day in the forest, breathing deeply, anticipating. The young women too, standing there proud and confident in their own power, looking magnificent. I wondered if they knew, just how much power, their naked bodies had.

How wonderful it was, that they could feel safe in this mixed circle. How privileged we all were, to be stood here, experiencing this controlled sexual power, basking in its magnificence. I could see it in their young eyes, this was something special here, something unique and they were honoured, to be experiencing this special moment.

But, I was now experienced in energy work and knew that special moments like this could not last long, so I needed to transform it. I suggested we all join in a chant, someone suggested 'cauldron of charges', as most of us knew the words by heart. We sang it in a round over and over:

> "We are the old people; We are the new people,
> We are the same people wiser than before.
> Cauldron of changes, feather on the bone.
> Arc of eternity, ringer of the stone"

Over and over we chanted. Then we started rotating slowly clockwise. Still holding hands, still chanting, gradually getting faster and faster, raising our core of power, and building the energy. It was so exhilarating, spinning wildly around and around. Such energy and power was generated, by our joyful chanting and dancing, that I thought we could go on forever.

But eventually, our core of power reached a crescendo of shouts and screams, then as one, we all fell to the ground, each one of us sending our power to the healing of our planet.

When we had regained our breath. I stood up and sombrely lead us to the entrance of the sweat lodge. As was usual, Lily had agreed to be the fire maiden, it was her job to bring the hot stones into the lodge, once everyone was inside. But before that she stood with me either side of the entrance hole.

We both lit up smudging sticks, of green sage. As everyone stood in line before the sweat entrance, we would smudge them before they went in. Lily smudged the back and I the front. Gary was the first in, he seemed keen to overcome his fear. Sherri followed, after smudging, she bent down on all fours and crawled into the small round entrance. Felix and Rubi followed, then Natali and Sam.

Alice remained at the end of the line, unsure what to do. Lily started smudging her back, while I prepared to smudge her front. She looked up at me, with her blue green eyes and light chestnut dreadlocks, and smiled up at me, she looked so lovely. But I could see a little fear there also.

Then she whispered very softly, "I'm sorry about before … you know with the paint."

I just smiled back and shook my head at the memory, it really was quite funny.

"Will you sit next to me," she whispered. "In the lodge. I'm a little scared, I'm going to faint or something. Will you look after me in there."

I was a little taken aback, as she seemed genuinely frightened, but I said, "Yes of course, I'll be coming in next."

Bradly was to help Lily with the stones this time, he was apprenticed to Lily, learning how to be a fire handler, as we needed a backup, if for any reason Lily couldn't come. So Lily smudged me all over and I bent down with my leather bag of ritual tools and crawled into the small womb like hole.

Inside was cool and dark, I was aware of the others in there, but only by the small sounds of shuffling, to get a comfortable spot and breathing noises. On the ground, we had placed straw, gathered from the dried grasses we had found in the forest. As I sat down, it felt dry and comfortable. Bringing out my small drum, I began a drumbeat appropriate to a song I was about to sing, it was a lively chant and quite fast and appropriate, I thought to a sweat lodge:

> *The rocks, the stones and the crystals*
> *Are the bones of the earth ….*

All the regular Cat Tribe members, joined in with the chant, repeating over and over, as I drummed. We were all sat with our backs to the canvas and either cross-legged or crouching, leaving a round stone pit, in the centre, free for the hot stones.

Outside, Lily and Bradly were raking through the fire coals, looking for the hot stones. One had a garden fork, the other a spade. The hot stone was shifted on to the spade and brought to the lodge entrance.

Inside, the chanting continued, unabated. Then we heard the shout from outside,

"HOT ROCKS."

The canvas across the entrance, was pulled back and the shovel with the red-hot rock, came through the door and into the stone pit in the centre. One of our tribe, had managed to get hold of some deer antlers, which we fashioned into a device, that could slide the hot stone, off the spade or move it in the pit.

The procedure was repeated, till there were three stones, for the first round. Then Lily and Bradly came into the lodge, and we all had to shuffle round a bit. I could feel Alice, snuggle close up to me, and could feel her body shaking. I wasn't sure if it was nerves, or that she was just cold. But that would soon change.

Once we were all inside and the canvas over the door, it was pitch dark. All we could see, was the red-hot glowing stones in the pit. We had stopped drumming and chanting now, everyone just looking at the amazing site of the glowing stones. I could feel the heat emanating from them. There were glowing tracks in the stones, some seemed to be cooler and others brighter and there were specks lit up at random. It wasn't hard to imagine, there could be salamander creatures within those stones.

Natalie was our water maiden. She had brought in a large bottle of water and a bowl to pour it into. She had made a sort of small broomstick, to splash the water on to the stones. As she did this, the water instantly turned to steam, emitting a great hissing sound as it did so.

Again and again, the steam hissed, as she sprinkled the water on to the stones. Soon, I felt the warm stream hit my body, and the warm vapour enter my lungs. The dome shape of the sweat lodge was getting warmer now, a pleasant warmth of a summer's day.

The ceremony we had devised, was in four rounds. The Earth round was the first and coolest round, then followed by the Water round, each round getting progressively hotter. Then Air round, and the hottest of all, the Fire round.

At the end of each round, we would send for more stones, which the fire maiden would facilitate, while everyone else stayed inside. Except at the end of the water round, where we all would come out, and go the short distance to the water pool. In the water gathered there, we could plunge ourselves into the Icey waters, to wash away the sweat we had accumulated on our skin. By the pool, were a few small buckets, that we could fill with the water and dash it over our heads

The earth and water rounds had gone well, everyone was enduring the heat. We had sung songs and chants. Made wishes and said prayers. Now we were in the plunge pool, the bravest of us, plunging into the Icey waters first, often this would be Lily.

She now stood in the centre of the pool, her stocky naked body, standing legs akimbo, her long straight brown hair, plastered to her head, looking around, like a wild woman. With a bucket of cold water in her hands, her piercing blue gray eyes, challenging anyone who seemed reluctant to plunge into the cold waters.

She seemed to take delight, in other people's reluctance. One time, she had unexpectedly soaked me, as I stood at the side, encouraging others to enter the pool. So, I was always carful to plunge myself first, from then on.

Back inside the lodge, we were now partly through in the Air round. It was really hot inside now, any moisture from the plunge pool had evaporated, adding to the humid air and I could now feel the sweat, rolling down my back. The water maiden, this time, had put eucalyptus oils, into the water she splashed onto the hot stones.

I took in deep breaths of the warm vapours; I could smell the astringent eucalyptus smell, as it enter my lungs. It felt good, as I could literally feel it clearing my air passages, allowing me to breathe deeply, to the bottom of my lungs. Around me there were bouts of coughing, as others were experiencing a similar expectorant effect.

Again and again, the water hissed on the red-hot stones, filling the chamber with hot steam. As it got hotter, I could hear a small whimper from next to me, and knew it was Alice, having a hard time dealing with the heat. I reached out and placed my arm over her shoulder to comfort her. She immediately clutched both arms around me, like a fearful child. I placed my hand on her wet dreadlocks and gently stroked and patted her head. She seemed to take comfort from this, and calmed down, as more steam welled up from the stones.

But it was Gary, who suddenly cried out in pain and anguish.

"I'm sorry," he cried. "I say sorry to all the trees, I have damaged or hurt, with the mechanical digger, I drove at the building site. I was ignorant, I was young, I didn't know any different then. I now feel your pain. Forgive me please, brother trees. Don't haunt me so, in my dreams, for I will repent and not work at clearing trees again." He then broke down into sobs of pain.

I could hear somebody comforting him, from across the lodge, and hoped it was Sherri, as I had seen them becoming close companions.

Alice at my side, was still clutching on to me, but seemed somehow strengthened by Gary's confession.

At last the Air round was over, and the small door was reopened, Lily and Bradly went out to the fire, to retrieve the last of the stones. A small draught came in, relieving the intense heat. Then more stones were brought through the door. There were about five or six of them, so I knew we would be in for a hot round, next.

When the last of the stones were in the pit, and the fire tenders back inside the lodge, we started the fire round.

Natalie's small broomstick, relentlessly splashed water onto the stones again, turning to steam, emitting a great hissing sound as it did so. I could feel, great swaths of hot steam wafting across my body. As I breathed in the hot vapour, I could feel it stinging my air passageways. It was hot. Really hot.

Every sweat lodge ceremony was different. It seemed this time, we had created the right circumstances, to make it a really hot one. There were a few manly groans coming from across the lodge. And the noise of people shifting about, attempting to get more comfortable.

Suddenly, I felt Alice moving, then a whispering in my ear, "I'm sorry Corin, I'm not sure I can take much more of this."

I could feel her warm breath on my ear, as she whispered this, it was incredibly arousing, especially as she clutched so close, that I could smell her womanly sweat. But I tried to overcome any feelings this induced. Remembering again, the control that Hazel had taught me, I was able to focus on Alice, and her problem.

I didn't want her to leave and think she had failed to complete the ceremony. I knew this could cause her problems, with her self-esteem. She was a strong woman, but was facing unusual circumstances, she needed to overcome her fears.

"Try putting you head low down," I advised. "Heat rises, it will be cooler near the ground."

So she let go of me, and I could feel her shifting about, to sit in a kneeling position, then she leaned forward, putting her head down low. I'm sure this must have helped her, for she reached out to my hand, in the dark and squeezed it. I took this as a sort of thank you.

By this time, the heat was getting intense. There were more moans from both woman and men. Then someone started the 'Aum' chant, maybe in a bid to gain strength from it. Several people joined in; it was wonderful. I joined them. In the darkness and suffocating heat, continuously chanting 'Aum', I could feel myself, raising above my physical body and its discomforts. Away from the restrictions, my physical body endured.

I felt myself floating free, in the darkness, but also joined by other souls close by, who were radiating a love and camaraderie and closeness, that we had not achieved before.

There was something special going on here, that I couldn't name. We all knew it. I was somehow aware of all the souls around me and how they felt, and how we were connected together. How we had, somehow, agreed to meetup in this lifetime, before we were even born. That all of us, had agreed that we would join up, and work together for a greater cause. And somehow, we had achieved what we had set out to do. It was an incredible feeling.

We had all worked together and helped each other, to raise ourselves up to this precise moment, when something touched us.

Out of the darkness, it was like the tiniest drop of pure sunshine, like a divine spark, or star seed of pure energy. But at that moment it touched us all. And we knew that each of us would be forever changed by it.

***

Touchwood smiled to himself, as he read over what he had just written. 'Yes', he thought, 'we had sweat lodges before this and some after, but this one seemed to stand out, as a pinnacle of connection to the spirit world'. With a warm heart he continued writing.

'… So connected were we at the moment, that each of us knew, that as we moved through our own individual lives, each of us would be committed to spreading an awareness of our connection to the natural world, and how irrevocably, we were a part of nature. And we all knew for certain, that by damaging the natural world, we were inevitably damaging ourselves too.'

'We would all move on, in our lives, not to great things, but dedicated to spreading that 'star seed' of wisdom, to whoever we met in the world. Once touched by that spark of divinity, we were like a stone thrown into a still pool, creating ripples that radiate out from the centre point and spread to fill the surrounding water.'

Chapter 22

The Sun and the Moon

Though I am old with wandering
Through hollow lands and hilly lands,
I will find out where she has gone,
And kiss her lips and take her hands.
And walk among the long dappled grass,
And pluck till time and times are done
The silver apples of the moon,
The golden apples of the Sun.

W.B. Yeats

Waves crashing onto the jagged rocks at the base of the cliff, provoked both fear and chaos. In contrast the silver goddess moon, hung high in a clear sky, shining like a great lantern, lighting a shimmering, silver pathway, onto the rippling sea.

Two human figures could be seen, silhouetted by the moons serene light. They were stood on a grassy mound, near the edge of the cliff. Deep in the centre of the earth mound, was a corbeled chamber. The chamber had been constructed, long before anyone could remember.

Some say it was made by the Faerie folk, others by a race of sorcerer's and magicians, before the coming of the Celts. A long thin passageway, linking the central chamber, with the outside, had been aligned to the winter solstice sunrise. On that day's dawn, a long shaft of sunlight, would penetrate into the womb of the earth and illuminate the chamber with glowing, golden light.

As we move closer, we can see the two figures on the mound, are a man and a woman, standing naked in the moonlight. The man kneels before the woman, his Priestess, his goddess saying:

"Blessed be thy womb, that have created all life on Earth," he leans in to kiss her sacred Yoni, her dark curly bush.

The Priestess is petit and slim and has well-proportioned body and limbs. A necklace of rough-cut gemstones and beads, hangs down to her petit breasts; her nipples standing out hard and firm. Her breasts are heaving, as she breaths heavily. Her eyes stare out to the far distance, along the silver pathway, on the rippling sea, to the silver goddess, floating in the sky.

The Priestess, her deep breaths, imbibing Luna energy, and that of the Sea Goddess, to bring about her transformation, as receptacle of the goddess.

"Blessed be thy breasts, that have fed and nurtured the children of the Earth," so saying, the Wiccan Priest stretches up to kiss the woman's heaving breasts, her nipples hard and firm on his lips.

The Priest too, has become a receptacle for the essence of the god, the Lord of the animals, the Green Man. As he now stands before his Priestess, she looks deeply into his eyes. A warm breeze brings with it the erotic, tantalizing smells of the forest. Bouquets of forest flowers, baskets full of ripe, forest fruits, and the pungent, but unmistakable smell of deer musk.

"Blessed be thy lips, that have spoken the holy words and breathed life into your creation." As he speaks these words, their lips meet, like the ocean kissing the shoreline. He wraps his muscled arms about her yielding, naked body. With his kiss, she blossomed for him, like a flower opening for the sun.

As her body completely surrendered, and relaxed, she drags him down to the grassy mound; his firm, young body pressing down onto her. She squirms in ecstatic ecstasy, as his now fully erect, firm, and hard manhood, finds her moist and secret temple. The god and the goddess, co-joined in divine bliss.

***

'The ritual on the earth mound had gone well ...'

Wrote Touchwood in his journal. He rubbed his aching hands; he was feeling cold. He turned round in his swivel chair and took a log from the basket beside the stove. Opening the stove front, he threw in the log, then a couple more as the fire was burning low. Turning back to his desk, he continued writing.

'... Hazel had told me she was very pleased with how I had progressed and applied all I had learnt to the Great Rite ritual, of my third degree.'

'It had been over a year since I had become Hazel's student. In that year, I had never worked so hard, at my magical path before. Hazel was an extremely obsessive and energetic tutor. And expected her charge, to work just as energetically. But I had worked through it all and eventually brought myself up to, the high standards she expected.'

'But it wasn't all plain sailing. There were bumps in the road, especially at the beginning. I recall in one of our first lessons, in Hazel's temple ...'

***

We were sat cross legged on the floor, she was teaching me in circle and wanted to be sure I understood the power of the Sacred Yoni, the female vulva.

"The woman's Yoni has been worshipped, all over the world," she explained. "In the tantric tradition for example, the Yoni is worshipped as the sacred symbol of the Divine Feminine, the Great Goddess, the source of all life. The worship of the Yoni, is the worship of the goddess, as well as the worship of women, as living expressions of the goddess."

"Yes," I added. "We often talked about woman, as the embodiment of the divine, during my previous Wiccan training."

Hazel nodded approvingly, "The magical powers of nudity, especially of the sexual organs, are strong and, in the case of the female, the Yoni gives off healing and protective energies. Its display, has the effect of a magical spell, used to turn away evil forces. Even in our own country, remnants of this knowledge can be seen, in the Sheela-na-gigs carved into old churches, often over the church doorway."

"Yes," I confirmed. "I have seen them carved in churches. But what about the man in these rituals, what part does he play?"

Hazel took a couple of deep breaths, perhaps I was distracting her from what she had planned to say. But the dutiful teacher in her, answered my question, "For many modern Pagans and in

Wicca the consort of the goddess, 'the god', is seen as the masculine form of divinity. He is the polar opposite but equal to the goddess. The Green Man has often been used as a representation of the god, along with the Horned God, a syncretic deity that incorporates aspects of, the Celtic Cernunnos and the Greek Pan, among others.

"But surely you must have been taught about the aspects of the god in your coven, I know that Doyle is big on the Green Man and enjoys talking about him."

"Yes, he did, he even took some of the novice men to see a Green Man carved into a church near him, we were on the way to the pub, to discuss the male mysteries," I revealed.

"Yes, he would," retorted Hazel. "But sadly much of that ancient knowledge, has been lost to us. However to get back to the Great Rite ritual. At the centre of Wiccan ritual and theology, is an ancient idea; the 'hieros gamos' or sacred marriage. It is a ritual of sexual magic, involving intercourse between the Goddess of fertility, embodied by Her Priestess, and Her Consort, present in the Priest. The sacred marriage in Wicca, confirms and seals the highest level of religious initiation, the third degree."

I was stunned. I wasn't sure if I had heard her rightly. It sounded like she was saying that to get the third degree, we had to … in circle.

I had to clarify, before we went on. "Sorry Hazel, forgive me if I've misunderstood, but it sounded like you are saying, that to get my third degree, we had to do … intercourse … an actual ritual, of sex magic?"

"Yes of course. I thought you understood that." Hazel said, looking genuinely puzzled.

"But I thought the Great Rite was symbolic," I bleated like a schoolboy. "I've seen it performed by my High Priest and Priestess. The chalice of wine represents the womb and is held by the High Priestess. The Athame is the phallic representation and is held by the High Priest. The male holds the Athame above chalice. Female holds chalice with wine below. The Male lowers Athame into chalice saying, 'co-joined they are one'. That's what everyone talks about, as the Great Rite."

Hazel looked at me in disbelief and shock. She seemed lost for words. Never had I seen her look that way before. Never had I seen her lost for words before. A myriad of emotions seemed to pass over her face. Still she said nothing.

Then suddenly an anger, seemed to well up inside her. She stood up and burst out through her clenched teeth, "Wait till I see Doyle again!" She was shaking her head in anger.

Then suddenly looked at me accusingly, "Are you *sure*, they hadn't schooled you in this?" she said, managing to reclaim some calm.

I shook my head miserably.

"Because, I know for a fact, that this coven, do perform the … 'an actual ritual, of sex magic,' for the third degree. I myself, was initiated by Doyle himself." She took some more deep breaths, looking from side to side, like a caged animal, unable to look me in the eyes.

Then suddenly, she looked offended and said stiffly, "Of course … if you don't wish to continue with me as you High Priestess … in the Great Rite… then we can always … find you a younger …"

"No! … no, no I don't … want that," I interrupted, holding up my hands, to halt her. "It's just that … it was a bit of a surprise.

I hadn't been prepared properly. They probably intended to …
but it was all … a bit confused when you took over …"

I looked at her, she looked so young and lost, I had never seen
her like this.

Gallantly, I went over to her and kneeled down, in front of
her. Looking up at her face, I smiled, "I don't want anyone else,
to teach me. I would be honoured, to take my third degree with
you, in a full enactment of the sacred marriage."

Her relief was palpable. She tried hard, to supress a sob, but
I could see there were tears forming in her eyes. Then she shook
her head and flung her hands to her face, wiping away the drops
of moisture.

She reached down and took both my hands, bringing me to
my feet. I thought she was about to hug me but stopped. Instead
she took in a deep breath, in an attempt to regain her composure.
Then breathed out hard and continued with her lesson.

"The Wiccan Great Rite is the sex act," Hazel continued in
as professional a way as she could muster. "That celebrates, the
union of the God and Goddess upon the sabbats. It is usually,
the central part of the Beltane ritual and is considered a form
of sex magic, that ensures fertility, blesses the growing season,
and brings a bountiful harvest. It could also be seen, as the
harmonious union of male and female energies within oneself.

"In ancient times, young lovers coupled in the fields, on
Beltane night, to send the energy into the ground, for a rich
growing season.

"As far as raising energy goes, it doesn't get much more
powerful, than actual intercourse. The rising of pleasure towards
climax, is probably the strongest form of energy-working known

to witches. Almost every culture in the world, contains traditions on how to shape and direct this kind of energy. To make love, is literally to generate the energy of love, which is powerful and transformative. It is one of the secrets of the sacred Yoni, that woman know instinctively when we make love."

***

Touchwood, sat back in his chair with a great sigh, dropping his pen onto his writing desk. He turned to look out of his window, it was a lovely late summers day. From here he could see the rows of apple trees in the orchard, each tree heavily laden with this year's harvest. His granddaughter Victoria was helping the younger ones to collect any apples that had fallen, before the chickens could get to them.

The vegetable gardens too, were laid out neatly and one of the young mothers was there with some toddlers foraging for the ripened beans. It was a sight which warmed his old heart.

The old man stroked his long silver beard, with a sigh picked up his large notebook to read what he had just written; he recited aloud:

'…. *I could hardly believe I had reached my goal, to have finally attained my third degree as a Wiccan Priest and was able to form my own coven.'*

'*Ten years ago I could not have imagined that I would be working in a magic circle in this way; it would have seemed like an impossible dream. Ever since I had witnessed the women's ritual on Silbury Hill, and been counselled by my guide, this had been my priority. I had needed to find a teaching group, that could guide me on my spiritual path. One, I could work in and learn about the goddess and her ways.'*

'However, I had searched and searched for years to find it: the Atlanteans and in particular Adrian, had taught me to meditate and so much more about esoteric matters.'

'Candra too, who I still missed dearly, had taught me that I had 'had potential'; I was fertile ground so to speak. She had sowed her spiritual seed in me, had nurture it and hope it would grow into a mighty tree. Candra the Rhennish girl, just before she had left, had bequeathed me the warrior's name 'Corin - The Spear'. And she had predicted correctly, when she told me: 'You are destined to lead, I can see that in you. One day you will'.'

'And that wonderful group of tree lovers and the mysterious whisperer Radu, I had learned so much from Radu. I had wanted to learn whatever he was willing to teach. But he too had left.'

'And of course the Cat Tribe. Together we had helped each other and spurred each other on to learn as much as we could about earth mysteries and energy raising.'

'Then finally, there was Doyle's wonderful Wiccan coven, which had eventually brought me to the High Priestess Hazel.'

'Each group had been a step on the way, a different aspect of that multifaceted crystal that is the spiritual world. I still remember vividly that incredible Great Rite ritual on the mound and thinking in a quiet moment afterwards. After the co joining of the Moon and the Sun, where does one go?'

Touchwood, at last had finished the first part of his book; now he needed a break from it. He turned to look out of his window again, at the young ones gathering apples in the sunshine, he opened the window wide to let in the warm air and could hear the joyous laughter of the young people. I am going out there to help them, he thought.

High in the sky above the orchard a raven could be seen as she glides effortlessly on the updraughts. She circles the boglands below, her keen eyes searching for carrion. She soars in flight, the raged feathers on her wing tips, hardly moving as she circles, in ever increasing radius.

She banked and turned in graceful spirals, leaning against the air currents. Now flying over bogland, now flying over a human farmstead. Her all-seeing eyes note, the neat rows of vegetables, and the polytunnels. She notes the apple orchards and the young people with their noisy chatter, while collecting apples and an old man with a silver beard carrying a laden basket to a waiting wheelbarrow.

Printed in Great Britain
by Amazon

23667631R00152